THE *dark* PRINCE
Les Fées: The French Fae Legend

BY: EMMA V LEECH

Copyright © 2013 Emma V Leech

Cover Design by Keevs & Alys Arden

Cover Photo by istockphoto.com/profile/zhenikeyev

Floral Brushes by lileya.deviantart.com/

Published by Emma V Leech

All rights reserved.

ISBN-13: 978-1507785546

ISBN-10: 1507785542

No part of this book may be produced or transmitted in any form or by any means, electronic or mechanical, including copying, recording, or by any information storage and retrieval system without express permission from the author.

This is a work of fiction. Names, character, places and incidents are either the product of the author's imagination or are used fictitiously. Any resemblance to actual events, locales, or persons, living, or dead is coincidental.

THE DARK PRINCE

PROLOGUE

The Dark Prince by Océane DuBeauvoir.

Once upon a time mortal and Fae lived side by side. The gates between the worlds were open and trade existed between the two races.

The Fae were divided into three royal houses; the Light Fae, the biggest and most powerful race were known for their music and artistry; the Dark Fae, though far fewer in numbers, were revered for their intelligence and fierce natures, and it was the warriors of the Dark Fae who were called upon if trouble was upon the land. The Elves, the third house, were a tricky and powerful race, and the rest of the Fae had never trusted them.

Time passed and the mortal world grew to such an extent that they began to cut into the wilderness, both in their own world and in Faery. The Fae, whose lives are integrally bound with its land, began to feel the loss as a pain in their souls and requested a stop to the ever increasing consumption of the countryside ... but man in his hunger for knowledge and advancement, refused.

The Dark Fae spoke of war but the Light counseled against it; instead the Fae decided to retreat to their lands and close the portals between worlds. Those humans already settled could stay but they would never again return to their own world, as no Fae would again set foot in the mortal realm. Their history was to be wiped from the planet; all writings or belongings of Fae origin would be destroyed or brought back from the human realm until nothing remained. A spell would be cast and humanity would forget that they had ever been.

It took many years to gather every scrap of writing, every artifact, and on the day when the gates between the lands closed the King and Queen of both Light and Dark came to witness the historic event. One of the last mortals to pass through the gate to Faery was a young woman; her hair was flame red and her beauty captured the heart of the dark King. His desire for the mortal woman was soon the talk of the land, and broke the heart of his wife; who died suddenly from a mysterious illness that no healer could mend.

The Dark King lost no time in marrying the mortal woman, and in doing so hardened the heart of his young son, still grieving for the loss of his mother.

The Prince silently swore vengeance on his father and the mortal world ... and bided his time.

Chapter 1

Océane's first thought as he strode into the great, brightly lit room of the museum was that he was much taller than she had imagined him in her book. Actually he was far more, well ... more. Her second thought was more along the lines of, 'Oh shit!'

She had been engrossed in her work as always. It was early yet, the museum had just opened and she was alone in the room and contented to be so. Dark-rimmed spectacles that drove her mad by sliding constantly down her nose were firmly in place and a scruffy bun kept her hair out of her eyes. There was something in the delicacy of the writing that drew her. Even though she hadn't a clue what the words meant the beauty of them spoke to her. She was so captured that she didn't hear the slash of a metal blade, not dissimilar to the one in the glass case she sat beside.

Too late she looked up to find the figure of a man bearing down on her with fury in his eyes. Though, he was like no other man she had ever come across. Long, white blond hair fell around his face, paler than any she had ever seen, yet it seemed to glow with a vibrancy that no human possessed. She wondered vaguely if there was some kind of theatrical exhibition in the museum but his clothes were so exquisite …

As he got closer she noticed writing as it danced across the surface of his skin. Intrigued, she tried to focus, to make out the words, not noticing the blade in his hand or the body of the security guard whose life was draining away along with his blood on the museum floor.

Too late the words on his face became clear...

Run!

And then there was darkness.

***

"Have you taken leave of your senses?" Aleish demanded. Prince Laen looked at the shabby creature curled up like an unwanted bundle of clothes at his feet, and then back to his sister Aleish, a fragile-looking blonde who currently wore an expression of pure fury.

"There was no other choice ... Have you seen the book?" He pointed an accusatory finger at the delicately bound volume he had thrown down into the long meadow grass in disgust. Aleish glanced at the book and the gold leaf of the title as it glinted in the sun, and was clearly unimpressed.

"And there was no other choice than to hit her over the head?" Her startling black eyes were wide with disapproval and Laen avoided her gaze. He may be her older brother and able to strike terror into the most hardened soldier's heart but Aleish was tougher than her looks suggested. "What were you thinking, you damn fool!" She persisted as he gritted his teeth. "How could you do such a thing?" The uneasy feeling that he had not taken the best course of action had begun as soon as he'd reached the gates, but the disappointment in Aleish's eyes was illuminating his decision with the colourful clarity of a stained glass window on a bright day. "I begin to think I do not know you at all," she finished and the disillusioned look on her face made him uneasy.

"There was nothing else I could do!" Though in truth hurting the girl had not brought the satisfaction he'd expected. In fact it had pained him to strike her but she had been about to scream. Besides, he had managed the whole thing with only one mortal life on his blade – though he was now unsure whether that pleased him or not. The desire to go and fight something tangible rather than the insidious slow death that was creeping quietly around the realm was burning as fiercely as ever. "The dagger had to be retrieved for the safety of the lands!"

Despite his protests, Aleish's anger flared, unabated. "No one has disputed that, not even our father, but why bring her here? It was agreed that you would go and retrieve the blade with as little fuss as possible, but no, you have to go and abduct a woman on your way. Excellent choice!"

Laen scowled at his sister as she bent to examine the wretched thing again. "Read it and see why I brought her. She knows something!" he insisted, trying to reassure himself of his own motives as much as Aleish. "The humans will find their way back here sooner or later ... The gates are weakening, more and more of their filth and disease is contaminating our land. How long before they realise they have irrevocably damaged their own world and decide to take ours instead? They will destroy us and everything we care for! You know they are capable of it, Aleish."

She rolled her eyes, sitting on the ground to better examine the bump on the girl's head, and Laen cursed to himself. He knew Aleish didn't want to hear his rant against the humans. It wasn't that she didn't share his concerns as she had been affected by the situation as badly as any, but she was a gentle soul, and his ideas of how to deal with the problem nauseated her. She glared up at him, all gentleness hidden behind an expression of contempt.

"I have always supported you, Laen, but this is taking things too far. What exactly do you propose we do with her?"

He paced up and down, his hand clenched around the dagger he had dispatched the museum guard with, and knew there was nothing else to be done. "She will have to come with us."

"Gods!"

Laen stopped his pacing and raised his eyebrows; his sister rarely swore.

"Well are you going to just stand there, you fool?" She huffed, her usual patience clearly having been long spent on him. "We cannot take her to the inn, can we? We will have to go straight home. You had best go and get the horses and borrow an extra one."

Laen strode off muttering something dark, and left Aleish to keep watch on the unconscious human.

By the time he returned, he found his sister looking anxiously at the creature, who groaned and reached for her head.

"She's waking!" Aleish looked at her brother with panicked eyes.
Laen grimaced, knowing that his life was about to get a damn sight more complicated. "So I see."

He looked at the girl with distaste. Her clothes were cheaply made and shapeless, her hands ingrained with ink, the nails bitten to the quick. Next to his sister, comparably a bird of paradise, the girl looked like one of the tatty pigeons he had seen in the human city. He snorted at the thought, which drew her attention, her eyes flicking open and staring at him with undisguised horror. He thought briefly that he had done her a disservice, as her eyes were actually rather beautiful once open, very large, heavily lashed and a deep muddy brown ... rather like a cow.

Before he had time to congratulate himself on the comparison, the girl had lashed out and kicked him in the knee with the heavy-soled leather boots she wore. He bellowed in pain, wondering if she made a habit of this sort of thing, as he could see no other reason for a woman wearing something quite so ugly, before grabbing hold of her by the hair.

Océane clawed at his hands. "Let me go, you freak!" She struggled and screamed, trying to scratch him with what remained of her nails. A savage expression crossed her face, and she twisted so she could sink her teeth into the exposed flesh of his arm.

Laen yelled again and was torn between trying to calm her down and sticking a knife in her chest and having done with it, but then his sister would believe he truly was a heartless brute, and he had done his best to keep that fact from her. In the end he took the middle road and slapped her hard enough that she let go but not so hard as to do any damage.

"Laen!"

His sister looked at him in horror, and so he dropped the thrashing human and presented his bloody arm for inspection.

"She bit me!"

"You abducted her," she shouted, hitting his broad shoulder with more anger than effect. "What did you expect, a thank you note?"

***

Océane spat blood on the ground frantically and wondered with a pounding heart if the terrifying man standing over her was likely to have AIDS, though it didn't look like she'd have time to die from anything so drawn out anyway, as he now had a dagger in his hand and was looking at her with hatred burning in his eyes. She screamed and scrambled to her feet, tripping over the thick, long grass as she searched around her for any signs of life. With a shaking hand to her head she turned in confusion as she discovered she was no longer in Paris but in the heart of some unknown countryside. There were no buildings, no cars - nothing but trees and a meadow filled with improbable flowers too jewel bright and lovely to be real.

"What the f--!"

She didn't have time to finish the obscenity as there was a thud to the back of her head and the ground rose up to catch her with alarming speed. Thick, strong arms caught her before she hit the ground and she thought she heard a woman screaming, but then the darkness welcomed her back once again.

Chapter 2

Océane came to and discovered the most nauseating swaying motion. She wondered briefly if her tormentor had decided to compound her agony by placing her on a boat. Her cheek rested against something coarse with an earthy, warm smell that she couldn't place and the swaying continued. She groaned. She had once travelled to England by ferry and had never been sicker in her life. Then, the thought occurred to her that boats aren't usually hairy, and she cracked open an eye to discover she had been lashed to a horse. She struggled to sit upright and stifled a scream. She had never been on a horse in her life, which was frightening enough on its own as the ground seemed an awfully long way away, but what kind of freak abducted women on horseback for the love of God? The worst kind, she decided, glaring at the figure riding beside her on the biggest black horse she had ever seen. The great animal looked at her in distaste, flicking its head in the air and rolling its eyes - Jesus, even his horse was a freaking psychopath. He looked her over in disgust before patting the great animal with affection. "Hush, Skylla. Don't let her upset you."

She raised her eyebrows in disbelief. "What do you want with me?" she demanded, deciding she had better get to the heart of the matter. From the look of him and his beautiful companion, she didn't think he seemed the type to need to abduct women for weird sexual motives, but what the hell did he want?

"I want to know about the book."

She looked at him in confusion and saw the words *mystification, astonishment* and *shock* flicker over his face like the words were illuminated with a delicate white light beneath the surface of his skin before disappearing.

"What the hell was that?" She pointed at his face, remembering suddenly that she had seen this before at the museum. He glowered and looked away from her in irritation.

"It is a part of our banishment."

Océane jumped at the soft voice as she realised the woman had spoken and was riding on her other side.

"Aleish!" Laen said.

"Oh hush! You have beaten and mistreated the poor girl enough for one day, the least we can do is answer her questions."

"Your ... what?"

"Banishment," Aleish repeated slowly, sounding out the syllables, obviously believing the blows to Océane's head had impaired her mental faculties.

"I know what the bloody word means, I just don't know what you're on about!" she snapped and then swallowed hard as her head began to throb and her stomach churned. *Bewilderment* scrolled under the woman's flesh and Océane shuddered.

Aleish flushed but continued with her explanation. "It is part of our punishment for speaking out against the King and his wife. We have been banished from the palace and the heart of his lands and now whoever speaks with us will see their own true feelings reflected back at them. It is one of the more ... subtle punishments but is nonetheless effective. It makes people very uncomfortable."

"No shit," muttered Océane before turning back to Laen and wondering if she had misjudged him as being the least mentally stable of the two. The girl was clearly madder than he was with her talk of Kings and palaces. She wondered if they had escaped from some kind of mental asylum as they were both obviously nutters; she was probably suffering some kind of trauma-induced hallucination, and they were going along with it, tying it in with their own personal delusions. She decided to get the conversation back on track in the hope that she might get to the bottom of things. She took a deep breath and tried to focus past her nausea. "What book?" she asked him.

"This one." He reached down into his saddle bag and held out her precious creation between his fingers as though it offended him, and she let out a small cry.

"Oh, please be careful with it," she begged, thinking of all the hours of work she had dedicated to this, her greatest achievement.

"Why?" He shoved it roughly back in the saddle bag and turned to her, anger flashing in his eyes. "What is it to you? How did you come to know of the things you have written here?"

Océane frowned and shook her head as she noticed the word *confusion* once again flicker under his skin. "What do you mean? It's just a Fairy story."

Laen glowered at her. "Fae, not Fairy!" he shouted, making her stomach clench in fear before she turned to Aleish. He held out his hand as if to illustrate his point with a smug expression. "You see, she admits it!"

"Admits what?" Océane looked from one to the other wondering what she could possibly just have confessed to but neither of them would say any more and her attention was taken by the surrounding view. They were heading into a valley now, skirted on one side by woodland, and for the first time it occurred to her that many of the trees, flowers and birds were unlike any she had ever seen before. She was no expert on the natural world, having lived her whole life in a city, but she was pretty sure the French countryside didn't look like this. The sky was blue but somehow the colour was more intense, like the artist had forgotten the water and just slapped the paint undiluted onto the paper. The light was fierce with every tiny leaf and blade of grass defined in sharper focus than anything she had experienced, though maybe that was her eyes as they had begun to water and the sun made her blink. Even the air was different - sweet and pure. She shook her head. That one was easy enough; it was just because she wasn't breathing in the usual grey soup of city pollution and dust and human detritus. The meadow before her was an extraordinary sight though and in any other circumstance she would have been begging to get down and draw what she could see and yet she couldn't identify anything.

She looked around her more carefully, trying to see if perhaps her eyesight was playing tricks on her as she didn't have her glasses on. One flower looked like a huge poppy but it was a deep vibrant purple and the petals were thick and velvety, not the frail silk of the ones she had seen before. She longed to reach down and touch them and see if they really were as soft as they looked. But there were dozens of others, all curious and wonderful and in every shade she could possibly conceive. Disturbed by the horse's passage, a butterfly flew up past her face. It was the size of her hand, the wings beating with slow and lazy strokes in the heated atmosphere and glinting with iridescent shades of green and gold. It couldn't be real. It simply could not be real - she had to be concussed. Glancing up she saw a flock of bright blue birds pass overhead, their shrill cries searing through her tender brain. She wondered how long she'd been out of it, and if the bumps to her head had done any permanent damage, as suddenly she felt very unwell. She swayed forwards, just stopping herself before she could break her nose on the horse's neck.

"Laen, get her down, she looks unwell. I believe she is going to pass out." The soft concern in Aleish's voice drifted through the pounding in Océane's head as she closed her eyes. She could hear Laen cursing her as he dismounted, and mentally returned his feelings with equal violence. The sun was too bright, too hot, burning her eyes even though they were now closed, and staining her vision a bright vermilion, a startling contrast against the previous lapis blue sky. It had been February in Paris and the days had been reassuringly familiar shades of dull and she had been dressed accordingly. Here, where ever the hell *here* was, it seemed to be the middle of bloody August. She tried to breathe deeply as acid burned the back of her throat and her stomach roiled again as she felt the ropes being untied and strong hands grasp her around the waist. She began to tell him to leave her be for a moment, but it was too late. The sudden movement was more than her constitution could stand, and with some small measure of satisfaction, she vomited all over him.

Chapter 3

"Disgusting!"

Laen's infuriated voice cut through the cotton wool in Océane's head more effectively than any paracetamol. She was lying on the ground in the shade of a tree and the grass felt blessedly cool beneath her cheek. She cracked open her eyes to see dappled patterns of light filtering through the leaves. It was soothing to watch the gentle touch of the sun burnish her skin with soft patches of sunlight and if she hadn't known the lunatic who had abducted her was close, she could have been quite content to lay there. She could hear birdsong, a gentle sound against the pounding beat in her head, the noise increasing in speed and volume as she pieced back together the moments before she had passed out. She forced her eyes open to look in his direction and swallowed down a scream. He was stripping off his soiled shirt, and she was confronted with a vast expanse of naked, muscular back. She let out an unwilling squeak of alarm that did nothing to help as the back became a chest, and the two definitely matched.

She pushed herself onto her back as he loomed over her and she noticed for the first time that his eyes were black, a stark contrast against the white blond hair that fell softly around his massive shoulders. His face was uncompromising with no hint of gentleness but all hard lines with a wide brow and high angular cheekbones. As a male specimen he was quite spectacular, if terrifying, and she cursed her idiotic luck that the only handsome man she'd gotten this close to in years was a complete frigging psycho. Nonetheless, when he leaned towards her, she had no reserve about bringing her boot into contact with his stomach and kicking him hard. Unfortunately he seemed to have learned his lesson the last time around, as he grabbed her foot and twisted her so she was face down on the ground; he then proceeded to sit astride her back with both her hands clasped in one impossibly strong fist.

"Where's Aleish?" she yelled, hoping that she might stop him, as at least Aleish didn't seem to like him beating her up. She groaned under the weight of him as the ground and every little stone beneath her jabbed into her flesh.

"My sister has gone to fetch water, she will not return for a few moments yet." His voice was low and threatening and her sore stomach clenched into a tighter knot. "So now we can have some time together ... alone."

His sister? She wasn't sure why but this didn't seem like good news, and although she couldn't see his face, Océane could easily imagine the nasty smile that had accompanied his statement. He pulled on her hair so that her neck stretched back at an uncomfortable angle.

"You vomited on me."

She could almost have laughed at the accusation in his voice, like *he* had something to complain about. "Well, *you* hit me on the head ... twice! You also slapped me and, oh yes, I almost forgot ... you abducted me, you bloody freak!"

Océane squirmed beneath him, cursing and screaming and trying to kick and get free of his grasp but he just pulled her hair harder. "My sister may have a tender heart but I can assure you I do not, so if you want to escape with your life I suggest you tell me everything you know about that book."

She stilled, fighting for breath and wishing she knew why her book was so bloody important. "I don't understand. It's just a book. I made it; I wrote it and illustrated it."

She felt sweat prickle over her skin as the weight of the sultry air clung to her, cloying and oppressive. His hard thighs pressed close to her waist to stop her from moving and as the heat of his body seeped through her clothes her heart stuttered with fear as she considered what his plans for her might be. She had to try and keep him talking ... try to reason with him, at least until Aleish returned.

"You admit you wrote it?" he demanded. "Now at least we are getting somewhere. The story, where did you discover it? Do you have contacts here, spies perhaps, or have you visited before?"

"Spies?" If she could have turned her head she would have looked at him in outrage. As it was, she contented herself with snorting and muttering about the state of his mental health. "There is a bookbinding competition in April for works of fantasy," she explained with as much patience as she could muster, "and that was going to be my entry. I would have bloody won too!"

***

Laen let go of her hair in disgust so that her forehead hit the ground with a thud. Lies. The girl was obviously an accomplished liar, but when he got her home he would find ways to get the truth from her, once he had her out of sight of his sister. He was sure there was a connection between the increased unrest and sickness in the Fae Lands and the discovery of the dagger, and to find her there with that book, with his story written down, it was just too much. How had the dagger come to be in human hands after all this time? It must have been taken there recently.

He did not believe that an item of such worth would have been missed by the powerful spells that had been used to hunt out their creations. It could not have been hidden and that meant it had been given by one of his kind as payment for some nefarious plot or it had been stolen. He did not trust the Light Fae, and the rumours about their King, Auberren, were increasingly worrying. He had always had ties to the human world and flouted the laws concerning the gates. Either way there was something deeply wrong in his world and he was going to discover what. He would not sit back and watch his people suffer and die as his mother had without raising a hand to help them. If the humans were tainting this realm with their filth then there would be a war, a war he had always been ready to fight, and he couldn't wait for it to begin. He left the woman on the ground and returned to his luggage where he yanked out a clean white shirt and pulled it on before opening a leather bottle. He unscrewed the top and drank deeply before looking back at Océane. With a grunt of annoyance he got to his feet and took hold of her under her arms, lifting her a little more carefully than before as he had no more clean shirts. He placed her sitting up with her back against a tree and held the bottle to her lips, sighing and rolling his eyes when she hesitated and looked at the bottle with suspicion.

"I am offering you water, not an end to your trials. I have already drunk from it as you saw yourself. When I want you dead I promise not to use anything as subtle as poison."

Her eyes flicked to the dagger at his hip but she was apparently reassured about the quality of the water if nothing else, and opened her mouth, swallowing gratefully as he tipped the bottle up. She wiped her chin on her shoulder where the water had spilled before looking up at him. "Thank you," she said.

He looked back at her in surprise, and she sneered. "Just because you're an ignorant pig it doesn't mean the rest of us have no manners."

He snorted and screwed the cap back on the bottle. "Manners ... from a human? Gods, whatever next!"

She seemed to frown at his word choice, but he heard someone coming towards them and turned to see that Aleish had returned, her own water bottle now full. She moved elegantly through the meadow grasses, her longs skirts making a pleasant swishing sound as she walked and Laen was once again reminded of the difference between the gently raised and beautifully clothed Fae women of his kind and the sharp-edged creature at his feet who seemed happy to dress like a farm hand. Aleish didn't look at him, reminding him that he was by no means forgiven, and she crouched down to offer some water to Océane.

"I gave her some already."

She looked at her brother in disgust. "Well, I am pleased to see your manners are making something of a comeback."

***

Océane smirked at the annoyance on his face but he just grunted before walking over and lifting her over his shoulder with no visible effort. She watched the ground swaying in and out of focus beneath her head as he walked and she closed her eyes. He deposited her, none too gently, back on the horse and she groaned as her head began to spin, and her stomach roiled. Laen backed off for a moment, watching her in alarm and she wasn't quite sure if she was grateful or disappointed when her stomach settled and he returned to tie her in place. The horse shifted impatiently and she grasped the saddle where her hands were tied to steady herself. He and Aleish mounted their own animals before they moved off.

She tried to make sense of what was happening to her as they travelled but could come to no sensible solution. They appeared to be deep in the countryside as they passed no roads and she could hear no traffic, nothing but bird song and the occasional scurrying of small creatures in the undergrowth. Occasionally she thought she heard the far off rumble of thunder but there wasn't a cloud in sight so she guessed there must be another explanation, a factory maybe or some sort of work going on. She wondered if they would pass by close enough that she could raise the alarm. She risked a glance at Laen and found he was staring at her with cold, emotionless eyes. The thunder, or whatever it was, rumbled again on the horizon and she scowled back at him before returning her attention forwards.

She moved her shoulders, stretching her neck out to try and ease her aching bones. Her skin was hot and clammy, her clothes sticking to her in damp patches and she could smell the musky scent of her own sweat on the still air. She glared up at the heavens wishing with all her might that there was a storm coming after all. But although the sky now seemed a rather strange colour, more indigo than the glorious Madonna blue of a Renaissance painting, it did not look like there was any respite coming as the sun burned as fiercely as ever.

The countryside they passed through was dazzling. Even in her miserable state she could appreciate that much; dense woodland skirted the edges of the valley they followed, and a river twisted tantalisingly close by, the cool water glinting in the sunlight. She licked her parched lips and tried to think of ways to escape, but her hands were tightly bound together and lashed to the saddle, the soft leather creaking as the horse swayed beneath her. She swallowed down the nausea that churned in her stomach and knew that even if she could get free, she was far too weak to get far; she would have to think of something else. This countryside could not continue forever, soon there would be people and then she would find a way to reach help.

They travelled for what felt like hours under the blazing sun and Océane felt sweat trickle down her back between her shoulder blades. She was groggy and listless, her loose grip on consciousness making it hard to keep track of time passing. She wondered if the blow to her head really had impaired her judgement as she felt increasingly that even the weather was angry with her, the sun was so fierce and unremitting. Hot and dirty, she had never felt sicker in her life, not even on the ferry. She had lost her glasses but for some strange reason she didn't seem to need them. Maybe the head injury again, she wondered. Speaking of which, her skull throbbed with a dull intensity that threatened to have her throwing up again. She wondered if she could arrange it so she could do it on Laen's clean shirt; it would be worth it to see the look on his face. In the end she couldn't be bothered and as the hellish journey didn't seem to have an end in sight she decided she could do worse than miss the scenery, and passed out with her face against the horse's mane.

Chapter 4

Océane awoke to yet another disconcerting sensation, this time of being carried in the arms of a man. All things considered, she preferred the horse. Unwilling to let him know she was awake, she tried to keep her limbs relaxed and heavy even though all of her senses told her to run screaming for the hills. Not that there would be any point. Laen, as that was obviously the man in question, certainly looked the outdoorsy type and would almost certainly outrun her. Her head rested against his broad shoulder and his long blond hair fell against her neck, tickling with the delicate touch of a feather as he moved. She resisted the urge to swat it away and opened her eyes cautiously, glancing up at the strong line of his jaw. She wondered if this was some kind of dream; she'd once seen a television program where the heroine of the story turned out to have been in a coma the whole time and the characters were all in her head. Perhaps the man holding her had actually been an ordinary kind of villain, and her head just mixed the details up with the story in her book. It was possible the blow to her head had addled her brain, combined with being in that museum surrounded by ancient swords and daggers and armour, all that metal work glinting under the unnaturally bright lighting like the sun reflected on water. Maybe he had actually been carrying a gun, not a sword, and she was presently in intensive care, hooked up to lots of machinery. It couldn't be more far-fetched than what she was actually experiencing. She strained her ears, listening for any tell-tale beeps to no avail.

She tried to think about it rationally. It simply couldn't be real, the countryside she had seen, the extraordinary and curious plants and birds. She knew nothing like that existed on earth. She may not have travelled much but she watched TV the same as everyone else, and as for the man carrying her ... she had never seen anything like him before, or his sister for that matter. They were beautiful in a way that she had never seen before, those black eyes for example with that Blanche Neige complexion and platinum blond hair that clearly hadn't come from a bottle. She had seen big men at home and on TV, the muscle-bound steroid fed kind, but he must have been six foot six and built like a bloody rhino too. She was taken past a vast tapestry of warriors fighting with swords and their bare hands. Their bare torsos were thick with muscle and they were all built like Laen but surely that had to be artistic licence - didn't it? You might find one man like Laen in a thousand or so at home ... maybe. Not all of them. The way the words appeared on their skin was simply not normal, not ... human, but if they weren't human, what the bloody hell were they, and where had they taken her?

She toyed with the idea of aliens but dismissed it almost immediately; she'd never really bought into the whole extraterrestrial deal. She began to reflect upon why he had been at the museum at all and fought down the urge to laugh at the idiocy of her own ideas. She had to consider though the curious thing about the discovery of the dagger, the very idea that had inspired her to turn the story into her competition entry. There had been speculation, in the more excitable press, about the possibility of another race - the Fae. Of course these were the same newspapers that ran with stories of alien abductions and Elvis sightings but, still, some people had considered it possible. Of course the scientists had dismissed the suggestion, but they had also admitted the metals that had been used were like nothing they had ever seen before. Once she had seen pictures of the dagger in the press, seen the strange and delicate characters that had to be some ancient form of writing upon the blade, she had simply had to see it for real. The desire had been overwhelming and the beginning of an obsession that had brought her to this point. A cold sensation began, heavy and disquieting in the pit of her stomach, as she considered everything and realised that Laen had been strongly of the opinion that she had written about him - and she had been writing a story about a Fae prince.

She looked about her with trepidation, acutely aware that her surroundings were beginning to back up her implausible story. She appeared to be on the inside of an enormous building - a castle? It was cool and dim inside after hours under the furious glare of the afternoon sun and she had to blink to make her eyes adjust. The walls were made of huge pieces of cut stone, yet they were adorned with many heavy, gilt-framed oil paintings of rather otherworldly people who looked remarkably like her abductors. The paintings were of obvious quality and age and their depictions of an aristocratic and powerful ancestry did nothing to soothe her growing alarm. Not that being abducted by a nobody wouldn't be terrifying enough but if he really was a Prince ... She stopped the train of thought abruptly before she succumbed to an attack of hysterics. She had to stay calm - and then she caught a glance of a painting of a huge man who bore a striking resemblance to the one carrying her, and in the picture he wore a heavy golden crown.

She felt her breath catch in her throat.

She was borne past dark wood doors, some of which were open and showed her tantalising glimpses of sumptuous rooms, and great tapestries with outlandish depictions of battle scenes, and Océane felt her eyes open wide as the idea took hold. She knew she ought to find it ridiculous, but after everything she had witnessed in the past few hours, what other explanation was there?

Océane cursed her dumb luck, of all the ridiculous things to happen. She had admitted to her friend, Carla, only days previously that she was fed up of living alone and wished she could be swept off her feet by a strong, handsome man. The phrase *be careful what you wish for, because you may get it* rang in her ears with an unpleasant clarity. She'd been swept off her feet all right and he was certainly strong. She had to admit he was also devastatingly handsome, in an unearthly, psychopathic kind of way. It just so happened he was not only an utter bastard, but also a freaking Fairy!

She sighed and thought every bad word she had in his direction, and then froze as she realised his eyes were on her. She was suddenly very aware that they were striding down an empty corridor and that his left hand was in contact with the bare skin of her waist where her shirt had ridden up.

"Where are you taking me?" She had hoped to sound strong and defiant and was irritated to hear her voice tremble and squeak like a little girl. He smiled down at her, a malicious glint deep in those obsidian eyes.

"Somewhere we can be alone."

Oh shit.

Océane used every vestige of energy she had left, which wasn't much, and thrashed, kicked, bit and screamed ... with no affect whatsoever. He just laughed and kicked open a door to his left. He walked through, slammed it shut, and threw her down on a large, four poster bed. She scrambled off of it as fast as she could, tumbling off the side and smacking her knees on the polished hardwood floor. As she pulled herself upright she saw a pair of glass doors with a small balcony beyond and a very high drop to the ground. For the moment at least she dismissed throwing herself over the edge. Finding her feet on legs that felt far too weak to hold her, she backed up into the farthest corner of the room with her heart pounding in her ears.

He stood looking at her, head on one side like a bird surveying a worm.

"Please," she said, holding her trembling hands out in front of her in supplication.

An amused smile played over his lips but his eyes glittered with hatred. "Please what? Please forgive you your trespasses? Please kill you quickly? Do expand a little, my dear, you must give me a clue."

Océane was appalled to hear herself whimper in fear. Why, oh why hadn't she taken those self-defence lessons? She'd been meaning to do it for weeks after she'd been mugged on the metro, but then she'd seen the dagger was on exhibition at the museum and all other thoughts had fled from her mind. It looked like she was about to pay for that decision with her life. Océane had never been one to back down or give up however and she wasn't about to start now. He would not get whatever it was he wanted, not without one hell of a fight. He took a step towards her and as she scanned the room, frantically passing over the beautifully carved four-poster and the luxurious rugs, her eyes fell upon a heavy silver candlestick. She snatched it up, brandishing it in front of her as Laen roared with laughter.

"Oh this is going to be fun."

Océane jumped out of her skin as the door opened, and almost cried out with relief as Aleish stepped through the door carrying a tray.

"I thought you might be hungry after ..." She looked up at Océane brandishing the candle stick, and then at her brother. Putting the tray carefully down on the bedside table she turned back to Laen, hands on her hips and fury in her eyes.

"Out!" She pointed at the door. Laen glared at her but to Océane's surprise he didn't argue with the delicate figure of his sister who was clearly made of sterner stuff than she appeared to be. Instead he turned to give Océane a charming smile that made her stomach clench with apprehension.

"Until the next time." He turned and left the room, shutting the door carefully behind him. She heard the promise in his voice though, and knew with complete certainty that there would be a next time.

Chapter 5

Océane dropped the candlestick and slid down the wall, gasping for breath. Her chest heaved, her lungs locked down tight as her throat closed, refusing to let any oxygen pass into her fear-frozen body. "Can't ... breathe ..." she rasped to Aleish, who rushed to the tray and poured some water into a glass. She then took a small vial from a bag slung across her chest and put a few drops in the glass. Holding it to Océane's lips she helped her to take a sip.

"It will help to calm you," she explained.

Océane sipped at the water as her chest relaxed with tiny gasps and released the cage around her lungs until her breathing returned to normal. Aleish reached down and got her to her feet, slipping one arm around her waist and helping her over to a small table and chairs which sat beside the large glass doors. Once Océane was settled, she opened the doors and a cool breeze blew into the room, fluttering the voile that covered the glass and caressing Océane's overheated skin with a gentle touch.

Aleish looked down at her. She was shaking almost as much as Océane, clearly appalled by Laen's behaviour. She passed Océane the glass of water and then stood before her, as though she was not the only one who had been taken from familiar surroundings and slung down in unknown territory. She wrung her hands together, her eyes troubled and full of concern. "I am so very sorry; I have never seen my brother behave like this before. He is ... an honourable man."

Océane choked on the water and gave a bitter laugh with just a touch of hysteria. "Yeah, honourable, that's the word. Kidnapping me, beating me repeatedly over the head, oh and threatening to kill me or-or worse. He's a real gent!" She slammed the glass down on the delicate, carved wood table beside her, splashing water over the sides onto the polished surface.

Aleish shook her head and looked like she was trying not to cry. "I know I cannot defend his behaviour but ... He does have reasons to hate your kind. Good reasons."

"My kind?" Océane looked at her with suspicion as that cold, crawling feeling returned to her stomach. As much as she had wanted answers, there was a part of her that really wasn't sure she wanted to know.

"Your kind," Aleish repeated. "Humankind."

Océane swallowed, knowing that the answer to this would change everything she had believed. "Then what are you if you're not ... human?"

"We are the Fae."

Although she had pretty much come to this conclusion on her own, it was nonetheless shocking to hear it said out loud. She tried to behave normally, to hide any reaction even though there was a part of her that really wanted to succumb to a good bout of hysteria and screaming. Instead she picked up the water with a hand that shook like she had aged a century in the past few seconds and took another sip. She wondered if Aleish was doing the same as she concentrated on the contents of the bag she was carrying and started arranging small glass pots and clean cloths on the table.

"Let me look at your head please." From Aleish's tone Océane knew she was not the only one holding onto normality with her fingertips.

Océane sat at the table and Aleish tended all of her bruises carefully, working with cool, gentle hands, cleaning away any dirt and adding a soothing balm. The calming scent of herbs drifted around her, easing the tension in her shoulders and allowing her to think with a little more clarity.

"Where exactly am I?" she asked after Aleish had finished her work.

"You are in the Fae Lands, on my brother's estate, at the farthest reaches of our father's Kingdom. Please keep still for a moment." She placed her hands gently on Océane's head and stood over her with her eyes closed.

Océane frowned. It was the strangest sensation. It felt like ... she was touching her, inside her head.

Aleish smiled. "No broken bones, no internal bruising or bleeding." She carried on silently as Océane wondered at the possibility of being able to diagnose internal damage in such a way. The sensation carried on until it suddenly changed. It was no longer investigating her wounds; it was investigating ... her thoughts.

"No!" Océane slapped Aleish's hands away. Aleish gasped and stepped back.

"I ... I am so sorry, truly, that was unforgivable. It is just that my brother is so sure that you are a, well, a wicked creature, but I cannot believe him."

"So you thought you'd just take a tour of my brain and find out for yourself!" Océane glared at her, astounded that she could just help herself to her most private thoughts.

Aleish sat on the bed and looked genuinely appalled at what she'd done. "Yes." She nodded and spread her hands out in her lap. "It was not my intention but ... your thoughts are so open and I just thought I would take a look. I thought you would not know."

"And? What was your conclusion?"

"That I am right, and my brother is wrong."

Océane sighed. Well maybe it had been worth the intrusion. "And you'll tell him that?"

"Yes, of course."

"And then you'll take me home?"

Aleish got up, not meeting her eyes, and picked up the tray of food she had brought. "Here, you must be famished, please eat something. We will go and sit out on the terrace and get some air."

"You didn't answer my question."

"I know. I ... I do not think I will be able to convince him. I will try, I promise. I will do everything in my power but my brother is a stubborn man and his hatred of humankind is deeply ingrained. It is no easy thing you ask, but then you know that, you know why he hates you so much."

"What?" Océane exclaimed. "I don't know any such thing!"

Aleish frowned, the gesture wrinkling her delicate nose. "But you wrote about it in your book, he showed me. In the first chapter you tell about why the gates between worlds were closed, and how our father betrayed our mother with a human woman."

Océane stared at her in astonishment. "What are you talking about? I just made that up ... I made it up! It's just a story, are you telling me it's actually true?"

She nodded. "It's true."

Océane gasped. "Shit. This is like something out of a film; I keep thinking I'm going to wake up."

"It is no dream."

"No, it's a fucking nightmare!" She saw Aleish flinch at the obscenity and sighed. "Sorry, I'm a little upset." She was quite impressed that she'd said that with no trace of sarcasm but Aleish smiled all the same.

"Just a little?"

Océane huffed and rolled her eyes. "No, actually. Actually I'm a lot upset and I'm thinking seriously about having a nervous breakdown, if I can just summon the energy." She leaned her head in her hands, elbows on the table. Her head felt much better since Aleish's care but she was still exhausted.

Aleish had put the tray down again and come to sit beside her. She leaned over, placing her hand on her arm. "If you want my brother to believe you, you are going to have to help me convince him, and to do that you need to be in control. You have to stay calm and reason with him. He is by no means stupid, far from it, but he is very stubborn; you will have to use your wits, and your charm."

Océane snorted. "My what?"

Aleish smiled and got up, taking the tray of food out through the glass doors onto a stone terrace. "Your charm," she said over her shoulder.

Océane stepped out and was momentarily speechless at the view laid out in front of her. "I don't have any charm," she muttered as she watched a vast red sun drowning under the edge of a molten landscape. Every curve of the valley had been painted in shades of gold and copper and bronze, as though the whole scene had been eternally preserved with precious metals.

Aleish chuckled and gestured for Océane to sit down at the table where she had placed the tray. "Of course you do, you just need to find it. Now please have something to eat."

Océane sat, feeling more miserable than she ever had in her life despite the glorious vista before her and thought that she would never be able to eat. The smallest morsel of food would likely stick in her throat and choke her to death and maybe that would be for the best. Then she looked at the tray and her stomach made an audible complaint. She smiled ruefully at Aleish.

"Well, maybe I could eat something."

There were wonderful moist sandwiches made with a dusty black bread which looked odd but tasted divine. To her relief the filling was nothing more bizarre than chicken salad with some kind of mayonnaise and herbs, and then to follow, a bowl of fruits, none of which she could name but all were utterly delicious. She watched curiously as Aleish bit into a large black apple, the red juices staining her fingers but Aleish warned her away.

"I think you would not like the side effects," she said with a smile. "Some things that are quite harmless for us are not tolerated by your kind. The reverse is equally true."

Océane shrugged and had no problem with clearing the other delicacies on offer. To her dismay she soon discovered she had devoured the entire tray and far from choking to death, she had swallowed every bite with relish.

Chapter 6

"Feeling better?" Aleish looked at her, eyes twinkling with amusement.

Océane nodded, her hands resting on her full stomach as Aleish wiped the sticky residue of what had apparently been an Ebony apple from her own fingers. "Much."

Aleish smiled and it was a good smile, genuine, at least Océane wanted to believe it was. She realised that for all she knew Aleish could be working with her brother, doing some sick version of the good cop-bad cop routine. Though to what end she could only guess.

"You still have not given me your name," Aleish said.

"You never asked," Océane replied with a little acid in her tone, which she instantly regretted. She didn't really believe Aleish was a bad person, or perhaps she couldn't believe it anyway; Aleish was her only ally at present. She needed the possibility of someone being her friend, and after all it wasn't Aleish who had abducted her; she had been nothing but kind, and was probably her best and only means of escaping. She sighed and tried to make her mouth sit in some estimation of a smile. "My name is Océane."

Aleish's eyes widened. "Oh, that is quite lovely, it suits you."

Océane snorted. "It does not! Océane should be a cool blonde with blue eyes and a turned up nose ... More like you for instance. I don't know if you've noticed, but I'm neither blond nor blue eyed."

Aleish laughed and the sound rang out across the valley, echoing among the hills so that it sounded as if the trees were laughing softly with her. "Océane, you are far more than that, you just cannot see it at present, but I think you will."

Océane frowned, not liking the tone of the conversation, she hated talking about herself. She knew she wasn't bad looking but looks meant nothing. In fact they tended to bring you attention, attention which she neither wanted nor needed. That kind of attention had brought her trouble in the past, the kind that made her shut herself away in her flat and daydream about Fae Princes rather than join the real world. With a shudder that made her skin feel damp and defiled she remembered an old brown car belonging to one of the men who worked in the orphanage she had grown up in. It smelled of stale cigarette smoke and the little green tree hanging from the rear view mirror endeavoured to smother it, perfuming the air with pungent chemicals masquerading as the fresh scent of a pine forest. Even today the smell made her heart thud and her skin crawl like the hand she had found on her knee, ostensibly placed to comfort but lingering long enough to dispel any hopeless notions of security and trust. Coarse grey hairs had peppered those wide knuckles and the soft, white skin patterned with pale brown spots. She had felt as though those faded brown freckles had infected her and marred her own skin as she had seen them again every time she looked in the old foxed mirror in her room to confront the hollow-eyed girl reflected back at her. Her best friend, street savvy Carla, with her quick, bright gaze and her sharp tongue had saved her from disaster then and ever since. She forced the soiled memory from her mind, keeping the comforting image of her blue-eyed saviour and only friend in that awful place behind her eyes instead. Drawing courage from the familiar image she changed the subject.

"Tell me about your brother," she demanded, her eyes fixed on her hostess.

The smile died on Aleish's lips and her expression became wary. "What do you want to know? After all, he says you have written it all down."

Océane frowned and bit her lip, her finger tracing the path of a delicate design of cobalt blue peacocks, their tail feathers interlocking all around the plate her sandwich had been on. It reminded her of a Russian design she had seen in the museum. "Has he read it all?" she asked, trying to sound nonchalant under Aleish's sharp gaze.

"No," she said. "Not yet."

Océane sighed inwardly. That was something. "And you?" She watched as Aleish shook her head, making the delicate silver earrings hanging from her earlobes dance at her neck.

"Just the first chapter."

She paused, wondering how on earth she had managed to write something so fantastical and have it come true. "So your step-mother," she asked, curiosity burning. "Is she the wicked bitch I wrote about in my story?"

Aleish's eyes flicked to the door as though she was afraid someone was listening and took a breath before nodding.

Océane frowned. If that was true, then ... "Did she treat Laen as badly as I wrote, when he was a child and ... And what of your father? I mean ..." She paused as she considered the story in her book. "Oh, Aleish, the terrible things I wrote." She blanched as she remembered just how cruel he had been and sat forward, whispering herself now. "Did he really beat him and do the dreadful things I described?"

Aleish looked out at the last rays of sunlight that sank behind the tree line. The warm glow cast by the setting sun did nothing to soften the shadow of long borne sorrow etched on her face. "I know not what you wrote, Océane, but I do not believe you could capture with pen and ink the pain they both caused him."

"Oh." Océane sat in stunned silence as the appalling things she had written about returned to her mind. Just writing about them had made her weep for days but to actually live through it as a child, it was unthinkable. The beatings had been cruel enough, so cruel that she hadn't wanted to write them ... only her fingers would not stop hitting the keys as the story poured forth. The aching loneliness, though, that had been the most devastating. Her own childhood had been grim enough but if what she had put in the story was true...

"Mother was pregnant with me when Seline arrived." Océane looked up, her thoughts dragged back to the present as Aleish's soft voice took her attention, her words laden with sadness. "She died a few weeks after I was born, so I have no memory of her but Laen adored her. He believes ... He believes Seline murdered her."

Her heart became heavy in her chest at the expression on Aleish's face. "Oh my God, Aleish. That's appalling, I'm so sorry. Truly."

Aleish smiled, though the pain was still clear in her eyes. "It was a very long time ago now, and in truth it is only a small part of the story, but perhaps you can begin to understand why Laen feels the way he does. His world was torn apart by a human woman and now for some reason the gates between the worlds are beginning to show signs of weakness, and your pollution, your diseases are seeping through. Our only experience of the human race has been one of violence and greed and now your world has become so toxic that it is poisoning our own. It is affecting our lands, our crops ... our people. The Fae are dying, Océane. We are not immortal as a race but we have very long lives, yet now for the first time we are dying from disease. This is something we have never seen before." She paused, her lovely long fingers placed on her lap. There was a gold band on her finger, and Océane assumed the Fae must have the same tradition of ring giving for a marriage. Now those elegant fingers turned the ring around and around, her eyes focused on it, her voice heavy with regret. "Our kind has never before been sick like this and ... for a long time now we have had difficulty having children. Our lands used to ring with the sound of children's laughter and now ... Now they are so few." Her voice broke and Océane could see tears sparkling in her eyes as she stared at her, open-mouthed with shock. There was something in the way she said it that spoke of a desperate need and somehow Océane knew that she was longing for her own child.

"Truly?" she whispered. "This is our fault, you're sure?"

Aleish blinked away her tears and nodded as she began gathering the plates and bowls together on the tray. "There is no doubt of that. Our healers can do nothing, our father the King is powerless to fight disease and the people grow more and more angry. I have heard rumours now from the artisans who trade with the Light Fae that over the border even the land itself is sickening. If things do not change, the Fae Lands will die and we will die with it."

Océane reached forward and put her hand out, covering Aleish's. "I had no idea of the suffering we were causing and I honestly don't believe mankind has even the slightest idea of your existence, let alone the affect we are having on your world." Océane squeezed her hand, willing her to understand what she was saying. "You have to believe me."

Aleish looked back at her, the words *compassion, sorrow* and *guilt* flickering briefly under her skin. "Perhaps I do but I'm afraid it is not me you need to convince, Océane."

She held onto Aleish's hand tighter. "Do you really think he would kill me?" she asked, hearing the fear in her own voice.

Aleish hesitated, seemingly unwilling to answer the question. "I have never known my brother to be anything but kind and gentle to those he cares about and those over whom he rules. He has never raised his hand or even his voice to a woman in our world and if you had asked me before this day I would say that he never would. It is true, he is a warrior, and he is not afraid to take a life in defence of our kingdom or for what he believes to be right. He would have no problem with executing a traitor, but I have never, ever known him be in any way violent towards a woman. His behaviour to you ... disturbs me. His hatred for humankind is clouding his judgement and he sees you as a part of everything he despises. I do not believe he sees you as a person at all, Océane, but as some creature without thought or feeling. So the honest answer is, I would hope not but I think you must take great care. We have to find a way to make him see you as an individual, as a woman, and not just as part of a race responsible for all of our problems."

"No pressure then?" Océane smiled but it was half-hearted to say the least.

Aleish sighed, obviously finding no humour in her words, and gestured to a door opposite the bed. "I ordered a hot bath to be drawn for you, through there. You'll find everything you need."

"Thank you," Océane said with real gratitude. The idea of soaking her aching limbs in a bath was as close to heaven as she felt likely to get any time soon.

"I will have some clothes brought to you as well," Aleish added with a sniff of disapproval. "It's about time we got you out of those filthy ... garments." She eyed

Océane's outfit with obvious distaste, and Océane in turn regarded her long, elegant gown with equal horror. Bloody hell but these people had fancy tastes, what on earth was wrong with jeans and a sweat shirt? Océane looked fondly down at her red Doc Martins. Some people just had no taste. All those silks and velvets were all well and good for a party but for everyday ... No way.

"I could do with some clean things, if that's OK," she agreed with a cautious nod, "but nothing fancy please, some trousers and a shirt maybe?"

Aleish looked scandalised. "Women do not wear trousers!"

Oh crap it was worse than she had feared. "Why ever not?" Océane demanded as she crossed her arms with an indignant expression.

Aleish returned a pained glance at the offending items. "Who wants to look like a man?" she asked, and headed for the door bearing her tray.

"What? Trousers don't make you look like a man!"

Aleish turned and looked her up and down with raised eyebrows. "Oh really?"

Océane flushed and caught a glimpse of her dishevelled appearance in the glass doors. "OK, well I admit I'm not looking my best but ..." She turned back to see Aleish heading out of the bedroom door. "Aleish, just nothing frilly ... OK?" Océane yelled as she shut the door behind her.

"Bugger." As if things weren't bad enough, now she was going to have to wear a bloody dress as well. She sank down on the bed feeling exhaustion pull at her bones. Her head was full of questions that she needed to answer and her mind span with the implications of everything she had just discovered; there really was another race of people, another world within the world and it was extraordinary and terrifying and ... not as dreadfully surprising as she felt it ought to be. She considered the endless news reports and documentaries about global warming, wars and disasters and contrasted it to the little she had seen of this world so far. If the human race were really responsible not only for destroying their own world but the Fae's too, well it was little wonder that they were hated.

She thought about what Aleish had told her of Laen, of what he had suffered as a child, that he was a good man and he was just protecting his people. Then she remembered what it had felt like to be trapped alone in a room with him. She shuddered and prayed she wouldn't have to repeat the experience. Aleish would talk to him, she told herself. She would make him see that she could not be held responsible for the sins of a whole race. *But what about the book* ... The question circled with no easy answer to which she could cling.

Her head had always been filled with daydreams and nightmares, Fairy stories of love and deceit, of magical wars and battles for power, and Kings that fought and died with fire as the land burned around them. She had long since accepted that her imagination was vast and fantastical. It was a defence mechanism against the real world and a childhood that had been bleak and lonely. It was easier to get through the day if it was filled with handsome Princes and spent in a place where anything was possible. She would just have to make Laen see the truth. She had made it up; she would make him believe it.

Océane reached down and undid the laces on her boots, sighing as she let them fall to the floor with a heavy thud. She headed for the bathroom, padding across the polished wood floor in her socked feet. Just as Aleish had said, a steamy hot bath full of bubbles awaited her. As she stepped into the room she was enveloped in the damp scented air, heavy with lavender and something else exotic and beyond identifying. She slung her clothes down with as much care as Aleish would have given them and sank with a groan into the hot water as the grime and the stresses of the day began to fall away. Suddenly things did not seem quite so bleak and she toyed with the idea that there was magic in the water, as she had surely never been in so much danger before in her life. Yet as she reflected she found that today had been one of the most terrifying but also the most interesting of her entire life. She wondered how on earth she was going to convince Laen of her innocence. She would need to think of something and fast or her continuing existence was likely to become the only thing she could no longer believe in.

Chapter 7

Océane regarded the dress laid out on the bed with utter disgust. To be fair, it was simply cut with no frills or bows, so it could have been worse ... but not much.

"It's pink."

"It is dusty rose," Aleish corrected with a haughty sniff.

"No." Océane shook her head slowly, quite unable to tear her eyes from the horror on the bed. "It's pink!" The words were spoken with as much disdain as she could manage and she still didn't think it conveyed just how much she hated it. Though judging from Aleish's expression she'd done pretty well.

Aleish raised her eyebrows to the heavens before heading for the door. "Well it's all I have in your size at the moment. You are much ... curvier than me," she said, shaking her head at Océane in exasperation as she went out.

Océane stood in her new underwear, which thankfully had been simple, white, and fitted perfectly. She glared at the dress as though it had personally insulted her. Moments later the door opened again and she turned, hands on hips. "I'm not wearing it and that's final!"

To her dismay she discovered it was not Aleish who stood in front of her but Laen. His huge presence loomed in the doorway as he stopped dead in his tracks. He was wearing what appeared to be his usual attire of black leather trousers and a simple white linen shirt momentarily combined with a slightly stunned expression. It didn't last, however, and was quickly replaced with an arrogant smile.

"As you wish," he said with a sneer.

Océane shrieked and snatched the dress up off the bed. It may have been pink but it was better than standing in front of a mad man in her birthday suit. "Don't you knock before you enter a woman's bedroom, you pervert!" she yelled, trying to ensure she was covered by the slippery pink silk and failing miserably as it slid between her fingers.

"Not when that woman is my prisoner and is afforded no such courtesy." His voice was harsh and it sent fear prickling over her skin. "Now get dressed, and fast. I wish to speak to you." He strode over and sat down in the chair by the French doors. Océane moved as he walked past her, turning in a circle, trying desperately to keep covered.

"Get out of my room!" she demanded, refusing to be bullied by the Neanderthal sitting in the fine oak chair which had creaked alarmingly as he sat down. She hoped it broke under him.

Laen simply reclined with a bored expression and inspected his fingernails on a hand that looked like it could bend steel. "The last time I checked, this was my room, my home, my land. Everything here is my property ... including you, so I will do as I please."

"Bastard!" she spat, fury and indignation pushing her temper past what was prudent in the circumstances.

He snorted, giving her an amused look from those disturbing black eyes. "Much as my step-mother may wish that was the case, my parentage has never been in question. If however you mean that I am a callous, cold-hearted brute ... then yes, quite so."

"I am not getting dressed in front of you," Océane said, her voice trembling with rage, "so at least have the decency to turn around for a moment."

She thought perhaps there was a flicker of surprise in his eyes but she couldn't be sure and he continued to stare unblinkingly back at her. "I'm afraid I have no *decency* where you are concerned, and frankly I am amazed you know the meaning of the word."

Fear coiled in her belly, cold and heavy as she tried to hold his gaze, and then she remembered what Aleish had told her. He was a good man at heart. "Laen, please ..." she pleaded.

He stood up abruptly, rigid with anger. "You dare to use my name?" he said in disgust. "It is Prince Laen to you, or your Highness, and you have the nerve to pretend you find my manners offensive? Impudent creature!" He stalked towards her and grabbed hold of her chin, forcing her to look up at him. Océane felt her heart stutter with fear at the anger in his eyes. "You have five minutes to get dressed and then my guards will come and fetch you. Do not keep me waiting or they will drag you through the castle in whatever state they find you." She saw the words *dread, horror* and *fear* curl up around his jaw and over his eyebrow before he let her go and he left the room, slamming the door behind him.

Océane's knees gave out and she sank to the floor, trembling and clutching the stupid dress as her heart threatened to break her ribs it was beating so fiercely. With trembling hands she shook it out and dragged it over her head. She had no doubt whatsoever that he had meant every word about the guards taking her whether she was dressed or not. Hauling herself back onto the bed she looked at the dainty, slipper-like shoes Aleish had provided which perfectly matched the colour of the blasted dress.

With a defiant smile she grabbed her red DM's and put them on instead.

Right on cue, the guards burst into the room and took an arm each, practically lifting her off the floor and ushering her through the corridors until she was standing, somewhat breathless, in a large room furnished floor to ceiling with bookshelves. She couldn't help but stare in wonder at literally thousands of beautifully leather bound volumes in front of her. Oh, but if she could only be granted a few hours to look at the skillful bindings, let alone read the actual books themselves. She didn't have time to consider the futility of her day dream however as Laen appeared, and dismissed the guards with a nod of his head.

The guards bowed and left the room.

***

Laen looked at her dispassionately. She seemed very small standing in the grand library and yet she stood straight, staring at him with fury burning in her eyes. He looked closely at those eyes now and determined that they were not actually brown at all. They were more a deep mahogany with small flecks of copper, like chocolate dusted with cinnamon. She also looked very different in the clothes that his sister had provided with her thick black hair now loose and falling over her shoulders. He could smell the scent of the shampoo she had used, the lingering fragrance of the bath oils his sister had no doubt provided for her curling around him with beguiling invitation. He recalled the way she looked standing in her bedroom in just her underwear. The shock of it had driven the words clean from his head and it had taken some time for him to gather his wits and return to the brutal demeanour he had deemed necessary.

Even now he found the sight of her anger something to admire. She would not let him know how afraid she was even though he knew she must be terrified. For a moment his resolve wavered as he considered just how afraid she must be, and then he remembered the state of his world, the plight that was befalling his people, the sorrow in his sister's eyes because she could not conceive a child. No. She had answers and he had to have them.

He stepped closer and her chin went up, the lovely chocolate-coloured eyes fearful and defiant. The word beautiful flitted nervously into his brain before being squashed with an iron resolve. His step-mother's beauty had brought disaster to his family; there was no way he would be seduced by a treacherous human woman. His gaze roamed over her until he came upon the toes of her hideous boots peeping out defiantly from under the soft folds of the dress. His lips twitched despite himself but it was a momentary reprieve.

He held her book out in his large hand before throwing it carelessly down on his desk. He heard her gasp and saw her fists clench with rage. Good, he wanted her to be angry. It was in anger that she would reveal her true nature.

"Where is the rest of it?"

He watched as Océane tore her eyes from her precious book to glare at him. "What do you mean? That's all there is."

"Liar!" he snarled, snatching up the board she had been working on at the museum. There was a half-finished painting of the dagger on it and a chapter heading: The Dark Prince is Lost.

"What is the meaning of this?" he demanded, his voice low and menacing. He watched her face fall as she saw that he had taken the illustration she had been working on at the museum as well as the book.

"It's just a story," she said, looking up at him with those big eyes and holding her hands out helplessly. "I had no idea it was your story." Her voice was pleading and to his disgust he found a part of him wanted to believe her. "I ... I thought I was making it up, honestly."

"What do you know of honesty?" He sneered. "Very well, and supposing I pretend to believe this ... preposterous idea, tell me, what happens next?"

He watched the alarm on her face and knew she was hiding something, that she knew something. Before she had time to come up with a decent story, to tell the lies that dripped so easily off the tongues of humans, he acted. He grabbed her by the wrists and slammed her up against the wall. He was so close; he knew she would feel his breath on her face, and he wondered if it were possible for her to actually die of fear as her heart surely could not survive at the rate it was beating against his chest.

"I can see your mind turn, trying to come up with a lie," he whispered against her ear. "Please do not bother. I will get to the truth, sooner or later, and believe me when I say you will not like my methods of reaching it." He deliberately looked her over, his eyes lingering on the low neck line of her dress, knowing full well what he was implying and despising himself for it. And yet he couldn't stop his gaze from raking over her. He looked back at the terror in her eyes and had to remind himself over and again of everything he was protecting. It was so much harder than he would have believed not to touch her with more gentleness than he was doing now. He wondered what it would be like for her to look at him with something other than fear and hatred.

Before he had time to question either his thoughts or his actions, there was a commotion outside the door of the library and raised voices. The door swung open and Laen cursed as the man who entered quickly took in the scene in front of him and the unguarded look in Laen's eyes.

A delighted smile played over the curve of the intruder's mouth. "Oh, my dear fellow, do forgive me the interruption. The guards told me you were interrogating a prisoner, but I see they were quite mistaken."

Laen dropped Océane as though she had burned him, and quickly arranged his face into a more suitable expression. "The guards were perfectly correct, Corin," he growled, glaring at Océane with hatred.

Corin scrutinised him, his interest piqued. "Well nonetheless, please do not forget your manners. Won't you introduce me to your charming captive?" He turned to give Océane the benefit of a devastating smile.

Laen's furious glare drifted from Océane and back to Corin, scowling harder as he saw the way his friend's warm gaze lingered on her and the returning gleam in Océane's eyes. He cursed with fury when he saw the realisation dawn on her face. She had finally found a powerful ally.

Chapter 8

The last thing that Laen had wanted, or expected, was the arrival of his oldest and closest friend, Corin. He was Crown Prince of Alfheim, the Elvish Lands, whose boundaries lay beside his own estate to the south. Corin's opinions on the human race differed greatly from his own and had been a constant source of friction between the two of them for as long as he could remember. The last Laen had heard of him, he had been up to his usual tricks in the human world after a run in with some witch's powerful boyfriend. That was also quite normal; Corin would always follow a petticoat into trouble. The greater the danger the more he wanted to play with the fire.

"Stay out of this, Corin."

Corin laughed, mischief dancing in his eyes. "Oh no, I wouldn't miss this for the world. Please do continue with your interrogation."

Laen watched Océane look from him to Corin as she became aware that there was a great deal of tension in the room and that, somehow, she was the root of it. The new arrival was very different from Laen, who towered well over six feet and was heavily made, like a body builder. Corin was a little smaller in comparison and more athletically built. He moved with a fluid grace, rather like a dancer. His hair was also long like Laen's but a dark chocolate brown and pulled back from his face with a series of intricate braids woven through with gold thread. The contrast between them was quite something, Laen's skin glowing paler still against Corin's warm honey tone, his white blond hair startling against the dark of his friend. It was Corin's eyes that demanded attention though and Laen cursed that he had chosen today of all days to turn up unannounced as he watched Océane's gaze fix on his friend and his golden eyes.

Anger flared in his blood and he turned back to the argument that was becoming ever fiercer between them whenever he brought it up. "You think this a joke do you? You think I do not know of your constant trips through the gates. Those gates are supposed to be closed between the worlds but you are as bad as the Light Fae! You are weak. You are seduced into wanting what is on offer on the other side, and in doing so you put all of us in danger. You think I have not heard tell of your most recent plot?"

Corin scowled, and the look he gave him made it clear that Laen's bulk was not something he found the slightest bit intimidating, and equally Laen did not underestimate his friend. He may be taller and broader than Corin, but he wasn't about to get into a fight with him if he could help it.

"We must make alliances with the human world, Laen. It is our only chance of survival."

Laen snorted in disgust at the familiar response and pointed at Océane. "Oh yes, to taint our own blood with that of a race of thieves and murderers, that is such a wonderful idea."

There was a flash of anger in the gold as Corin turned on him. "You have no idea of what you speak, you are so wrapped up in hatred that it blinds you to the truth ... The truth which appears to be right under your nose, I might add." He moved between Laen, blocking his view of Océane, who watched the exchange with rapt attention. "You really think this child is at the root of all the evil in the world?" His words were soft but there was no mistaking the thread of anger beneath them. "Wake up, you fool, before you do something you live to regret."

"You don't know what she has done!" Laen's fists clenched with anger and he stepped closer. But Corin just smiled at him, apparently unperturbed.

"Well then, Laen, why not behave as a host is supposed to when a guest arrives, and offer me some refreshment and a bed for the night. Then perhaps we can discuss matters in a civilized manner." The smile hardened into something rather more fierce. "Or have you lost all sense of honour?"

Laen's frown deepened. "Careful, old friend, before you overstep the mark. Of course you are welcome to stay, and be sure we will discuss this further in private." The warning in his voice was unmistakable but to his chagrin Corin ignored it just as he always did.

"Oh, but a meal would be so much more entertaining if your guest could accompany us."

Laen gritted his teeth as Corin turned to Océane and gave her his most charming smile.

"She is not a guest, she is a prisoner," Laen repeated, biting out the words and feeling increasingly like he wanted to beat his best friend's head against the wall.

"Yes, yes but nonetheless ..."

"No!" Laen shouted, his mind completely made up on this one. He knew Corin only too well, knew just how easily he could beguile a woman until she was so desperate for him she couldn't see straight. He would not let him loose on Océane or all hope of finding the truth would be lost. "I could not stomach a whole evening of watching you flirt with her, you might even try to persuade her to be the next Queen of Alfheim. I heard your last attempt did not turn out so well?" Laen sneered, well aware that he was pushing things past what was sensible with Corin but quite unable to stop himself.

"Laen ..." There was a warning note in his voice, but Laen continued.

"You think I am going to sit and dine while you agree with her about what a cold-hearted brute I am, when you have just tried to abduct a human woman yourself?"

To his satisfaction Océane looked at Corin sharply but he merely shrugged, looking uneasy. "It is not quite as he paints it, my dear," he said, scowling at Laen.

"Oh yes." Laen gave a derisive smile. "She only accepted two gifts before her lover discovered your plot and it takes three before you have them under your control. That is the truth of it, is it not, Corin?"

There was a prickle of power against Laen's skin as magic filled the room and he knew Corin was on the edge of what he would take. "There was far more to it than you know and that is entirely beside the point! I merely wanted to induce her to pay a visit to my lands in the hope it may be more appealing to her than the mess she was in at that point. She needed help and I need a wife. I had no intention of keeping her against her will," Corin said, his voice still calm but the expression in his eyes one of utter fury.

Shaking his head with disgust Laen pressed home his point. "The fact remains, Corin, that you tried to trick her into accompanying you. You could have just asked ... could you not?"

Corin's expression became cold and detached. "I am not about to discuss this with you now. I meant the girl no harm as you are well aware."

The two men stood glaring at each other and Laen gritted his teeth as the prickling sensation in the room increased. Corin was seriously angry and his magic radiated from him as though that anger had a presence of its own.

He watched Océane rub at her arms and frown, not understanding where the sensation had come from. She had watched the conversation between them with fascination and he had no doubt that after hearing Corin speak she would try to ingratiate herself to him. He doubted she would trust Corin any more than she trusted him, but she would know he was her best bet for getting away from here. She chose her target well before she struck and Laen could only admire her nerve. "At least he didn't feel the need to hit her over the head ... Your Highness," she said with a sly smile.

Corin looked at her utterly aghast. "He hit you?"

"Oh yes," she said, biting her lip with an anxious expression and deliberately turning big, innocent eyes on him. "Twice!"

Corin turned on him in fury and the sting against his flesh prickled with more heat. "Gods, Laen! What were you thinking? How could you?"

Laen cursed inwardly, knowing full well that there was little he could say to Corin to justify his actions. He hadn't been able to justify it to himself and he knew exactly what Corin would think of him. He gave Océane a cold, measuring look, well aware she was trying to play both of them against each other. "I had been dispatched to retrieve the dagger the humans discovered. She was standing right beside the accursed thing. I had just killed a guard with no witnesses and did not want her screaming the place down and bringing more, which is exactly what she was going to do."

"So you hit her?" The look of disgust on his friend's face made his guilt resurface and settle over him in heavy swathes. It was done now though, and for a good cause, he reminded himself once more. "I rendered her unconscious, yes. It was the most expedient way of silencing her, though now I admit, I wish I had just slit her throat and had done with it. I may yet decide it is my best course of action," he said, his guilt and anger making him lash out as it always did. He gave Océane a look that made her gasp and take a step back.

Corin cursed before taking Océane by the arm and steering her behind him. "That is quite enough, Laen. I do not pretend to understand what is going through your mind. I would never have thought to hear you treat a woman so ... prisoner or not. I admit I am shocked to my bones."

The fury and injustice of being made to look like a barbarian when all he wanted was to protect his people burned with white heat in Laen's blood and he returned a cruel smile. "Well then, perhaps you do not know me as well as you think!"

Laen felt a stab of regret for the doubt he had put in Corin's mind as his friend regarded him with a troubled countenance. "Perhaps I do not," Corin said, his voice low and uneasy. "Either way, I think this young lady has had enough of your company for one day."

"Fine," Laen agreed, wanting nothing more than to get the blasted woman out of his sight. "I will call the guards and we can talk in peace."

"That will not be necessary," Corin said, offering Océane his arm, and she took it with alacrity.

"Corin, let the guards take her." Laen's voice held a tone that Corin could not possibly mistake, but he gave Laen a cool smile.

"Please do not tell me you believe me incapable of escorting her to her rooms," Corin snapped. "You think she would overpower me perhaps?"

"I think you are incapable of escorting her without flirting and trying to make love to her, yes!" he roared.

Corin chuckled wickedly. "And this bothers you why ... exactly?"

"Because she is a prisoner, damn you!" Laen raged.

"Ah, yes," Corin said, looking at Océane with amusement in his eyes. "I'll bear that in mind," he added and escorted her from the room.

Chapter 9

Corin led Océane through the door and she held her breath, wondering frantically if she had just leapt from a house fire into a volcanic inferno. There was something about this man that invited her confidence in him but she had long since learned not to take things at face value, no matter how beautiful that face may be. This particular one defied any description she felt equal to giving, though she figured any definition of Adonis would probably fit the bill. She looked up as she felt those strange golden eyes on her like a heavy weight.

"That was very well played, my dear," he said with approval. He touched the hand he had placed firmly on his beautifully tailored sleeve with a reassuring gesture, leaving his own hand resting lightly on hers.

"Played?" she asked, glancing at his touch, a nervous feeling growing in the pit of her stomach as he began to lead her back down the gloomy corridor. She risked a glance back at the library door and wondered if Laen's open hostility wasn't easier to deal with, at least she knew where she stood.

"Don't fret so. You are quite safe I assure you."

She looked up at him in surprise and he gave her a warm smile. She wondered if all Fae men looked like the two she'd just met. This one could devastate the human female population single-handedly with a smile like that. "And yes, my dear," he continued. "Well played, you saw that I was useful to you and you backed me up. That is a very Fae way of doing things if I may say so. You'll fit in very well here."

She tore her gaze away from eyes that seemed hypnotic, and she shook her head. "Yes, well that's very kind of you but I'm getting out of here as soon as I can."

They turned the corner and he led her further into the castle along yet more dark passages that were occasionally pierced by narrow windows looking out onto a menacing grey sky. After yesterday's oppressive heat it was quite a contrast. "Oh yes, yes. Of course you are," he agreed before stopping in his tracks. "I am so sorry, my dear, Laen's manners really are appalling, I'm afraid I don't even know your name."

"I'm Océane," she replied.

A slow smile played across his mouth and he gave her an openly admiring look. "Oh yes, that suits you very well," he murmured.

Océane mentally rolled her eyes. "No, it really doesn't."

"Oh, really?" He quirked an eyebrow at her in amusement. "As you wish." They walked on again and he gave a heavy sigh. "Now as for getting you out of here, I fear that is going to take a little thinking about."

Now it was Océane's turn to stop dead. She looked searchingly into his eyes, trying to see if he was sincere or not. "You'd help me get out of here?" she asked, wondering if he was just thinking of grasping the opportunity to take her for himself or if he really wanted to help her.

The golden eyes looked back at her, utterly sincere and sparkling with amusement. "Help a damsel in distress? My dear, that is practically my *raison d'être*." He smiled at her before his face grew serious. "Besides, there is far more at stake here than just your pretty neck, I fear."

She began to relax a little, somehow reassured of his good nature despite her natural cynicism. "What do you mean, what else is at stake?"

He frowned as he led them down a long corridor lit with candle-filled sconces, the flickering light painting the walkway with eerie shadows, making the castle even more disturbing than it had been yesterday. The light danced over the thick tapestries and painted movement onto the portraits of terrifying-looking ancestors, giving their dangerous black eyes a disquieting lifelike quality and making Océane feel like she was being judged and found wanting. "The problem is this, you see, the Light Fae and the Elves have come to an agreement; Laen is quite correct of course, we have been using the gates for centuries, though only on a small scale. I myself am a regular visitor to your world. The Light Fae, I suspect, have been using them far more than they would like anyone to know but either way, we have agreed that they should be officially reopened and that there should be at least some selective trade between the worlds."

"Just trade?" she demanded.

Corin gave her an enquiring look, obviously noting the sarcasm in her voice. "Nothing gets past you does it, my dear? No, not just trade. We intend to find suitable ... companions to marry into our families. We hope that your bloodline will strengthen our own and give our children some immunity over the diseases that have come to plague us. The nobility will be the first to do this, to set an example to the people. It is this decision of course that has moved Laen to take such extreme actions as abducting you. I'm afraid to say that it is not an entirely popular decision. There are many who would share Laen's view of the world and believe it to be a terrible thing, to weaken our pure blood with other races."

"That's not exactly a new theme in our world either," Océane said in disgust.

"Quite so." He sighed and Océane started in alarm as the flames in the sconces leapt higher, sending bizarre shapes sliding against the cold stone walls and her eyes darting to the darkened corners and their uncertain shadows. She looked up at Corin and had the strangest feeling that he had made the flames erupt, but then he looked at her and smiled and the feeling dispersed. She gazed at his eyes as he spoke again. "And just as wars have been fought in your world, if we cannot make Laen see the mistake he is making, it will lead to war here. There is already much unrest in the land as the people begin to fear what will become of us and demand answers that none of us have. There are some who agree with him that we should move against your kind as you appear to be the source of our troubles. Laen's father may be the King, and with a human wife beside him a war with your world is the last thing he could support, but everyone knows the army will follow where Laen leads, no matter what the King decrees."

"He could do that?" Océane asked, wondering just how his despot father would react to that eventuality.

Corin nodded and traced his fingers over the back of her hand with a lazy touch that made her shiver. She scowled up at him but he seemed oblivious. "Laen has become popular and beloved by his people, far more so than his father who is a hard and disfavoured figure for many." He paused and she looked up to see an expression of real sorrow on his face. "Laen is my oldest and dearest friend but I would not ... could not allow him to take us into what would ultimately result in a war with the human world. Alfheim would have to make a stand against him and if that happens we need not worry about the fact that our people are dying, as we should simply kill each other a great deal quicker and have done with it."

Océane gripped his arm a little harder as the implication of what she was a part of presented itself. "That's just terrible."

"Yes it is." A deep frown marred his handsome face for a moment but he seemed to shake it off and he turned to her with a smile, though his eyes were still serious. "Which is why I believe you have been sent to us." He wrapped his long fingers around her hand on his arm and gave a gentle squeeze. "You are a gift from the gods in our hour of need."

Océane looked at him in alarm. She didn't like being thought of as a gift from anybody, let alone his gods, and the idea that she alone could be responsible for averting a war was horrifying, and more pressure than she was willing to take on in the circumstances. "Now hold on a moment," she began.

He chuckled at the panic in her eyes. "Calm down, my dear, I do not mean to place the entire fate of the Fae nation on your shoulders but it is the case that you could be very useful to us whilst in the process of securing your own release." He looked down at her, golden eyes intent and so focused on her she felt like blushing. "You do wish to get out of here I take it?"

"Absolutely!" she agreed with speed and enthusiasm.

"Well then." He nodded, apparently satisfied. "We understand each other."

They had arrived at the door to Océane's room at the same time as two massive and ill-tempered looking guards who glowered at Corin with obvious dislike.

"There you see, here she is safe and sound." Corin grinned at them.

"How did you know where my room was?" she asked him, realising there was no way he could have known.

He shrugged. "It is the most secure part of the castle; it is where I would have put you, if I truly believed you were a danger. Are you a danger to me, lovely Océane?" His beautiful eyes were almost amber in the dim light and full of humour. Océane swallowed and blinked, feeling hopeless under the heat of his attention and she wondered what the hell to say. She had never been any good at flirting. He just chuckled, obviously amused by his effect on her. "Now then, are you going to invite me in?" He seemed to be challenging her as his eyes still held a naughty sparkle and Laen's words rang in her ears. She knew she shouldn't encourage him, not that he seemed to need any encouragement, but then again, she really, really wanted to get out of this place ... preferably with her head still attached to her shoulders.

"I don't imagine it's up to me," she said finally, crossing her arms and giving the guards a pointed look. "I am a prisoner after all."

Corin glanced at her guards with disdain and sighed. "My dear, you may be Laen's prisoner, but to me you are a most charming guest whom I would like to get to know a little better, however I am a gentleman after all, and I would not presume to enter your rooms without an invitation."

Océane looked at him in astonishment, wondering if his manner was just a pretty front and underneath lurked a heart as black as Laen's. He waited, watching her patiently but with the air of a man who already knew what her answer would be. Oh what the hell. "OK then, would you like to come in, er ... I don't know your name."

He tutted and shook his head. "Oh, how remiss of me, I do apologise. Laen's manners are beginning to rub off I fear. My name is Corin Albrecht, crown Prince of Alfheim, the Elvish Lands." He executed a most elegant bow and took her hand, kissing it gently. "I am honoured to make your acquaintance," he said with a smile twitching at the corners of his mouth.

"Another Prince!" Océane said. "Bloody hell, you can't shake a stick around here without hitting a Prince around the head."

Corin chuckled. "Wishful thinking on your part I'm afraid, my dear." He opened the door to her room and stood back, politely gesturing for her to enter, just as though they were going into dinner and she wasn't about to be locked up against her will. Corin followed close behind her and she couldn't help but smile as he took great delight in closing the door firmly in the faces of the two scowling guards.

Chapter 10

Océane gaped at him as his words finally registered in her brain. "Wait a minute, did you say Elvish lands ... You're an Elf?" She looked at the delicious specimen of manhood in front of her and tried to reconcile it with big pointy ears and hats with bells.

"Guilty," he said, removing his jacket, which was a deep green, beautifully tailored, and clung lovingly to his broad shoulders. He threw it down on her bed in a careless manner and undid his waistcoat, which was exquisitely embroidered with climbing ivy that seemed to coil around his chest with such enthusiasm she almost felt envious. He then proceeded to undo the top buttons of his shirt. Océane was about to protest that he had gotten entirely the wrong idea, as he seemed to be making himself far too comfortable when he sank into the nearest chair with a deep sigh of contentment.

"Oh, that's better." He smiled, stretching his long, lean legs out in front of him and bestowing her with an utterly innocent expression. Océane scowled at him. He may or may not have been on her side but she didn't trust him as far as she could throw him.

"So," she continued, keeping a sharp eye on him in case he made any sudden moves. "Either I've lost my mind or you're an Elf and Laen is a Fairy."

To her surprise, Corin howled with laughter. "Oh, my dear, please I beg you, do not use such a term in Laen's presence or you may lose your head faster than you bargain."

Océane flushed as he continued to laugh at her. "Well what is he then?" she said with a huff of annoyance.

Corin took a breath and she watched him smother his amusement and try to regain his composure. "Very well, I will explain. You are in the Fae Lands." He sat up and leaned forward a little, gesturing for her to take the chair opposite him. "Now, Fae is a term that actually covers many races, though the High Fae would have you believe it applies to them alone."

"High?" she asked, dithering beside the chair and wondering if it might be safer to stay on her feet.

"I'm getting to that. So there are the High Fae who are the Light and the Dark, then come the Elves and after them various minor races or solitary Fae, like Pixies, Brownies, Dwarves etcetera. The High Fae are the largest of the races with the most land and therefore power, followed closely by the Elves and although there are far fewer of us we are individually gifted with the most magic."

"Magic?" Océane said with a sceptical expression. She watched Corin smirk at her before he made a negligent gesture with his hand. The room, which had become steadily darker as the black clouds gathering outside smothered any trace of daylight, suddenly blazed to light as every candle in the room lit and a fire exploded in the hearth. Océane squealed with surprise and sat down heavily in the chair after all.

"Magic," Corin confirmed with a grin before carrying on where he'd left off. "The High Fae are divided into two courts; the Seelie and the Unseelie."

Océane nodded automatically as she tried to assure herself she really was awake and he had created fire with just a flick of his fingers. The part about the Seelie and Unseelie she had written about in her book, though she wasn't about to admit that to Corin just at the moment. Some things were safest kept to herself.

He looked at her curiously and she wondered if like Aleish he had some way of accessing her thoughts. The idea was not a comfortable one.

"The Seelie, or Light Fae, are lovers of all things beautiful and artistic," he continued. "Music, poetry, fine wines and cuisine. They have a most romantic nature and a tendency to over indulge on all counts. They can be great artists, lovers and generous to a fault but at their worst they are greedy and power hungry. Like the Elves they are not so very tall as the Dark Fae and are often of rather more generous proportions. They would count themselves as Faeries in the traditional sense."

He frowned at her and she felt a shiver as the strange prickling feeling she had noticed in the library touched her skin once again. "Please do not consider any of us to have anything in common with the childhood stories you may have read of pretty winged creatures who sip from acorns and spend their days dancing and painting rainbows." His voice held a note of anger and she wondered if he had come across this comparison often. "You would be foolish indeed to believe us harmless, Océane, but then I think Laen has succeeded in making that point quite admirably, has he not?"

She nodded, mute, and he sat back again, crossing one leg over the other. He frowned for a moment and rubbed a mark from his long leather boot before carrying on.

"The Dark Fae, as you have no doubt surmised, are the warriors, the protectors of the Fae Lands. They tend to be rather more serious - to the point of being morose if you ask me - and could start a fight in an empty room. They are also very intolerant. Anyone a little different from what they judge to be normal would be in for a very difficult time." His voice rang with that dark, angry tone again and she wondered if he was thinking of the way the King had treated his son. He looked up and seemed to make an effort to shake off whatever feeling had clouded his thoughts. "Having said that, they are very courageous, loyal and brave. They are also the tallest and, speaking of the men, by far the most powerfully built of the Fae. The Elves are molded on slightly ... finer lines but, rest assured, are no less proficient." He said this with a flirtatious look, and winked at Océane, which made her flush as she had just been admiring the way his shirt fitted to perfection across his broad shoulders.

"And what are the characteristics of your race?" she asked, refusing to admit she was in the slightest bit flustered.

There was a low chuckle and he leaned his head on his hand, looking at her with heavy eyes. "Well now ... We are known for our charming and flirtatious natures. We are similar to the Light Fae; pleasure-loving, but our natures are not quite as indolent. Some of us have great magical powers and we are clever with words. You would be well advised not to bargain with us.

Never, ever take a gift from our hands, no matter how trifling, without our express admission that there is no tie attached to it or as Laen has told you, you will be completely and utterly in our power ..." He paused, the golden eyes fixed on hers. "To do with as we pleased," he added in a low voice that sent shivers running down her spine. "Never trust the Fae, Océane. It was always the advice your kind told each other in the days when you were aware of our existence."

"I had no intention of it I assure you," Océane replied, tearing her eyes away from his with difficulty. She got to her feet and crossed the room to stand beside the glass doors, feeling shaken by his words and needing to put some distance between them. "So what is your plan for getting me out of here?" she demanded, trying hard to sound confident and in control even though she was very clearly neither of those things.

He reclined in the chair, stretching his legs out once more and crossing them at the ankles with a thoughtful expression. "Well, I have to confess it is rather less of a plan and more an idea of how to proceed. I need to give the whole thing much more thought, but for now I think we will let Laen believe that I have admirably lived up to my reputation and see where that leads us."

Océane frowned. "I'm sorry, I don't follow."

He studied her face for a moment, and she was on the verge of looking away when he got to his feet with elegance and walked slowly towards her, never letting his gaze fall from her face. She felt suddenly like a deer focused upon through a hunter's sights and it was a most uncomfortable, if unaccountably thrilling, experience. She became transfixed by his eyes, which were slanted and now a deep tawny gold, rather like a lion. He stopped close beside her and her mouth felt dry. She searched for something to say to break the tension but found herself at a complete loss for words as she felt his breath flutter against her skin.

Corin moved closer still, his eyes intent, and tipped up her chin with one finger. To her astonishment Océane felt herself quite unable and worse than that unwilling to protest or move away as he brushed her lips with his own. It was the barest of touches that nonetheless had her heart skipping around like a mad rabbit.

"I mean, my sweet Océane," he said with his mouth still tantalisingly close to hers, "that Laen should believe that we have been lovers."

"Oh," was as complex a reply as she felt able to muster just at the moment, though she felt sure another, more pithy comment was just around the corner if she could only focus on it for a second or two. Sadly, with Corin's golden gaze looking at her like he could eat her in one bite, the pithy comment was destined to remain a mystery.

He traced a finger over her lips and trailed it down her neck to her collar bone as goosebumps quickly followed the same path. "Oh damn Laen to Tartarus," he murmured before kissing her again, this time much more in earnest. His tongue traced her bottom lip and to her immense surprise, Océane felt herself respond. With uncharacteristic wantonness, she opened her mouth to him, her hands sliding beneath his waistcoat to find a delightful landscape of hard muscle beneath the fine material of his shirt.

Although it was not in her nature to go around kissing men she had just met, in her defence it had been a very, very long time since she had been kissed at all, and to be frank, never in her life with such skill as Corin was displaying. He pulled her a little more firmly against him with one hand at her hip, the other cupping her face, and she went willingly as her hands moved over his broad back. His tongue toyed with hers, gently at first and then with increasing demands as he pulled her closer still and just for a little while she was lost in the feel of him. It was just such a relief to be treated with a little tenderness after all the brutality she had experienced since this whole nightmare had begun.

With a last gentle kiss, Corin withdrew, though he kept her close to him in his arms. "Why is it that my moral compass decides to make an appearance at the most inopportune of moments?" he complained with a frustrated sigh.

Océane looked up at him, feeling somewhat dazed and a little disappointed. "You mean to say you really aren't going to try to ... To ..."

Corin smiled and dipped his head to kiss her neck, his warm tongue making her gasp and squirm against him.

"To make love to you?" he murmured against her skin, making her shiver all over again.

"That wasn't an invitation, by the way," she said in a rush and pushed him away from her a little. A kiss was one thing, and in all honesty she was appalled by what she'd just done, but she wasn't about to fall into bed with a man just because he'd shown her a little kindness and that was certain. She looked up at him and swallowed hard. Yes, that was absolutely certain, she told herself severely but he was looking at her with a knowing expression that made her stomach flip and she had to admit that she didn't believe a word of it either.

He let her go without demur. "Let us just say ... not at the moment." He chuckled and went to pour himself a drink only to grimace with disgust when he discovered there was only water. "For the moment we will be supremely chaste and well behaved. I will stay and keep you company for, let's see, I suppose three hours should suffice."

"Suffice for what?" she demanded, feeling perplexed.

He sighed and raised his eyebrows. "After I am gone you will undress and take yourself to bed and pretend to be asleep with the air of a woman who is well satisfied with life, are we clear?"

With a glance at the bed Océane swallowed as she began to comprehend what he meant. She felt the blush creep from her cheeks, down her neck and across her chest. "I'm not sure I know what that looks like," she admitted as the blush deepened.

Corin looked at her sharply. "What?" he demanded, obviously appalled by her admission. "Gods, woman! Are there no able-bodied men where you live?"

She snorted with amusement at the horrified expression on his face. He seemed genuinely shocked. "The guys I know are lucky if they raise a smile, let alone anything else," she said, biting back a giggle as he gaped at her and she hurried on. "Well no that's not fair, it's just that I've not had a lot of luck with men so I've kind of given up on the idea and ... And I really don't get out much." She shrugged, looking embarrassed. "When I do it's usually museums ... you know. I'm really not very good at socialising. I tend to keep to myself," she mumbled, feeling idiotic as his eyes widened further.

He shook his head in disgust. "Well, my dear, one way or another that is a situation we shall rectify, you have my word on the matter." She felt her stomach do a little back flip and crossed her arms defensively as he gave her an appraising look. "You know, Laen really isn't a bad man," he said. "In fact, despite appearances, he is a very good one. He has been like a brother to me but I'm afraid his impression of you as a race has been coloured by experiences with his father and step-mother and the few humans with whom he has come in contact. We must endeavour to make him see the error of his ways."

She huffed at him, feeling flustered and quite out of her depth. "And just how am I supposed to do that?"

"Just by being your charming self," he said with a smile, taking her hand and raising it to his lips.

"You sound like Aleish. She said I had to charm him," she grumbled.

"Ah, now Aleish is a very wise woman," he said and Océane detected a fond tone to his voice.

Océane raised her eyebrows. "Oh, are you and her ..."

"Oh, no." He shook his head with a smile. "She's married, my dear. Though I have to admit we were once ... close." She smirked at the look in his eyes, knowing exactly how close that was likely to have been if he had anything to do with it. "Unfortunately she complained that I was not serious enough, and I had to agree, so we parted company. Her new husband is much more suited to her tastes, and very worthy."

"I take it that by worthy, you mean dull," she said with a wicked glint in her eyes.

He laughed, delighted by her comment and nodded.

"Really, my dear, we shall get along splendidly. That is exactly what I meant."

He spent the following hours regaling her with amusing stories and generally charming the pants off her, which of course was what he did best. He really was the most wonderful company, and made her feel both desirable and fascinating and as though there was no place he would rather be than spending time with her. Océane reflected that although she had never been close to a man even half as gorgeous as Corin was, he wouldn't usually be her type, which to her shame was rather more along the harsh, brutish lines of Laen's physic, if not his personality.

Despite that, she had to confess that he really was the most incredibly sexy man she had ever met. The time flew by and finally he got up to leave, and kissed her hand in a very courtly manner. "I dare not get any closer or I may not be able to continue to be such a gentleman," he confided in all seriousness, though his eyes crinkled with humour.

"And that would be a bad thing?" Océane couldn't believe the words had left her mouth but she had been so thoroughly charmed, she simply couldn't think of a good reason to let him go. Spending time in his company had been the most enjoyable thing she had ever experienced and she was more than disappointed that it had come to an end.

He looked at her with such a regretful expression that she almost laughed. "For me ... No," he replied with the utmost sincerity. "It would be an exquisite way to pass the rest of the day and I wish more than anything to remain here with you. For our cause, however, I would have to admit that it would be a mistake." Océane blushed as she saw the desire in his eyes and he sighed heavily. "Understand me, my sweet Océane. Laen will accuse us of being very naughty indeed and we need to be able to take the moral high ground. I need to see his reaction, both to the fact he believes we have been intimate and to the news that we have not and then I will have a better idea of how to play him."

"What if he doesn't believe you?" Having spent some time in his company Océane was quite prepared to admit she probably wouldn't believe it either if she was in Laen's position.

He shrugged. "I will give him my word. That he knows is beyond reproach and he will have no choice but to believe me. We have known each other since we were children and he understands that if I give my word, I keep it, and if I tell him it is the truth, he will believe me."

Océane reflected that he had given his word to her that she should know what a well satisfied woman looked like, and bit her lip as the implication made her heart pick up. Corin seemed to be well aware of her train of thought as he kissed her lightly on the lips and whispered, "A promise is a promise," against her mouth with a tone that made delicious little sparks of desire light up over her skin and warm her far more thoroughly than the fire in the hearth had done.

He retrieved his jacket from the bed, shrugging it on before reaching forward and grabbing hold of the bed covers. He swept them back with one brisk movement, sending cushions flying to the floor. He caught Océane's eyes and gave a wicked chuckle before heading to the door where he paused and turned with a smile. "Until tomorrow, my dear. Now remember, I know Laen better than I know myself, and sooner or later he will come in search of me. Don't forget what I have instructed you to do and we shall see what we can make of him." He opened the door and was about to step through when he turned again and said over his shoulder, "Oh, and nice boots by the way." He winked at her and was gone.

Chapter 11

Once she was alone, Océane did as Corin had instructed. She undressed and made sure to scatter her clothes as though they had been dropped in a fit of passion. She raked her hands through her hair until the heavy waves were tangled and unruly and then set about laying herself on the bed in what looked like a state of abandon. Trying to present herself in such a manner whilst ensuring everything was covered from the neck down wasn't the easiest of things to arrange, especially as her experience of such things came mostly from television and films.

Hearing a deep voice addressing the guards outside her door, she realised her time was up and tried her best to look as though she was in a deep, contented sleep. Belatedly, she took a moment to wonder if she was doing the right thing in putting her trust in Corin and playing Laen in such a way. He had made threats of a very unpleasant nature and to allow him to view her in such a light was far from prudent. Her heart began to thud as she began to realise the implications and dangers of what she was about to do, but it was too late now. The door swung open and the game began.

She heard someone enter the room and walk over to the bed and she supposed it was Laen. Keeping her breathing deep and even, she tried to still the desire to scream and run as far from him as possible. Corin had made her believe she was in no danger and both he and Aleish had gone to great pains to explain that Laen's actions were totally out of character. Stupidly Océane had begun to come to the same conclusion as it was exactly the kind of behaviour she would have written for the hero of her story. She knew it was foolish to imagine that he had anything in common with a fictional character but there it was ... In her mind they were becoming one and the same man and she was probably not nearly as afraid as good sense should have allowed her to be.

It was still only early afternoon but whoever it was standing by her bed, they blocked the light from the glass doors and she felt a great, predatory shadow cast over her. Her lungs tightened, trying to keep the rise and fall of her chest steady while in truth she could hardly breathe at all. The room seemed to darken further as thunder rumbled overhead and the storm that had been threatening all day made itself known.

It was the hardest thing to lay there looking relaxed while he stood watching her for what seemed the longest time, though it was probably no more than a few seconds. Eventually though she heard him turn and leave the room, punctuated by the violent slamming of the bedroom door, then Laen's voice roaring at the guards in fury and instructing them to find Corin without delay.

Océane sat up in bed while thunder shook the windows and doors and hail clattered against the glass with such violence she feared it would shatter. Lightening brightened the sky beyond the battered glass, an eerie luminescent purple, the strange light casting the room with a mysterious hue. With relief she exhaled as her tension ebbed away and she began to laugh. Thunder exploded overhead again and she jumped and then laughed harder still. She wondered if she should perhaps enroll in some kind of acting class if ever she got back home as she obviously had a talent for it.

***

Laen searched every room in the castle, some of which he'd doubted he'd even been in before, looking for Corin but he seemed to have disappeared. A wise move, he reflected with a bitter taste in his mouth, as in his current mood he wanted nothing more than to choke him to death. The nerve of the man, he could scarcely believe it. Slamming the door shut on yet another empty room he wondered who he was kidding. Corin couldn't help himself, and the most irritating thing about it was that no matter how outrageously he behaved, the women seemed to love him anyway. If he were completely honest with himself at this point, Laen would have admitted that he was no better when it came to women, except his conquests tended to confine themselves to longing and tearful looks in his direction when they thought he wasn't looking, and Corin's simply adored him. He was even invited to the damned weddings when they settled down with a more sensible choice. By the fires, but it was unfair. He looked out of the window. The hail had turned to rain which fell in unrelenting torrents, slicking the castle walls until they shone and turning the paths and walkways into abrupt rivers that burst their banks and saturated the gardens around the castle. He dismissed the idea of looking outside as lightning split over his lands, the white light crazing the skies like ancient porcelain. Corin hated rain. Where ever he was to be found, it wouldn't be out there.

Laen clenched his fists as he looked at the storm

lashing at the world outside. He was well aware that he was becoming more and more bitter and alone but he didn't know how to stop it. He was consumed with a nameless anger that seemed to eat away at his insides until everything good in his life could only be viewed through a veil of cynicism. The only person besides his sister that he had ever confided in, had ever counted as a friend, was Corin. Now his absolute refusal to see the danger that the human world presented to them was pushing Laen to a point where he would have to take a stand against him for the good of his people. Fury blazed in his heart at the injustice of it. Why couldn't Corin see that a pretty face could not put to one side the retribution due for the destruction of their race?

Returning to his rooms, he found he was far too angry to concentrate on his work and spent the rest of the evening staring out of the window in a mood so black that his staff didn't dare call him to dinner as thunder rumbled the castle to its foundations. The unlucky serving girl who lost the toss tiptoed into his study and wordlessly left his meal on a tray beside him where it remained, untouched, for the rest of the night. He hardly noticed it was there.

He really couldn't fathom why he was so devilishly annoyed. So Corin had taken the wretched woman to bed, so what? If she allowed herself to be used in such a way, why should he care? It was just the kind of behaviour he would expect from a human female. He could not decide quite why he was so angry with Corin, though, as his behaviour was hardly out of character either, far from it, except he reasoned that Corin had taken advantage of his hospitality. No doubt his prisoner was now feeling safe in the knowledge that she had a champion to defend her against his brutality. Well he would show her that that was far from the case. He took a moment to wonder if he had started off on the wrong foot with Océane and if perhaps he should have acted as Corin had and seduced her, maybe then he would have found the truth and had a rather more enjoyable time in doing so. The thought did not improve his mood.

***

By the next morning Océane had decided that she had to trust Corin and believe that he really was sincere in his desire to help her. Besides she really had very little other choice, and once she had stopped worrying about whether or not this was a good idea, she felt able to relax a little. He would keep her safe from Laen and she felt sure something was being done to get her out of this weird, frightening and beautiful place.

Aleish had come to see her very early, scolding her for still being in bed despite the fact it was barely dawn. She'd brought a great pile of dresses, this time all far more suited to her tastes. She had settled on a deep green velvet, which she had to admit fitted her rather well. It was long-sleeved and simply cut, with a deep neckline slightly off the shoulder and tight at the waist. It showed off rather more cleavage than she was comfortable with but Aleish had nodded with approval and seemed to think it wouldn't hurt her cause, so Océane wasn't about to complain. It wasn't jeans and a top but it would have to do. At least it wasn't pink. She even decided that she'd go the whole hog and abandon her DM's in favour of the elegant shoes that obviously matched the dress.

Now she sat, suffering in silence as Aleish had taken it upon herself to bring her own make up to complete the ensemble.

"There," Aleish said, apparently expressing her satisfaction at a job well done.

"That's it?" Océane asked in surprise as she had expected far more than the few simple touches that had been given.

Aleish shrugged. "It is all you need." She hesitated for a moment as she began to put her belongings away before asking, "You saw Corin yesterday?" with a note of enquiry, despite the fact she must be well aware that she had.

Océane nodded, wondering if she should tell her the truth or if she should be played as Laen was. "I did, yes."

Aleish got up and smoothed out the folds of her dress. Today she was wearing a delicate pale blue that worked well against her fair skin and blonde hair. She looked elegant and ethereal and every inch a Fairy princess. "He is very charming, is he not?" she asked, sounding far too nonchalant.

"Yes, very," Océane agreed and wished she could pull off such a look, perhaps then Laen wouldn't feel so angry towards her. Aleish had the kind of fragile beauty that usually made men trip over themselves in an effort to open doors and throw their coats over puddles. She snorted at the idea of Laen acting in such a way for her. He'd probably push her in head first.

Aleish gathered her things and gave her an encouraging smile. "I had best be gone, Laen will be bound to come early he ... He was in such a frightful temper last night, I doubt he slept." She jumped as a crack of thunder exploded over the castle. "Do try and be polite to him, Océane ... I know he does not deserve it but ..."

"But I have to charm him, yes. Yes, I know." Océane rolled her eyes and sat down on the bed, crossing her arms and looking mutinous. Aleish bit her lip and looked increasingly anxious.

"Well ... just try, please?"

Océane glowered, harbouring dark thoughts of giving Laen a taste of his own medicine as her eyes fell upon the heavy silver candlestick, but Aleish frowned back at her. "All right, I promise!" she huffed.

"Good." Aleish put her hand on the door knob and hesitated once more. "Do ... Do be careful with Corin, won't you?"

"Oh?" Océane felt a moment's alarm at the serious look in her eyes but then Aleish flushed and looked at the floor.

"He is most dreadfully easy to fall in love with," she said in a hurry, and left the room with equal haste.

Océane chuckled to herself. Oh yes, Corin had left a mark there, that was for sure.

A gust of wind rattled the glass doors and she shivered as she looked outside. The temperature had dropped further overnight and although the rain had gone, a thick smoky fog had engulfed the castle. The trees on the horizon all but disappeared in its heavy, damp embrace and made her feel that she was lost among the clouds. Océane turned her back on the chilly scene beyond the glass and went to stand by the fire to warm herself up.

She didn't jump this time as Laen swung open the heavy oak door and stood glowering at her. "You are awake then," he stated.

The moment he entered the room the idea that she had to make herself agreeable to this overbearing oaf made Océane's blood boil. Instead she made a great show of looking around herself before replying. "Why yes, it appears I am."

He snorted at her, his face set with a haughty sneer of derision. "Yes I have no doubt you are in a good mood this morning. I confess I find myself astonished that you had the energy to haul yourself out of bed. I do hope you found everything to your satisfaction?"

Océane was surprised at how much the accusation stung, after all she had been prepared for it, but she returned his glare with an innocent expression. "I'm so sorry, what ever do you mean?"

"I mean the fact that you entertained a man you had just met in your bed yesterday. I always knew humans lacked any kind of morals, but I have to admit you surprised even me with your cheap behaviour!"

She saw his fists clench with anger but instead of being alarmed Océane was gripped with such fury at his words that before she had time to think about what the hell she was doing she had crossed the room and slapped him hard across the face.

"Bastard!" she exclaimed with rage. "I never knew it was possible to hate someone quite as much as I hate you. I did no such thing yesterday but frankly I don't care if you believe me or not. I can't do anything to change your mind as you've already painted my character in the blackest of colours. And that being the case I might add ... What's it to you?" she demanded as she glared at him, defiance etched in every line of her body.

***

Laen took a moment to catch up as he was still in shock from the fact that she had actually hit him. She was half his size and by rights ought to be terrified and intimidated, and she had stood up to him and slapped his face. As a Prince he was used to being treated with a great deal of deference from women, and whilst she had attacked him the day she was abducted, that had been out of fear. For her to stand there and slap him out of pure anger was something he had never encountered before in all his life. As for the question she had asked, he still hadn't come up with a good answer for that one himself.

He looked down at her feeling quite as perplexed and angry as he ever had in his life, and wondered why the hell he hadn't just killed her when he'd had the chance. If he did it now his sister would never forgive him as she seemed to have taken a liking to blasted woman and had threatened that she would return to their father's palace and take the consequences if Océane was harmed in any way. On top of that was the very unpalatable fact that he now knew without a doubt that he couldn't do it. Océane didn't know that though, and he took a little grim satisfaction at the fear evident on her face as he took a step closer.

Her eyes widened and his gaze fell on her mouth as she

gasped, her lips parting a little, and the sight almost made him catch his own breath. He grabbed the hand that had slapped him and made a point of standing over her, using his imposing size to intimidate her. She still glared at him with anger burning in her eyes despite her fear and he could not help but admire her courage. Nonetheless he leaned down until his mouth was against her ear, feeling her soft hair tickle his cheek and cling to the stubble. "Do that again and I will have you removed to the dungeons to end your days with the rats," he whispered. Unaccountably he then raised her hand to his lips and kissed the palm, making her jump as if his touch was electric.

Before she had time to ask him what he was doing, he turned and left the room, slamming the door so hard it rattled on its hinges.

Chapter 12

Laen stalked the corridors of his home with a burning anger that scattered his staff like frantic chickens with a fox at large in their domain. What the hell had he been thinking? The wretched woman made him so furious and yet the sight of her anger had been ... glorious. He had wanted nothing more than to pick her up and throw her on the bed and ... And he refused to let his mind wander down that particular road. This was undoubtedly the madness that had possessed his father's mind when he had come across the red-headed she-devil that had ruined his young life. Well he was not his father, and he would not be taken in by it. He would be the master here, and what's more he'd make sure she knew it.

Trying hard to forget the vision he had been confronted with yesterday afternoon, the sight of her tumbled in the sheets of the bed, he headed for the breakfast room with his thoughts in turmoil. That being the case it took him a moment to react to the sight of

Corin sitting at his table, tucking into a hearty breakfast.

"Good morning, Laen. I must say your cook is a wonderful woman. I really should try to poach her from you but then again perhaps not. If I ate like this every day I might get mistaken for a Faery! I seem to have a tremendous appetite this morning though ... can't think why," Corin mused absently, apparently unaware of his impending demise, all the variations of which were parading through Laen's mind in glorious shades of scarlet.

Laen gritted his teeth until his jaw hurt and wondered if the Fae laws of hospitality would object to him running his best friend through with a sword, in the circumstances. Surely seducing another man's prisoner came with some kind of punishment? The thought of Corin in that bed, with Océane, filled him with a blind fury that had every muscle taught with the desire to cause him serious injury.

With difficulty, he forced himself to sit down at the table across from Corin, who passed him a basket full of warm muffins that were filling the room with a tantalising smell, but Laen continued to stare daggers at him. Corin put the basket down and sighed. "Good grief, man, spit it out whatever it is. Your face is giving me indigestion."

"You just cannot help yourself can you?" Laen said in disgust.

Corin shook his head apologetically and helped himself to another muffin. "No I'm afraid I can't. I'm ashamed to admit this is my fourth." He shrugged, popping another piece of the delicious cake into his mouth and chewing contentedly.

"I am not speaking of the wretched food, man," Laen roared in frustration, slamming his fist down so hard the china cups chinked in their saucers. "And you damn well know it."

Corin glanced at him with a slight frown. "Oh, really? I do apologise, what else is it I can't help?" Corin looked up as a maid came into the room with a tea pot and proceeded to refill his cup. She cast him a covetous look from under her lashes and Corin winked at her. She blushed and giggled before sashaying out of the room while sending what could only be described as a *come hither* look towards him as she went. Laen watched his friend's eyes follow her and it was all he could do not to reach across the table and wring his blasted neck.

"I am talking about Océane," he said through his teeth.

He watched Corin nod and smile at him. "Ah, delightful girl, simply charming ... but I still don't follow."

A nerve was ticking in his jaw, he could feel it leaping under his skin as he took a deep breath and with every vestige of patience that remained he reminded himself of all the reasons Corin had been his friend since they were small boys. "Corin," he said with a voice that was dangerously calm. "I am warning you, my temper is fraying and you acting the fool is enough to make me forget my duties as host and take you outside." The last part of the sentence was spoken a little more forcefully than he had intended but at least it got his attention.

Corin wiped his mouth with his napkin and folded it carefully before placing it on the table and turning to face him. "Laen, am I to understand you are calling me out?" he asked with a deeply reproachful tone.

"Not yet," Laen replied, feeling his blood pulse in his head, "but if you do not stop speaking in riddles and trying to evade me, I will!"

Corin huffed and shook his head, looking perplexed. "I assure you, my dear fellow, I am doing no such thing, and I am quite at a loss to understand why you are so hot under the collar."

Laen stood up so quickly that the fine wooden chair he had been sitting on took a lurch sideways and hit the floor. "Because you took advantage of both my hospitality and my prisoner!" he yelled.

Corin looked up at him with a perfectly innocent and wounded expression. "I most certainly did not."

Laen's expression was one of complete incredulity.

"You dare to deny it?"

"I not only dare, I completely deny it!" Corin retorted with some heat. "Not only that, I think you should consider the fact you have just maligned a lovely young lady's reputation. Frankly, Laen, I believe it should be me calling you out!" He crossed his arms and glared back at Laen, looking indignant and very much the victimised party.

Laen's head was beginning to pound in earnest and his hope of having some means of venting his anger seemed to be slipping away from him. "You mean to sit there and tell me you didn't take her to bed, on your word of honour?" he demanded.

Corin stood up and pushed back his chair. "On my word of honour, Laen"

Laen was beyond puzzled, so he did what he always did when he was unsure of himself, and retreated to anger. "By the fires, Corin, the guards said ..."

"The guards said ...what?" demanded Corin with an icy tone.

Laen stared at him and knew he looked utterly bewildered but he just didn't know what to make of the situation. He did know that Corin's word was beyond reproach though. He had to back down. "You have given me your word and I accept I have made a mistake but ..." He shook his head.

"What?"

Laen sighed with frustration and picked up the chair he had knocked over. "I went to her room yesterday, the guards said you had not long left and that you had been there for hours and she ... She was asleep in bed in the middle of the afternoon and she looked ..." He swallowed hard and looked away from Corin's knowing gaze. "Well, never mind how she looked."

"Ah yes, the poor girl was complaining of a headache, that is why I left. Probably as a result of all those blows to the head you delivered. Child's probably got a damn concussion! I offered to heal her but she's so terrified of all of us she wouldn't let me near." He sighed, looking wistful. "I'm glad though, I'll admit. I did wonder if she had feigned it to get rid of me."

Laen scowled. "Why would she do that?"

Corin sat back down and picked his cup up. "Well, I think she found my advances a little hard to take. I'm of the opinion she is quite an innocent." Laen felt Corin's gaze on him, searching his expression for something.

"You gave me your word!" Laen exploded, thumping the table with enough force that a plate bounced from the surface and shattered in a star-burst that sent pieces scattering across the floor beside him.

Corin turned to him with wide eyes. "I gave you my word I did not take her to bed, I never said I didn't try," he clarified with a perfectly straight face.

Laen massaged his temples and reminded himself that Corin was his friend. He could not kill him ... unless he gave him a reason. Nonetheless the admission was interesting. He could not remember ever coming across a woman who could resist Corin once he had set his sights on her. "She rejected you?"

"As gratified as I am to hear that tone in your voice - why are you so surprised? My dear man, I really cannot believe you still think all human women are harlots. If you cannot see that girl is quite inexperienced in such matters, I do despair of you."

Laen frowned. He hated to admit it but Corin usually knew what he was talking about when it came to subjects like these but he just couldn't accept what he was hearing.

"You're sure?"

Corin snorted with amusement. "Not completely sure, no, but rest assured I am at your disposal if you wish me to make ... deeper enquiries."

"That will not be necessary." Laen returned to massaging his temples; suddenly he had a pounding headache and the strong desire to bash his friend's face in.

"As I said before, you really cannot help yourself can you?"

Corin stood up abruptly as anger turned his eyes a deeper shade of gold. "If you think I'm going to sit here and listen to you bemoan the way I live my life you have another thing coming," he said with some asperity. "Frankly, Laen, given the choice, I would rather be one of my conquests that one of yours. I may bruise the occasional heart a little but I do not leave them frozen to the core as you do. Neither do I feel the need to terrorise innocent girls and treat them as abominably as you have treated Océane. That you then make out as though I was doing something reprehensible when it is clear to me you are simply jealous is more than I can stand." Laen glared at the fire in the hearth blazing brighter as Corin admonished him. The flames flickered and died a little and he glanced up to see that Corin was doing his best to get his anger under control. He looked at Laen, his face calm though his eyes still held the heat of his words. "Now if you'll excuse me, I think I shall leave you before one of us says something he will live to regret."

Laen watched his friend stalk out the door and wondered what in the fires of Tartarus had just happened. He was the one who got angry and ranted, not Corin. Corin rarely lost his temper with him, no matter how provoked, but the human question was coming between them more and more. Now he had to add Océane to the list of things that were tearing at the fabric of a friendship that had lasted for decades. More frustrating was the fact that Océane was not living up to his preconceived notions of what a human woman was, and it was most aggravating. But if he was wrong about that, and he was yet unconvinced of that, but if he was wrong … Gods he had a headache!

Chapter 13

Corin left the breakfast parlour feeling unaccountably irritated. Something was not quite as it should be and he could not decide exactly what. He had gone out of his way to rile Laen, and had received exactly the reaction he had hoped for. He knew Laen as well as he knew himself and perceived that he had been right in his estimation of how things would proceed. Unfortunately the discovery did not give him half as much satisfaction as he had thought it might, which concerned him immensely. He looked out of the window at lowering, wolf grey skies as the wind buffeted the landscape and tore around the castle with a morbid howl. Cursing, he turned away. Somehow he didn't think Alfheim would be faring any better. He had the distinct feeling that trouble was following him, a dark shadow that lingered on the edge of his mind and whispered to him when he was alone. He was becoming increasingly unsettled by what the future would bring. Somehow Laen's feelings towards Océane were crucial but the knowledge brought him no peace.

Heading back to the rooms Laen always left ready for him, he was lost to his troubled thoughts and almost didn't hear the squeal of protest as he passed by the open door to a large linen cupboard. Peering inside, he discovered Aleish trying in vain to push a large box back onto the shelf above her head. Rushing over, he took the weight of it from her arms and slid it back onto the shelf.

"Oh, no I wanted it down!" she exclaimed. "It was just too heavy so I had to push it back."

Corin rolled his eyes. "Well do make your mind up." Obligingly he lifted the box down for her as the scent of Rosemary and Lavender drifted up around them. "Darling, what on earth are you up to?" he asked with a reproving tone as he brushed a cobweb from her hair. "Surely you have maids for this sort of thing."

"Oh!" she huffed. "The place is going to rack and ruin since I left. I only came to find some dresses for Océane and found the place in such a state ... Well I couldn't leave it like that. He really must get a housekeeper. I've tried myself but I can't find anyone who isn't scared to death of him." She looked up to see him smiling at her affectionately. "What?"

"We've hidden in here before," he said, mischief dancing in his eyes.

Aleish blushed and brushed her skirts down self-consciously. "Yes, well ... that was a long time ago. Before I was married."

He shrugged and leaned against the shelves of linens and pursed his lips. "Well we're here now ..."

Aleish frowned. "Oh do behave. I simply do not have the energy to fend you off today what with Laen in an almighty fury and Océane trapped here." She rubbed at her forehead in a weary gesture and grimaced. "By the fates, what will happen to us?"

He sighed and crossed his arms with a truculent expression. "You're no fun anymore."

"Oh, Corin!" She snorted and shook her head at him. "What am I to do with you? I suppose you have been making that poor girl fall in love with you."

He shrugged and affected a wide-eyed, innocent expression that he knew Aleish wouldn't be fooled by for a moment. "I thought I behaved admirably ... in the circumstances."

"In what circumstances?" She pouted and gave him a knowing look. "You mean alone with a beautiful girl and you resisted the urge to take her to bed?" She raised her hands in mock astonishment. "What a martyr you are! They will dedicate ballads and erect statues to your great sacrifice. You'll probably be made a Saint."

He nodded with great sincerity. "And quite right too, I'd say."

She burst out laughing, hitting his shoulder with a playful smack. "Oh, you are quite impossible."

Catching her hand, he held it to his lips, kissing the knuckles with soft lips. "It is so lovely to hear you laugh, darling."

She stopped abruptly, her eyes wistful. "No, you must not ... please." She blushed again and moved away from him, busying herself with rearranging the linens but he could see how her hand trembled.

He sighed heavily and leaned against the shelves once again. "I'm sorry, Aleish. Forgive me."

She glanced up at him and smiled. "As if you think I wouldn't forgive you most anything." He smiled in return but his heart wasn't in it and she frowned at him.

"What is it? Each time I see you I feel more and more that you're carrying some burden. I cannot see what it is but I can tell the weight of it is laying heavy on your mind." Her face was full of concern for him and not for the first time he wondered what it would be like to be married to her. The thought was too disturbing though and he crossed his arms and looked away. For a moment he considered telling her everything, everything that was keeping him from sleep, making him drink more than ever and raise hell at every opportunity. He desperately wanted to. Before he would have confided in Laen without hesitation, but now things were too tense between them, he was too afraid of losing his oldest friend for good. So instead he did what had become second nature and ignored the voice in his head that called him and tormented his conscience in the darkest part of the night. He forced it away and turned to her with a mischievous grin and a twinkle in his eyes. "Why, darling, you know I am considering how to lure you away from that husband of yours. The loss of you weighs heavy on my heart."

She tutted at him. "Do not try that on me, I am by no means stupid. You are just trying to divert me!" She stepped closer to him, her black eyes intent and he knew he could never delude her, of all people. "You can put on an act for everyone else but I see the truth of you and you had best not forget it. You are a good man, Corin, but you squander your talents and your life. You cannot carry on this way forever. You are terribly lonely, we both know it and no amount of one night stands and torrid affairs are ever going to ease that." She sighed and her expression softened. Reaching out, she laid a hand on his arm. "You should not be so afraid to love someone. It doesn't have to be like that for you."

He snorted, suddenly becoming terribly interested in the variety of fabrics folded neatly on the shelves. Anything other than look her in the eyes. "Yes, between our two families we have such wonderful examples of how these things can work out for the best," he replied, his tone caustic and full of bitterness.

She shook her head and gave his arm a reassuring squeeze. "Laen is nothing like our father, thank the gods, and there is no reason to think you will follow the same path as yours. You are not him and if you carry on ..." She paused and he knew she was unwilling to put into words what she could see coming. She looked him in the eyes and her care for him only made everything seem more desperate. "You simply cannot live like this, Corin. Find something real and true, something worth fighting for, and hold onto it."

He was quiet for a long time, not knowing what to say but in the end he leaned over and kissed her cheek. "You know I can't." He wondered if she could hear the regret in his voice as clearly as he could.

***

After Laen had left her room, Océane had stood for some considerable time staring at the palm of her hand as though she hoped to find the answer to the universe written there - or at least the answer to what the hell she had just experienced.

Stockholm syndrome, she decided, sitting down with a thud in the nearest chair. She'd read about it in the papers, where victims developed feelings of affection or even love for their abductors. She frowned and considered how she felt about Laen. Fear - yes, intense dislike – absolutely. Hate - no doubt in her mind. Not Stockholm syndrome then. She sighed. She hadn't needed to see the words that had flickered under his skin to identify the feeling she had experienced when his lips made contact with her palm but it had been mortifying nonetheless. She had even wondered if she might be about to have a seizure of some kind as in her innocence she had never realised that a man's lips on her skin could cause such a violent reaction.

It was also a very unpleasant revelation to discover that she could have such an intense reaction to a man she hated with every fibre of her being. Why couldn't it have been Corin; that would have been a much nicer experience.

Magic then, she decided with relief. Of course, that was it. In books the Fae were supposed to have all sorts of weird and scary powers, and she knew Aleish could read her mind when she touched her. She gave a sigh. Thank

God! She really wasn't losing it completely. The wicked bastard had played with her mind to make her feel like that, to make her want him. Just wait until she saw him next, she'd give him a piece of her mind all right and he wouldn't have to touch her to get it.

She heard thunder rumbling in the distance. The rain was coming down in earnest still and the damp cold clung to her dress and chilled her even by the fire. She shut the balcony doors that she had opened in the hope the fresh air would wake her sanity up and give her some peace. That at least, seemed to have worked. She sat back down in the chair and stared out at the grim day outside of the windows. God but she was sick of being stuck in this bloody room, they could at least give her a book to read. She was just wondering if she should take a nap to try and while away some time when she heard the door open, and her heart both sunk and began to pound frantically as she saw Laen stride through it. She leaped up out of her chair and took refuge behind the bed post. Like that was going to protect her!

She looked at him critically; his white blond hair fell straight either side of his face until it just brushed his shoulders, and his skin was so very pale but seemed to have an opalescent glow that came from within him. He was dressed in his usual soft, black leather trousers and boots, and a simple white cotton shirt that was tied loosely shut with a lace and afforded her a tantalising glimpse of that fine chest. Damn it but he was gorgeous and she hated him all the more for it.

He walked in, his presence appearing to force the air from the room until she could barely breathe. He sat down on the edge of the bed and those disturbing black eyes lifted to hers.

"Well then, Océane, have you decided to tell me more about the book?" He smiled at her pleasantly, which was the most unnerving thing he'd done yet.

She shook her head, momentarily having lost the ability

to speak.

There was a flash of annoyance in those dark eyes but the pleasant smile remained. "Perhaps you would like to explain 'The Dark Prince is Lost' then? How do I come to be lost? Tell me, am I merely misplaced or did you perhaps have something more permanent in mind?" He watched her, waiting for her to reply but once again no brilliant answer could be found no matter how hard she tried. She knew she was trying his patience but ... she didn't know what to say.

He got up from the bed and moved closer to her. Océane stifled a shriek of alarm and began backing up, knowing that she was going to run out of room at any moment. She held her hands out in front of her as if warning him to stay back even though there was really no point. "K-Keep away from me, you ... You freak!" she said in fury. "Don't you dare touch me!"

Laen only smiled at her again, amusement glittering in the gaze that never left her. "Really, Océane," he said, his voice soft. "That was a silly thing to say. I never have been able to resist a dare."

He kept moving forwards and she kept retreating until she found herself backed up against the bedroom wall. There was simply nowhere else to go, so she snatched up the silver candlestick that she'd threatened him with before. "Just back off!" she shouted, anger that he should make her feel this way giving her courage she never knew she'd had. "God, I knew you were a sick bastard but I never believed *even you* could sink so low."

One eyebrow quirked and his lips twitched. *"Even me,"* he repeated, not trying to hide the laughter in his voice. "Oh really? Please ... do enlighten me."

She quailed a little as he was standing close now and the size of him made her feel a lot less brave than she had felt when he was on the other side of the room. Nonetheless she put up her chin and stared at him defiantly. "I mean your Jedi mind tricks, you creepy bastard. Bloody hell, as if it's not enough to abduct me and knock me about!"

A look of puzzlement crossed his face and he frowned at her. "My ... what?"

She snorted in disgust. "Oh don't act all innocent. You know exactly what I mean." She tapped a finger against her temple and sneered at him. "You got in my head ... Like your sister can, and you're not doing it again or before I know it I'll be flat on my back agreeing that *they're not the droids I'm looking for*," she yelled, brandishing the candlestick and wishing it was possible to melt into the wall at her back.

Laen's expression was momentarily one of complete bewilderment. "What in the name of the gods are you talking about?" The idea began to sink in, as she watched his confusion, that he really didn't know what she was referring to, which meant ... he hadn't used any weird mind bending powers on her after all. She felt the blush burn her cheeks and spread down her neck as his expression cleared and he began to laugh. It was a soft, low sound that made her heart pound faster.

"What are you laughing at?" she demanded, stamping her foot, though she knew damn well, and 'mortified' did not even come close to how she was feeling. She had no choice but to bluff it out though. "I suppose you think manipulating innocent women is a fine morning's entertainment?"

He took a step closer to her and she held the candlestick up a little higher. She looked up and up and could feel his breath on her face as he spoke.

"I didn't do anything to your mind and I am far from believing you are innocent yet, my dear."

With a movement too fast for her to take in, he snatched the candlestick out of her hand and threw it on the floor where it landed with a clatter. She screamed but had nowhere to run as he leaned over her with his hands braced on the wall either side of her head. He was so close that she could smell him and was infuriated to discover he smelled wonderful, fresh and clean like a cold winter's day.

"I don't believe you!" she said, not looking him in the eyes, her voice barely more than a whisper.

She glanced up to see that he was smiling at her and she was aware of a softer look in his eyes that hadn't been there before. "I am really not interested in whether or not you believe me, Océane." He paused and one hand moved to touch her hair, a delicate caress as one finger stroked and then tucked the lock behind her ear. He lowered his head further so that his mouth brushed her cheek. "I am however deeply interested in the fact that you desire me."

"I do not!" she objected and was horrified to hear her voice sound so unconvincing. The man was a complete and utter bastard, the kind she had spent her life running away from. She was not about to go weak at the knees for a domineering Neanderthal like him. She really wasn't. But now his eyes were fixed on hers and she couldn't look away from him.

"I do not wish to hurt you, Océane. I only want to know the truth."

She frowned as she wondered if that was really sincerity she could see in his eyes. "I've told you the truth," she said, and he sighed, his breath fluttering against her skin and making her shiver.

"We both know that is not the truth though," he said.

She risked a look up at him and saw his face soften.

"If you are truly innocent you have nothing to fear from me. I only seek to protect my people."

She bit her lip, wondering if she could try to convince him that what she had said was the truth ... just possibly not the whole story.

"Things do not have to be so ... unpleasant between us." His voice was low now, seductive, and she began to feel alarm. This was a bad, bad situation. "I know you want me."

To her relief, indignation at his arrogance brought

anger flooding back with a vengeance. "No," she said, grateful beyond measure that he could not see the words she could see on his face. "I do not."

To her fury he chuckled. "Hmm." He brought his body a little closer to hers. "Well then, let us see."

Before she could make any objection he had dipped his head and begun slowly kissing a trail down the side of her neck to her shoulder and what she had intended to become an expletive came out as a gasp. His lips were warm and soft as they gently caressed her skin and when his tongue added to the assault she had to clench her hands to stop them from fisting into his hair and pulling his head against her. With a teasing bite, he stopped at her shoulder and raised his head, watching her like a bug under a microscope. Heart pounding, she took the opportunity to duck under his arm and rush across the room to the French doors. Maybe if she got outside she could scream for help ... Maybe Aleish would hear her.

She was tugging at the doors when two strong arms swept around her waist and he pulled her firmly against him. "Not yet, I have not finished my interrogation." She felt his breath coming fast now, cool against her burning skin, and tried to convince herself it was fear making her heart pound. With one hand he lifted her hair and placed it over her left shoulder leaving the other clear for his lips to return to their delicate torment. He nipped at her ear lobe and she was horrified to hear her breathing hitch. With the gentlest of touches he returned his attention to her neck. "So very lovely," he murmured against her skin.

Oh God, oh God, Océane repeated over and over in her head, though whether she was praying for Him to intervene and stop Laen or make sure he continued, she simply couldn't decide. How could a man who had gone out of his way to frighten her now treat her with such delicate attention. In a last ditch effort she tried to get away from him, trying to break his hold on her body and - despite his denial - she was sure he had possessed her mind as she could not possibly be sane. However he simply grasped her hips, pulling her tight against him, and the feel of his hard body pressed against hers was enough for all reason to finally up stakes and flee. Instead she gave in to sensation and leaned into him as his hands started to move over her. One large hand splayed over her belly as the other swept up past her waist to cup her breast where it remained to give a gentle squeeze. To her everlasting shame Océane moaned, and tipped her head back to lean against his shoulder.

***

"Océane," Laen murmured, her name spoken with a yearning he was too absorbed by to hide. It never occurred to him to stop and wonder why her name felt so right on his tongue, so consumed was he by the feel of her soft body against him. He forgot that he had come with every intention of terrorising her into giving him the information that he needed. He forgot that he needed to know if she was aware or even master of some plot to kill him. At this precise moment he didn't care if she had been plotting to overthrow his father's kingdom or have an assassin murder him in his bed; all he could think about was how much he wanted to taste her lips on his. How much he wanted to see her smile at him instead of turn away in fear or rage.

The hand on her belly moved up to her face, caressing her cheek before turning her head towards him and he didn't even try to disguise the longing he felt sure was in his eyes as his mouth moved towards hers. But before he was able to satisfy his craving, the door opened and he heard Corin's voice speaking to the guards.

"I'm quite sure he is in the middle of an interview but I wish to see him."

Laen let go of Océane so quickly that she almost dropped to her knees and had to grab hold of the door handles to steady herself. He could see she was trembling.

For his part Laen was feeling more than a little flustered himself, though outwardly it was in no way visible. As part of a royal dynasty he was well used to having his every expression scrutinised, and had perfected the blank face at a very early age. So by the time Corin stepped in the room he was standing a discreet distance from Océane, looking perfectly calm. She on the other hand looked flushed and was breathing heavily. Laen looked at her with satisfaction. Her cheeks were pink and she was clinging to the door handles like they were the only thing holding her up. He did wish however that she didn't look so obviously in turmoil in front of Corin's sharp eyes as for some reason he didn't want him to know what had been going on. However, he watched as Corin took one look at his own carefully composed expression and Océane's look of bewilderment, and knew his friend was in no doubt whatsoever of what he'd interrupted.

Chapter 14

Océane looked from Corin to Laen and sincerely wished they would both leave her to suffer captivity alone. She was beginning to think she deserved to be locked up - tucked up nice and safe in an insane asylum. She was quite obviously losing her mind.

It was perfectly clear that Corin had guessed what he had interrupted, and her embarrassment was only compounded by the self-satisfied smirk on Laen's face. The smug bastard. God, but she hated him.

Corin fixed her with his golden gaze until she couldn't bear it, and turned back to Laen who had now returned to his normal dark and brooding persona. She wished they'd both just bugger off and leave her in peace. Between the two of them she didn't know if she was coming or going, although she was pretty sure which it would be if she spent any more time alone with Laen. The thought made her blush, which Laen noticed, and he snorted with amusement.

Hated. Him. So. Much.

"So, Laen," said Corin, finally breaking the torturous silence. "How did the *interview* ... go? Did you discover anything of interest?"

Laen gave a bland smile and turned to look out of the window at a sky that was somewhat lighter than it had been half an hour ago. "Oh yes, it was most ... illuminating."

"Really?" Corin was not sounding quite his usual suave self and Océane's heart sank. "Perhaps you would like to share your discovery?"

Laen pursed his lips as though he was considering the question. "No. I do not believe I would."

"I see," Corin replied, his voice clipped and his eyes never leaving Laen's face.

Océane rubbed her arms as a prickling sensation began to sting her skin.

They stood glaring at each other until she could bear it no longer. "Oh for heaven's sake! Would you please take your pissing contest elsewhere, you're giving me a headache."

Corin was the first to respond. He smiled at her, though she felt it wasn't such a warm smile as he normally sent in her direction and the thought made her uncomfortable. She wondered if he was angry with her. She had followed his instructions just as he had asked ...Wasn't this what he had wanted?

"Quite so, my dear, my apologies," he said, turning his attention to Laen, whom Océane refused to look at. "Laen ... a word." This request was accompanied by a dark look that boded ill for their future friendship but all Océane wanted was for them to leave so she could gather her wits - if she had any left to concern herself with.

Laen followed him out of the room but not before sending a look in Océane's direction that made her stomach do a somersault. He would be back.

The door closed and Océane collapsed into the nearest chair. Her heart was still thudding in her chest and she could make no sense of what had just happened. Laen was probably just trying a different tactic, she assured herself, like the good cop, bad cop routine except he was obviously bipolar and had taken both roles upon himself. Yes, she thought, worrying at a finger nail with her teeth, her thoughts snarled up in a tangle. That had to be it. Except she had seen the soft look in his eyes, heard the tender tone of his voice and ... And she was completely and utterly certifiable.

***

Laen and Corin walked in silence to the library that served as Laen's office. Laen went to stand by the fire that blazed in the hearth and looked down at it, one foot on the fender as he studiously avoided Corin's eyes. "Well, Corin, what do you want? I have things to attend to."

Corin sat himself down in one of the large leather armchairs with all the appearance of being quite at ease. "So," he began with a conversational tone, "you decided you would test my little theory yourself, how interesting. Tell me, do you agree?"

Laen looked up from the fire to glare at him. "Let us just say the results were ... inconclusive." In truth he didn't know whether he should truly be as cross as he was or be thankful that Corin had come in when he had. Much longer in the company of that witch and he may have been altogether undone. He wondered if he was onto something, that maybe she truly was a witch and she had bespelled him. There was no other reason for his reaction to her. His court was full of beautiful women more than willing to share his bed and nurture the hope that he might one day choose a wife from among them but none of them made him feel like this. No one had ever provoked the anger or desire that she could command with little more than a glance in his direction. Not just desire either, he noted with a stab of alarm. She interested him. He wanted to know her, know more about this strange, bold creature that would look him in the eye and talk to him as an equal. More than that, she would curse and chastise him for being a fool and a bastard. No woman had ever spoken to him in such a manner. He should be furious, but he knew he was far from angry - he was intrigued. Witchcraft, he decided firmly - either that or he was losing his damned mind.

"Perhaps your feelings towards the human race are not as clear cut as you thought," Corin pressed, his gold eyes fixed on Laen with interest. "Are you wavering, old friend? Ready to admit that you may have made a grave error in judgement? Really you can tell me, you know I am not one to say *I told you so.*"

Laen gritted his teeth. Damn him. Corin knew him too well. The bastard always had an uncanny knack of knowing what was in his mind. At least Aleish could only do it if she touched him. Corin just seemed to know. "Not in the slightest," he said with as cool a manner as he could manage though it irritated the hell out of him that Corin had managed to grab onto the little sliver of doubt that had begun to worm its way into his mind. "You may not be aware of this but she is not only here because she was human and in my way. There is far more to it than that."

He watched as Corin tilted his head, his eyes narrowing. "Well then ... do please explain."

Laen went and picked up the book from his desk and threw it to Corin, who caught it deftly in one hand. Turning it carefully, he traced the delicate design of dark green bindweed and thorns that had been inlaid on the soft black leather. Corin was a great lover of books and he knew quality when he saw it. "Exquisite," he murmured and then his expression froze as he saw the title of the book. "The Dark Prince?" he said, so quietly that Laen thought he spoke it to himself.

Laen frowned, sure that he had seen Corin shudder. He told himself he was glad Corin was as disturbed as he had been. There was every reason to be concerned.

Corin looked up at him. "You mean to say she made this?" His voice held an edge to it that Laen could not quite understand but he was obviously struck by Océane's talent. "It is beautifully done," he added.

Laen nodded. "Yes, she made it, but it is not the quality of the binding that concerns me. If you look at the inside you will also discover that she wrote it, and the subject matter is the reason I brought her here."

Corin paled and stared at the book. He looked horrified and held it in his hands as though it might explode in his face. "Well perhaps you would like to précis the contents?" he said to Laen, sounding shaken.

Laen leaned back against his desk and sighed, folding his arms. He refused to admit that he was disappointed to see how troubled Corin was, that he had wanted Corin to come up with an explanation, a reason to prove the girl was innocent. "It is my story, Corin. I am The Dark Prince of the title."

Corin closed his eyes and let out a breath. It looked as though a great weight had fallen away from him and Laen scrutinised him with a frown, wondering what had disturbed him so. When Corin looked up again he seemed perfectly calm and spoke as though it was simply a curious occurrence. "Fascinating, and what was her explanation?"

"She says that it is simply a story, that she made it up and had no idea it was about a real person," Laen exclaimed, disappointed to find that the explanation seemed just as unlikely to him now as it had the first time he had heard it.

To Laen's surprise Corin did not look as shocked at the obvious lie as he thought he might. He felt sure that this revelation would cast doubt on her innocence, even in Corin's eyes. Instead his friend just smiled at him.

"My dear fellow, she is quite likely telling the truth."

Laen looked at him in disbelief. "You cannot be serious? Read it, damn you, and tell me how you can think that?"

"Oh don't worry I will read it but you forget I have far more experience of the human world than you, and I'm afraid this is where your lack of knowledge makes you jump to the wrong conclusions."

Laen narrowed his eyes at him, his face set in stone. "Oh, really?"

"Yes, Laen, really." Corin tucked the little book safely into his jacket pocket. "You see there are thousands of books of this type in the human world, romances mainly, though some are a little nearer the truth of our fair lands."

Laen widened his eyes, and crossed the room to his desk, a big, heavily carved affair scattered with paperwork where an elegant, silver tray awaited with a crystal decanter and glasses. "Romances? What the devil are you talking about?"

Corin got up, joining him beside the desk and taking the decanter from Laen's hands before he'd had the chance to serve himself. He ignored Laen's protests as he always did and sloshed a generous amount into a tumbler before handing the decanter back to him. "I am trying to explain to you that for the women of the human world, we are something of a ... romantic fantasy."

Laen's hand stilled with the decanter poised over his glass, and gaped at him in astonishment. "Oh, please!"

Corin laughed at the expression on his friend's face. "The next time I am there I will be sure to pick some out for you. You'll find them fascinating reading I assure you. I certainly do. I picked up quite a bit of useful information too." He chuckled and raised his glass to Laen before draining a good portion of its contents. "You see, many women dream of being carried off by a brooding, dark and dangerous Fae Prince ..." His gold eyes glittered with amusement and Laen could not believe the fool wasn't just making the whole thing up but as he continued it only became worse. "You, my dear fellow, have probably starred in many a woman's erotic night time fantasy. In fact," he added with a grin, "I'd lay money on it"

Laen just stared at him - dumbstruck. It was undeniable that Corin had far more knowledge and experience of the human world and its people but what he was suggesting was simply preposterous. "You think to mock me perhaps?" he said in disgust. "The idea is utterly ridiculous."

"I promise you that I speak the truth, and whilst I cannot guarantee it, I would suggest there is the possibility that Océane has told you everything she knows about the book and that she really did make the whole thing up."

Laen shook his head. He could not deny, to himself at least, that he wanted to believe her but the very idea was quite outrageous and he was wholly unconvinced.

Corin downed the rest of his glass before pouring himself another large measure. Laen scowled at him and took the decanter away, placing it back on the tray as Corin rolled his eyes at him and went to stand by the fireplace. The flames flickered and sparked, burning brighter and leaping higher up the chimney as Corin got closer.

"I have a suggestion, Laen, since I assume your investigations did not bring you any closer to your answers," he said with just a hint of acid in his tone. "I think you should let me try. Océane trusts me, at least up to a point, and I am more likely to get her to tell the truth if she is not afraid she will have her throat cut the minute she reveals it." He paused and looked down at the flames and Laen tried hard to suppress the feeling he got at Corin's suggestion. "Let me take her for a little walk around the grounds," he continued, and Laen gritted his teeth. "I can show her the beauty of the place and make her feel relaxed. Then I will get to the heart of the matter and we shall see."

Laen clenched his fists and turned away to look at the increasingly dark clouds that gathered overhead. The thought of Océane alone in Corin's company for any length of time was not something that brought him any pleasure, and it was for that reason alone that he agreed. He had to break whatever hold the little witch had over him and if Corin got himself ensnared, more fool him. Jealousy raged in his blood and he was infuriated to hear a rumble of thunder as the temperature began to drop again. He really was losing his damn mind! The only thing that mattered was finding out the truth. Who got to it and how really wasn't important. It really wasn't.

Maybe if he kept repeating it to himself, he'd believe it.

Chapter 15

Damn him. Laen cursed Corin, his jaw clenching so hard his teeth hurt. He stared out of the window at the glowering clouds hanging low in the sky and held on tight to his anger. It was harder than he would have credited not to let his attention wander and remember the softness of Océane's breast beneath his hand, the feel of her nipple peaked and taut under his fingers. Oh gods. It was everything he could do to keep himself from running back to her room to see if he could coax her into his arms again. He would be kinder this time, he vowed. He would make amends for his brutality. The thought of seeing the fear in her eyes again when she looked at him made him feel sick to his stomach. He had to ... He needed to ... Damn. What the hell was he thinking? She was a prisoner and here for good reason. He had no business thinking about the desire he had received from her, about what it would be like to taste her. He swallowed hard and tried instead to focus on the crop yield his farm manager had predicted this year, but found the only yielding he could think about was hers as she had leant her head against him with a moan that had set his blood on fire.

"Laen!"

He jumped as he remembered he was not alone and tried to remember what the hell they had been talking about.

"Have you been listening to a word I said?" Corin asked in exasperation.

Laen turned away from the sight of the dismal weather and went to sit down behind his desk. "I said you could take the woman out, did I not?" he growled, reaching for his glass once more.

Corin tutted and tried to reach for the decanter again but this time Laen was too quick for him. He scowled at Laen and put his empty glass down with a thud. "No actually, you just grunted. Am I to take that as a sign of approval?"

Laen groaned and put his head in his hands. "Yes, yes, anything. Just go away and leave me alone will you." Why, why? Why was this going so badly wrong? It had been the first time in years his father had actually spoken to him - to entrust this task to him. It had given his ego something of a boost to know that there was no one else in the Kingdom his father would trust to get the job done. Of course it had occurred to him that it had been chosen as a perfect opportunity for him to get himself killed but he preferred not to consider that.

He snorted inwardly. He had suffered a lifetime of hatred from the man whose blood ran in his veins and yet still he clung to the grain of hope that he would one day be seen as a worthy heir to the throne. What a fool he was to believe that. Well, any hope of that was gone for good now. He tried to convince himself that he didn't care what the old bastard thought of him, not anymore, but he did care whether the King came to hear how he had made a mess of the whole thing. *Idiot,* he cursed himself. His father had done nothing but abuse and humiliate him since he was a boy.

He looked up and stole a glance at the man who had saved him from the misery of his childhood. Corin was a good man, a good friend. He alone had saved him from the hell that had been his existence from the moment his mother had died. He had never let him down, had never stopped being a friend despite the fact that Laen's father despised him and made it dangerous for them to be friends, despite the fact that Laen had often not deserved his friendship. He gave a heavy sigh. So what if he had botched the job, it wouldn't change a thing in his father's eyes, just as it wouldn't change anything if it had been a complete success. And after all, he *had* retrieved the blade. He just hadn't bargained on Océane...

Once again his thoughts wandered, and he groaned anew.

***

Corin looked over at Laen, who was quite obviously in turmoil, and shook his head. He was beginning to deeply regret having played any part in this farce at all. Things were going exactly as he had planned, and he was not at all sure he was pleased about it. In fact he was fairly certain he didn't like it in the least. He should have just seduced the girl when he'd had the opportunity. Then he could have discovered the truth about the book so that Laen would have let her go home and all could have returned to normal. Of course sooner or later Laen would have started a war with the rest of the Fae Lands and the human world and Corin would have been forced to stand against him. He simply had no choice in the matter. He may have a well-deserved reputation as a hell-raiser and a womaniser but he was not entirely irresponsible.

He looked out at the appalling day beyond the window and cursed inwardly. Laen's lands had always been subject to violent storms whereas, up until more recent times at least, it had rarely rained in his own. *It's coming for you*, a malicious voice whispered in his head. He shut it off abruptly as the cold feeling began to grow inside him. He cast a longing look at the decanter and closed his eyes. He could not take Océane out if he was drunk. The words circled in his brain though, snide little whispers that hissed and spat with venomous enthusiasm and he wondered just how much longer he would be able to shut them out for before he had to act or simply lost his mind altogether.

"Very well, then we are agreed," he said, tutting again as he realised Laen wasn't attending him in the slightest, so he raised his voice. "But I do hope the weather clears as I'm certainly not going out in this!" He gestured outside in disgust and received a glower from Laen in return. Corin was well aware that he was baiting him. It was a dangerous game and he wasn't entirely sure it was the best way forward but he was extremely irritated, and well past caring.

Giving up on the idea of getting a response to any further enquiries, he left Laen to brood and stalked out of the room, muttering about idiot friends. Once away from Laen's eyes he took the book from his pocket and looked at it again with a strange feeling in his chest. He smoothed the soft leather between his hands and heard again the resentful murmuring of the voice. His heart began to pound as he traced the words of the title, *The Dark Prince*. For a moment he had been terribly afraid that...

He put the book back in his pocket and steadfastly ignored the way his hand trembled. It was Laen's story, not his. It was fine.

Gods he needed a drink.

By lunch time the weather, whilst not exactly glorious had cleared up enough for Corin to ask the kitchen staff to prepare a picnic and to go and save Océane from another moment languishing in her room. He tried to ignore the anticipation that stirred in his blood as he approached her bedroom door. She wasn't for him, not this time. He had to follow the plan. Of course if he had been following the plan it would be Laen who was taking her out for a walk around the garden and not him. It should be Laen. This was his land after all. Corin gritted his teeth and suppressed a surge of jealousy. What the devil had gotten into him? He stopped in his tracks as the uncomfortable realisation spread, because he knew full well what was wrong with him. Aleish was right, he was lonely. Oh gods he was lonely. He was tired of taking a different woman to his bed every night. He wanted ... He wanted...

He remembered the distant look in Laen's eyes as he had sat thinking about Océane, and he knew it had been her on his friend's mind. There was no doubt of it. Maybe, finally there was a woman Laen could care for and who could love him in return as he deserved to be loved. Maybe they could be happy together. Corin closed his eyes as his chest began to ache.

Anyway, for him she would have been just a woman, just another woman who would come and go. Far better that she love Laen. Corin would never fall in love. He wouldn't allow it.

***

When Corin arrived to say he'd persuaded Laen to let her out for a walk, Océane could have wept at his feet. As prison cells went, it was luxurious in the extreme but she was bored out of her mind. Worse than that, however, was the fact that her enforced solitude meant she had plenty of time to torment herself with thoughts of Laen and whatever it was that had happened between them.

What *had* happened between them kept going round and around in her head and she simply didn't know what to make of it. She did know that she had to get out of here, however, before she did something that would get her certified for life, and she sincerely hoped that Corin had come up with an idea.

Of course that would mean never seeing Laen again.

The thought popped into her head unannounced and she rejected it immediately, if reluctantly. That was the whole point, the man was a psycho! She refused to allow herself to believe there was a single part of her that regretted that fact.

She glanced at Corin as he led her through the endless corridors of the castle and gave him a grateful smile for ending her captivity. The look he gave her in return was enough to make her cheeks heat and she turned away. She wondered if she was foolish to go wandering the grounds with him, but then if he had any nefarious ideas he could have easily made use of the fact she had been locked in a bedroom. There was no need to go traipsing the countryside. In fact, she thought as her blush deepened, at the time she had been more than willing to give him anything he wanted. She swallowed, feeling his eyes on her and she had the uncanny sensation he knew what she was thinking. Well anyway, she didn't believe she had any reason not to trust him, although ... She stole another glance at the gorgeous man at her side. She really had never seen anyone so beautiful in all her life, not even in films but ... But there was something about him that did worry her, disturbed her, something that she couldn't put her finger on. Laen was brutal and violent and very obviously someone she should not trust. Corin though ... *Never trust the Fae.* His own words echoed back to her and she shivered and wondered whether Laen were truly the more dangerous of the two of them.

They reached the bottom of the staircase that brought them into the great entrance hall and she cast aside her concerns as the vast scale of the building took her attention. She looked up and up at ceilings that loomed over her, taking in the beautiful designs wrought upon the heavy stone. They swirled and twisted, elegant and deceptively graceful against the sombre grey granite and she felt her breath catch as she stood still, drinking it all in. It was certainly a very beautiful place. The castle itself was stark and imposing but in places it still managed to attain a homely feel, though there was evidence of neglect as her eyes fell upon dusty furniture, and furnishings that showed signs of wear. It appeared as if this was being taken in hand, however, as they passed an open door to see Aleish scolding an uncomfortable gathering of housemaids and making obvious reference to the state of the castle.

"She's a scary woman," Corin whispered, and Océane grinned as they crept away.

She returned her attention to the building and found that there were many wonderful paintings once you got past the terrifying relatives, though the family resemblance to Laen was uncanny. They were all tall and white blond with fierce dark eyes that seemed to bore into your own until they reached the truth. She wandered from painting to painting until she came across the largest and most forbidding yet. A great mountain of a man looked back at her through the paint and even this two dimensional representation made Océane want to cower at his feet.

"Laen's father, the King," Corin said, and Océane looked up, startled by the anger and disgust in his voice.

"You don't like him?" she ventured, and turned to follow Corin as he walked away with a bitter laugh.

"Don't worry, my dear, the feeling is entirely mutual."

Océane glanced back at the furious-looking King and wondered just what kind of father could treat his son with such callousness and cruelty. It certainly explained a lot about Laen. She shook her head, wondering why on earth she was trying to make excuses for him. "What is he like then, the King?" The words were out of her mouth before she could consider her motives any further, and Corin turned back to look at the painting of the monarch in all his royal finery. Even in paint the King exuded power and menace as the promise of violence lingered in his black eyes, in the harsh sneer that might have passed for a smile, in the meaty hands that held on to the hilt of a fine sword in the manner of one who was well used to wielding it. Océane took a step back as she saw the hatred in Corin's eyes.

"I have sworn that I will kill him one day, if that answers your question."

She took a breath before fear stopped the question on her tongue. "Why--"

When Corin replied his voice was soft but no less angry. "Because of what he did to Laen, to us both." He looked up as if remembering himself and who he was talking to, and he shrugged apologetically. "Families," he said with a wry smile. "Come on, Océane." He paused in the doorway and gestured outside. "I think we had better make haste or we will get wet."

Océane looked at the ominous clouds that mottled the sky like bruises on a pale face and couldn't help but agree with him. She wished that she could ask him more about Laen but something told her that he didn't want to say anything else, and she felt it was perhaps too much like prying to pursue the matter, no matter how much she wanted to know.

"I wish I could show you my lands," Corin said, sounding rather wistful as he led her down the steps and onto a graveled path. "I think you would like it there. This is very beautiful but rather wild and unkempt. Laen is not much interested in the land. I have beautifully landscaped gardens, lakes and waterfalls, oh and you should see the rose gardens, the scent is divine when they are in bloom."

Océane looked at him in amusement. The two men were obviously used to competing with each other over everything, women included, though she could tell by the pride in his voice that he was sincere about his gardens. She wasn't sure she would agree though. She had always found formal gardens a little claustrophobic, like nature was being bound to the will of the gardener. She much preferred this landscape, where nature was being held gently in check. They walked up to a high brick wall with a door in it and as Océane stepped through, her breath caught in her throat. It was stunning.

"This used to be an orchard," Corin said as he led her through the trees. "It was planted by Laen's mother but when she died, the orchard sickened and died with her."

Océane gasped. "How is that possible?"

"We are Fae, Océane, our lives and the fertility of our land is one and the same. He or she who rules over the land influences how it looks and the health of the land is tied to our well-being, both mental and physical. This was his mother's land, and when she died it became Laen's. The rest of the Kingdom is subject to the King alone."

He smiled as she gaped at him, trying to understand what he was telling her. "That's incredible."

Corin nodded. "When his mother died, Laen could not bear to destroy the orchard. It was a place that she had loved very much. So instead he planted wisterias to grow up the dead trees and make it seem as though they lived again." She watched as he reached out and touched one of the plants. Its head hung heavy and dejected, beaten by the recent storms. As his fingertips touched one of the blooms, the whole plant seemed to sigh like a woman beneath her lover's touch and the petals smoothed out, their bruises fading away until they were fresh and unblemished once more. New shoots thrust out as more buds appeared and bloomed before her eyes and all around him birds and insects gathered, the lazy drone of bees mumbling softly as they searched and flew away, dusty with their golden treasure. She watched with tears in her eyes as he moved slowly, from tree to tree until the whole orchard was like a scene from an impressionist painting but too perfect, too vibrant to be real. She had to be dreaming.

Océane looked around and tried to reconcile the Laen she had experienced so far with the man who could create a memorial of such beauty for a loved one. The ground was carpeted with fallen blooms in delicate shades of purple and lilac through to white, and as the heavy drapes of flowers tumbled around them Océane thought she had never seen anything so exquisite or so touching in her life.

***

Corin stole a glance at Océane and sighed, knowing that she was thinking of Laen and not of him. He shouldn't have shown her his powers, shouldn't be able to do that at all. Not here. This was Laen's domain not his and he certainly shouldn't touch the land without permission. Just for a moment though he had wanted to show her, even though he knew she would not be impressed with his parlour tricks. Her thoughts were with his friend, just as they should be. He had known it was just the sort of romantic story that would warm her tender heart. The story was also entirely true, but suddenly he wished he hadn't told her.

"Come, Océane. This way." He took her hand and she followed him out of the orchard, though he could sense that she didn't want to leave. He led her along a little farther and paused as she stopped, turning to frown into the distance.

"What's that?" she asked, rubbing her arms as though she was cold.

Corin looked back at the menacing shadow that sullied the horizon like an inky smear on a clean sheet of paper. "Dark wood," he replied before turning quickly away. "Never go there."

Océane didn't move, as though she was unwilling to turn her back on the place. "I wouldn't!" she exclaimed. "Not willingly at least but ... why? Is it evil?"

He laughed and shook his head. "No. No the place is not evil but the things that live in it ..." He hesitated, his voice dropping to a whisper as though he was afraid to be overheard.

"They are?" she finished for him.

"It is not as simple as that, Océane." He looked back at Dark Wood and pushed away memories that would have sent him to his knees if he let them, nightmares that were not just in his head, but existed in the gloom of the trees, abiding in mouldering obscurity, lurking in the shadows, walking the dark places - the dwelling of old gods. "Not evil but ... ancient. Powerful." He shook the lingering gloom that talking of the place seemed to cast over him, and he forced a smile to his face. "These trees however are rather less threatening." He gestured to a well-worn path that led them into the woodland that skirted the gardens where the floor between the trees was thick with bluebells, their tiny bells covering the ground with a haze of colour as intense as a Mediterranean sea.

"Oh!" she exclaimed and pointed at the flowers. Dozens of tiny hummingbirds no bigger than a large moth darted back and forth between the blooms with sharp movements like they were tugged by strings as they collected the nectar. Their feathers glittered brightly in the dim light of the forest. The tiny, fluttering, airborne jewels glinted in shades of deep ruby and amethyst, and Corin watched Océane with pleasure, glad that he could share in her discovery of their world. "So pretty," she breathed. Corin held out a finger and a tiny bird came and alighted for a moment, allowing Océane to gently touch its downy feathers before it flew away. She grinned at him in delight and he smiled back, finding that he wanted to show her everything, wanted to make her happy. A little farther along on the trail a young deer bounded out onto the path before stopping dead and staring at them, ears twitching back and forth nervously. Océane was transfixed.

"Oh how beautiful," she said.

"You've never seen one in your world?"

She shook her head and he thought she looked sad. "I live in a city. You don't see this kind of thing there. I've always wished ..." She trailed off and shrugged and instead took a tentative step forward. Corin grabbed hold of her arm and she looked at him in surprise.

"No closer, my dear, they can be vicious creatures."

She laughed at him, her eyes alight with humour. "A deer? Vicious?"

"This is not the mortal realm, Océane," he cautioned. "Things are not always as they appear."

She turned back and the deer suddenly bellowed at her, showing double rows of nasty sharp teeth before bounding away. She shrieked in alarm and stepped backwards so quickly that she lost her balance. Corin stepped forward and grabbed her, and didn't pass up the opportunity to pull her into an embrace. She fell with her hands pressed against him and he watched as she was confronted with his golden eyes, knowing what effect they had, knowing there was something between them.

"Are you falling for me after all, sweet Océane?" He gave a low chuckle and watched in amusement as she swallowed nervously.

"Sorry," she said, failing to break away from the intensity of his eyes on her, "it made me jump."

Corin looked at her in his arms and fought very hard to behave himself. Every instinct was raging with the demand that he pull her closer, that he kiss her and make her his own, but then there was a deep, angry rumble of thunder and he looked behind them, glaring into the forest.

"Come," he said in a dull voice feeling regret sweep over him before he had even let her go. "We had better keep moving. I fear the weather is not going to be kind to us."

He led her even farther down the winding path, past wild honeysuckle that tangled and twisted in the trees, the pretty white and yellow flowers perfuming the damp air with their heady scent, past rhododendron bushes that towered over them, blocking the light and engulfing them in a darkness so profound only the white glow of their flowers lit the path like stars glittering in an icy night sky and finally out to a little stone folly that stood on the edge of a grand lake. It was ancient and ivy clad, the skill of the mason all but obscured by the lush green coat, leaving just glimpses of the beauty that lay beneath, like a Victorian lady revealing an ankle. It was sheltered with a roof and closed in on three sides, giving complete privacy and a fabulous view over the glistening, black surface of the lake. With the dramatic skyline of thunderclouds as a backdrop it was stunning in its harsh beauty, and dreadfully romantic. The staff had laid out a wonderful picnic for them and it was quiet and secluded. At least here they should be free from prying eyes.

***

Laen swore to himself as he realised where Corin was going.

Damn him.

Now he would have to tear the folly down stone by stone with his bare hands. Anything rather than look at the place again and consider what had gone on there ... what was probably going on right at this minute. Thunder crashed overhead and the first heavy drops of icy rain began to plummet from the skies as he promised himself the pleasure of beating Corin black and blue in the very near future. He had seen his friend take advantage of the situation when Océane stumbled and a fury had come over him that he simply could not understand. After all he knew better than most exactly what Corin was about, what Corin was always about, and exactly how he would try to get Océane to tell him the truth. He would have been foolish indeed to believe Corin wouldn't seduce her. Why in the name of the gods this bothered him so much he didn't know, but now at least he had to admit to it.

It bothered him.

It bothered him very much indeed and he was now deeply regretting agreeing to Corin's scheme. Like the fool that he was he had gone and given out permission for another man to seduce her. It should have been him sitting next to her in that folly. Not to seduce her but ... to try to make her see that he wasn't the bastard she believed him to be. Not completely at least, not to her.

More than anything he was furious that Corin had taken her to his mother's orchard. He couldn't figure out why but he realised that he had wanted to show her that place himself, one of the last places he had ever been happy. He wanted to show her everything.

All of it.

He wanted ...

He raged at his chaotic thoughts internally. She was driving him insane. The sooner they found out what Océane had been up to with that book and got rid of her, the better. Then things could return to normal. He thought the words with vehemence, but he knew he was lying to himself. The idea of returning to his normal life filled his heart with dread. And the idea of his home without Océane in it ...

With fury he returned to the castle, his heart full of rage and regret and with no other thought in his head than of beating something or someone to a pulp.

Chapter 16

Corin had given Océane the most wonderful afternoon. As usual, he had been charm itself and amused her with stories about his life. They were mostly stories that made her laugh at his expense, and she liked him all the more for that. He made her feel as though there was simply nowhere in the world he would rather be and whether it was true or not she was happy to believe it. The picnic had been delicious, and far from looking at her with disgust as she ate like a glutton, he seemed to enjoy her enthusiasm, and encouraged her to try everything on offer. Now they sat, replete, looking out at the rain sheeting down on the lake in front of them. The thunder storm that had been threatening all day worsened with every moment and the rain had begun in earnest the moment they had entered the folly.

There was a lull in the conversation, nothing awkward, just the comfortable sort where both parties were at ease and willing to admire the scenery for a moment. Océane sighed, feeling it strange to find such contentment given the circumstances. She listened to the rain as it hit the deep, cold water and smiled as thunder rumbled overhead once again. She had always loved storms, even when she was a child. Somehow knowing that everyone must submit to the power of nature, that no matter if you were a lonely, dependent child or a successful adult you could do nothing to stop the onslaught of the tempest was a thought that had comforted her. Everyone was equal in the eye of a storm. Turning a little, she stole a glance at Corin out of the corner of her eye. He was sat back in the corner of the folly, angled towards her but with his head turned to look out over the dark water. His gaze lifted to the troubled sky overhead and she felt suddenly afraid for him as the glowering clouds seemed to reflect in his eyes. She wondered just what it was that made him look so lost and she wondered if he would allow her to be his friend, to give him someone to confide in. She remembered what he had said when they first met, that Laen was his oldest and dearest friend but that he would stand against him if he tried to start a war with the human world. Perhaps that was what made him look so sorrowful.

She considered the tension between the two men earlier when Corin had interrupted something and she hoped he hadn't misjudged things. As far as she could see, she was only making things far worse for them both. The thought of the two of them fighting each other made her hands sweat, and she rubbed them on her dress. Though why she should worry about Laen was quite beyond her, she only knew that she did.

Corin looked up, obviously feeling the weight of her gaze on him, and he gave her a smile that made her breath catch. Not because it was flirtatious or seductive but simply because he seemed to sense her concern and was grateful for it. She returned the smile and watched his expression change, saw desire darken his eyes, and she looked quickly away. She was well aware that he had been on his best behaviour, although she had to admit to a moment's alarm when she had seen the secluded setting for their picnic. She knew now that he was a terrible womaniser; or perhaps it was a wonderful womaniser. So far, however, despite her misgivings it had been delightful. She couldn't help the suspicion, however, that there was an ulterior motive at work somewhere and she wished she could figure it out. Her instincts told her there was something inherently good about Corin and she had decided to trust in the belief that despite his sly nature, his actions were motivated by the best of intentions.

She would just have to wait and see.

***

So far, Corin congratulated himself, he had behaved impeccably in very trying circumstances. A picnic in a folly, in the pouring rain seemed to him to be the most perfect of settings for seduction, and yet he had kept his distance and his flirting to a minimum.

Frankly it was killing him.

Worse than that, the girl seemed to be at ease with him, which was troubling to say the least. Generally speaking a woman found alone in his company would either throw herself at him with no encouragement whatsoever or was as tense as an antelope in a lion's den.

This was new and would be rather puzzling if not for the wistful expression on her face. He knew with no question in his mind that despite everything he had done, she would rather be sat here with Laen than with him. It seemed grossly unfair, but then you couldn't fight chemistry. On the one hand he was glad; he would give anything to see his friend happy and if it meant he could see that the human race really was just the same as the Fae then he should welcome it with open arms ... and he did.

He did.

Truly.

He watched the rain tear at the treetops like a lover shaking his mistress in a jealous rage and he tried to smother the feelings that threatened to bubble up and overwhelm him. It was getting harder, so much harder to keep everything at bay. To carry on laughing and presenting this shallow façade to the world, to his family, his lovers ... to everyone he cared for.

He wondered how long it would be before he was swallowed up by the jaws of a fate he could do nothing but run from, when the burden would finally drag him down into madness or worse - destroy everything he loved. He almost wished it would happen now... He was so tired, tired of running.

He looked up to find Océane watching him with such concern in her eyes that his heart ached. He wondered what it would feel like to be loved by someone like her and to spend his life loving her in return. He imagined his home filled with their children, laughing and shouting and causing chaos, and he felt overwhelmed with longing. He watched as she saw the need in his eyes and quickly turned away, and he knew it was not something he was ever destined to have. He swallowed down the bitterness that followed the realisation and focused on the job he had been given. That, at least, he could accomplish.

"Do you trust me, my dear?" he asked.

He watched her eyes widen and could almost see the words *not as far as I could throw you* flicker through her mind but then her expression changed and she seemed to consider her answer more thoroughly.

"Yes."

Corin sighed inwardly. "What, no *maybe or I'm not sure,* a definitive yes?"

Océane chuckled, clearly amused by his demeanour, and she nodded.

He huffed and sat back, folding his arms. "You really shouldn't, my dear. I've warned you before, the Fae are a tricky race and most untrustworthy." He sat forward again, looking at her intently. "Are you quite sure?"

She snorted with laughter. "Would it please you if I changed my answer?"

"No, no ..." He waved his hand dismissively and sighed. "I'm just not sure how I feel about being trustworthy. On the one hand I'm very glad, as I need you to trust me but on the other it makes me feel like I'm your favourite Uncle or something, and that is most discouraging."

Océane reached out and patted his arm in a consolatory manner. "I've never had an Uncle, favourite or otherwise, but I'm quite sure if I did he would be nothing like you."

Corin's lips twitched in amusement and he took the hand on his arm in his and kissed the knuckles gently while looking deep into her eyes. It was an old-fashioned move but one that never failed to steal a woman's breath - human or Fae. But he found nothing in her eyes aside from affection and friendship. He was taken aback by just how much that hurt. He let her hand go and busied himself for a moment by putting the picnic things back in the hamper.

Friendzoned.

He had heard the expression the last time he had been in the human world and had been puzzled as to its meaning. He felt he had just been given an example that explained it in stunning clarity.

He ignored the look of surprise Océane gave him before she helped him pack the things away. They both knew if he had been going to make a pass at her, that would have been the time and he tried hard not to notice her relief. She looked puzzled, as if she was aware she had hurt his feelings but couldn't figure out how.

By the time the picnic things were packed away, Corin had his charming smile firmly back in place and he withdrew her book carefully from his jacket pocket.

Océane bit her lip.

"You are a very talented young woman; it is the most

beautiful binding I have ever seen, and I have quite an extensive collection," he told her, stroking the delicate design with a careful finger.

"Thanks," she muttered and looked at her feet.

Corin took hold of her hand and gave a gentle squeeze.

"Don't worry, my dear, I'm not going to interrogate you but I would like you to tell me the absolute truth." He used his free hand to turn her head so she could see the sincerity in his eyes. "Will you do that? Please?"

She looked up at him and he could see the fear in her eyes. "You won't believe me." She snorted and shrugged hopelessly. "I don't believe me! It's ... preposterous!"

He returned the book to his pocket and clasped her hand between both of his as though he was giving her his word. "I promise you that I will."

She looked out over the dark water and he did the same. He would not pressure her into speaking. She would tell him when she was ready. He suppressed a shiver, the only warmth in his body the place where his hands held onto Océane's and watched as the rain beat down upon the surface of the lake with fury, as though envious of its voluminous depths. Océane sighed and was silent for a moment more before she blurted out her answer. "I made it up."

Corin nodded. "How?"

"What do you mean?" She looked at him, her expression one of incredulity and disbelief that he could simply accept her answer.

He turned her hand and traced a pattern on her palm. "I mean did you sit down and think about what you wanted to write, did you dream about it, did you wake up one morning and the story was there in your head? What made you write about him like this?"

Océane frowned and looked back at the lake. Corin thought she looked uncomfortable, and gave her hand another gentle squeeze before letting it go. "It will be our secret if you prefer, my dear, but I really have to know."

She slumped back against the wall of the folly and stared out at the same view. "To tell the truth I can hardly remember. I've always made up stories you see ... in my head. Day dreams I suppose but ... But I don't often write them down." She lifted her hand to her mouth and chewed at a nail as Corin waited for her to continue. "As far as I remember I made him up when I was a teenager," she said, her cheeks flushing as she spoke. He could sense that she really hated talking about her past. She clasped her hands in her lap, the fingers entwined so hard her knuckles turned white. "I--I was very unhappy. You see I was orphaned when I was a baby and I had just been rejected by a possible family. I had stayed with them for a few weeks but ... it didn't work out. They thought I was too old to fit in with them. They said I was too difficult." His heart contracted as he saw a tear slide down her face and she brushed it away with an angry movement. He didn't know what to say to her. More than anything he ached to take her in his arms, to hold her and promise that he would never let her be alone again, that neither of them would be alone again, but he knew she would not want that, so instead he stroked her hair gently, tucking a strand behind her ear. "I am so very sorry, Océane, truly. I had no idea."

She shrugged as though it was unimportant, as though it hadn't shaped her whole life. "It was a long time ago."

"And so you made up the story of The Dark Prince, about a boy who was hurt by his family and swore to take his revenge?"

She nodded and smiled at him gratefully as though she was relieved that he had understood and she didn't have to explain it to him. "I ... I would lose myself in books and make-believe worlds. My mind was always full of these most amazing Fairy stories." She laughed and shook her head. "I have no idea where they came from ... Some of the things I came up with were ..." A strange expression lit her eyes, as though she was afraid but she shook it off and gave a sheepish grin. "And I just ... made him up." She took hold of his hand this time, looking at him with wide eyes. "Do you believe me?"

He squeezed her fingers gently before getting up and pulling her to her feet. "I believe you."

Océane looked at him as though a weight had been lifted from her shoulders. Hope glistened in her eyes and she leaned forward and kissed him on the cheek. "Thank you, Corin. Thank you so much."

Corin smiled at her and nodded, and thought that a kiss had never made him feel so very sad in all his life.

"Come, my dear, it appears the rain has eased for a moment so let me take you back before Laen decides to try and drown us again."

She stopped in her tracks, frowning at him. "Before Laen decides?"

Corin looked down at her and was glad for the sting of the cold air against his face. "Why yes, have you still not understood?" He gestured to the unhappy scene around them as the wind and rain beat against the landscape. "The land is tied to us in every way and the weather in our land is no exception. It reflects the mood of the ruler."

There was a dissonant growl of thunder in the distance and lightening branched out across a sullen sky that grew darker by the moment.

He heard Océane gasp as another clap of thunder assaulted their ears and vibrated up from the ground so hard it made his teeth rattle. "Shit," she whispered, but the wind tore away her obscenity.

"Quite so, my dear," Corin said over the din. "I think we should make haste."

They set off back through the woodland. Corin knew exactly what he would face when he got to the castle and he welcomed the thought of it. He felt suddenly that he wanted to go home, back to his own land, even though he felt sure it would be raining there too.

Chapter 17

Océane ran behind Corin, trying in vain to keep up and not tumble face first into the undergrowth. Rain obscured her vision an icy sting that made her flesh burn with the chill as the wind lashed against the countryside with a fury that threatened to tear up trees and snap them to kindling. What on earth had happened to make Laen so very angry? The idea that his emotions controlled the weather was extraordinary but now that she knew, it made a strange kind of sense to her. She accepted that this was how it should be - though she couldn't fathom why. At least he couldn't be angry with her. She wasn't even in the castle so she couldn't be the cause unless ...

She remembered the tone of his voice as his strong arms held her trapped against his chest, the tender look in his eyes, and the tension that had made it impossible to draw breath when Corin had walked in on them. Her heart was already hammering, her breath coming in gasps from running in the storm, but now as the possibility presented itself she felt a new burst of energy and began to laugh as she ran.

She was out of Laen's sight with Corin and he just couldn't stand it. It was driving him crazy.

He was jealous.

Lightening cracked and split the sky, illuminating the castle like some kind of Gothic nightmare against the purple horizon as they ran back through the gardens. She was cold and wet, her clothes soaked through and she didn't care in the least. They ran in through the great doors of the massive building but this time she saw nothing of her surroundings. She was lost in thought, wondering about the strange, dangerous man who had brought her to this place. Trailing her hands over the dark grey, stone walls, she followed as Corin led her back to her room and watched the water drip from the heavy material of her dress, leaving a trail all the way to her bedroom door.

To her surprise Corin left her the moment they reached her room and she thought he seemed preoccupied. She had thanked him for a wonderful afternoon but he seemed anxious to be elsewhere. He didn't even try to kiss her and once again she worried that somehow she had upset him as he didn't usually pass up an opportunity.

Once he was gone she stripped off her wet clothes and hung them up to dry before taking a bath. The weather was certainly very different from when she'd arrived, she mused, sinking her chilled skin into the deliciously hot water. Thunder rattled the windows in their frames and the wind made a lonely keening sound as it tore past the castle walls, and Océane smiled and sank deeper into the water.

After her bath she spent some time investigating the dresses that Aleish had brought to her and for the first time in her life spent an age agonising over which one was best. She had washed and dried her hair so that it shone and fell in gentle waves over her shoulders and admired herself in the mirror. She was beginning to get used to dressing in such a way and had to admit that the new frock in a deep shade of chocolate brown was really rather becoming to her complexion. The colour matched her eyes almost perfectly and she wondered what Carla would have made of it. Talking of her time in the orphanage had brought her friend sharply to mind and she hoped she would be able to see her soon. They had been best friends since they were very small and Océane knew she would not have survived the dreadful place if her ever optimistic friend had not been there to keep her going.

Carla had always been on at her to make more of herself, nagging her to dress nicer, put on some make-up, go out into the world and live before it was too late, forever wagging her finger and intoning dire warnings that if she wasn't careful she would end up becoming a recluse; old and alone with nothing but her pot plants for company. Thinking about Carla made her sombre though. She really did have to get back home as soon as she could. Carla needed her. She was probably worried sick wondering where she had got to, and that wasn't good for her friend's already fragile health.

A scream and clashing metal broke her from her thoughts, and she raced to the balcony. What she saw when she opened the glass doors brought her mind to a grinding halt.

Océane looked down at the scene below her and lost the ability to breathe. It took some moments for her mind to catch up with her eyes and register what she was watching. She had never seen a fight like this before except on the TV and she didn't think anything that she'd seen there had captured the power, the primal violence or the sheer terror of it. She hoped to God it was just her inexperienced eye that made it look more frightening than it was and they were just letting off steam but she was pretty sure Corin and Laen were trying to kill each other. They were both stripped to the waist and what she had come to recognise as magic rose up from around them and made her skin burn, the hairs on the back of her neck standing on end as she held onto the balustrade with fear spreading like a sickness in her heart.

The scream, it appeared, had come from one of a group of servants from the laundry room who had been chatting in the courtyard when the fight had found its way there. Océane watched them drop everything and flee to safety, leaving baskets of washing where they fell, the clean linens dropped carelessly in dirty puddles that collected on the treacherously wet cobbled floor.

"Stop it!" she screamed and the wind ripped her words away but she repeated it anyway. "Stop it! Stop it, you stupid bastards!" But the wind howled around the courtyard still, plastering the men's long wet hair to their heads and blowing the wayward baskets back and forth, the roar of thunder the only sound that could muffle the metallic clang of their blades.

The cacophony rang through her ears as the two friends fought, sword meeting sword in a relentless clash of power. She had been wrong to assume Laen would have the greatest advantage with his staggering size. Corin moved with the grace of a dancer, far quicker and more agile than the big man and seemed always to be just out of reach. It was in fact rather like some strange and violent dance as the two of them moved around each other, their eyes locked as though no one else existed on the earth.

Océane wondered if there was any way for her to climb over the balcony and scale the side of the building, but before she could try Corin stumbled over an empty basket of linens that the wind had blown in his path and she stilled. Laen took advantage of his momentary lapse and suddenly Océane could see a stream of blood running from a deep wound on Corin's shoulder. She screamed uselessly but knew she had to put an end to this before one of them died.

Shocked into action, she ran to the door of her room and pounded on it, shouting at the guards to let her out. They opened the door to her and she tried in vain to run past them, to try to explain to them what was happening but they gave her stony looks and told her to get back in her room. She screamed and shouted to no avail and they were about to slam the door in her face when Aleish rounded the corner.

"What in the world ..."

"Oh thank God!" Océane wept. "It's Laen and Corin ... outside ... They're trying to kill each other."

"Gods!" Aleish cursed, though she didn't seem as surprised as Océane might have expected. "Well it wouldn't be the first time. Come on." She grabbed Océane by the hand and told the protesting guards to shut up and go and talk to her brother about it- that is if they dared interrupt him.

"Do they do this a lot?" Océane asked as they picked up their skirts and ran through the castle.

"No, but it has happened."

They took the stairs two at a time, rushing towards the back of the building and the courtyard. "So this is normal?" she persisted. "They're not really going to kill each other?"

Aleish gave Océane a look that made her heart sink. "I've never seen Laen as angry with Corin as when he returned today. No, this is not normal."

They rushed out of the courtyard to find the two men still standing, much to Océane's relief, though they both had the clear intention of remedying the situation one way or another. Corin had obviously got his own back for his injury as blood dripped freely from a wound on Laen's arm. Both men were breathing heavily and their muscular bodies glistened with sweat and blood and the rain that continued to fall unabated. If she hadn't been so frightened for them, Océane would have taken a moment to enjoy the spectacle as they were simply magnificent. They put her in mind of ancient gladiators and would have made a wonderful illustration for her book. All other thoughts fled, however, as she saw Laen lose his footing on the slippery cobbles. Corin allowed him the briefest second to right himself but Laen was in no mood for mercy and spun around with astonishing speed to hit Corin in the face with the hilt of his sword. Corin fell heavily and Laen raised his blade as though he would finish the job.

Before she had time to consider the wisdom of her actions, Océane screamed and covered the distance between them to throw herself in front of Corin, whose sword had fallen from his hand, too far away to reach.

Laen stopped in shock at the sight of Océane covering Corin to protect him, and lowered his sword.

"Stop it," she screamed as hysteria turned to anger. "Stop it, you bloody mad man ... Do you really want to kill him? He's supposed to be your friend!"

He looked at Corin and back to Océane and they could both see the words flickering under his skin.

"He is no friend of mine." He turned in disgust and flung his sword to the other side of the courtyard before storming away.

"Laen!" Aleish called but he didn't turn around, so she ran after him.

Océane watched them go before turning to Corin with shaking hands. "Are you OK? Did he hurt you?" she demanded.

He sat up with a groan. "My pride is a little dented but I will live ... thanks to you," he replied and leaned forward, resting his head in his hands as his breathing calmed. "That was very brave, Océane, if very foolish." He looked up and smiled at her, leaning forward to kiss her forehead. "Why did you do it?" he asked as he moved away, his eyes intent on her.

Océane put her hand to her mouth to stifle a sob. "I thought he meant to kill you."

"For a moment there I thought so too," Corin said, his voice rather shaky. She saw the sorrow in his eyes and felt angry at Laen all over again. He was an ungrateful bastard who didn't deserve such a friend and yet ... her heart bled for him.

"I'm so glad he didn't!" she sobbed, and threw her arms around him, her hands sliding on his slick skin.

Corin sighed and held her for a moment. "Well I find I am rather pleased about it myself but ... The thought would really trouble you, my dear?"

She hit him in annoyance and then felt guilty as he hissed with pain. "Of course it would trouble me, you idiot, you're my friend!"

Corin snorted. "Ah yes," he said, sounding weary. "Friends."

Océane reflected on the words she had seen on Laen's skin and finally realised why Corin had been so put out. But before she could make any comment her eye was taken by the steady stream of blood coursing down his chest.

"Oh, God. Corin, you're bleeding!"

He looked down and grimaced. "It is merely a scratch," he replied, and then grinned. "Do you know I've always wanted to say that to a woman? Isn't that what the hero always says in your human films?" Océane laughed, knowing she sounded hysterical but he really was impossible. He groaned again as she helped him to his feet. "Unfortunately I rather feel I was cast as the villain in this one."

"What are you on about?" she huffed. "Come on, you'd better come back to my room and I'll clean you up."

Five minutes later she had him sitting in her bathroom while she cursed and swore about idiot men and cleaned up the nasty cut on his shoulder along with a few other minor nicks and cuts up his arms.

"Laen is a bloody maniac, he should be locked up!" she said in fury as she inspected a cut on his wrist that had come perilously close to severing the vein.

"Don't judge him too harshly, Océane."

She looked up at him in astonishment. "He just tried to

kill you!"

"Yes," he said, golden eyes watching her every move. "And I'm afraid I asked for it."

She frowned at him, kneeling at his feet. "What?"

Corin sighed and leant his head back against the chair, closing his eyes for a moment and once again she felt desperately sad for him. She had the strangest feeling that he was standing alone on the edge of a big black hole with nowhere else to go but down. "Océane, I knew how he felt about you right from the first moment I entered the library and saw you together, and I have done nothing but bait him and go out of my way to make him jealous. I have tried to tell myself that it was for the good of the land - my noble cause, but I'm afraid it was rather more base than that."

Océane shook her head. "I don't understand, what do you mean? I know you went out of your way to make him jealous, that was the whole point, but it isn't as if he actually cares for me. He's just a spoilt child and he thinks you've taken his new toy. If you didn't have it, he wouldn't give it a second thought."

He smiled at her and reached forward, touching her hair with a gentle hand. "You are very wrong, my darling girl, which is just as well as I know you have feelings for him too."

She opened her mouth to protest but Corin sat up and placed a finger to her lips to silence her.

"I have been foolish to try and stand in the way of you both. If I had been truly doing what I should, I would have found a way to bring you together sooner but ..."

She felt her eyes prickle as she saw again the longing and loneliness in his eyes. She moved to take his hand but he took it away before she could, looking away from her as he spoke.

"What were the words you saw on his face when he looked at me, my dear?"

Océane hesitated.

"It's all right, I know you saw them," he said with a sad smile.

"Desire, jealousy... love," she whispered, and the expression in his eyes as he looked back at her made her heart twist. "Oh, Corin."

"Oh gods, please don't pity me, darling, or I shall be quite undone." He got up out of the chair and walked away from her, out of the bathroom.

She gave him a moment before following back into the bedroom to find him standing, looking out of the window as the rain continued to lash the countryside although the thunder seemed to have burned itself out.

"You see how tormented he is?" He gestured to the wild scene before them and leaned his head on the glass. "He's falling in love with you, Océane, and he's scared to death."

Océane gaped at him. "Don't be so ridiculous."

Corin sat down heavily on her bed looking exhausted. "Believe me I wish I was. I swear I will never meddle in other people's love lives again, may the gods strike me down. I have caused nothing but trouble all around." He pulled the band from his hair and shook it out, scratching the back of his neck irritably. Océane swallowed and looked away. He may not have affected her in the same way as Laen but he was astonishing in his beauty.

"Laen has never before met a woman like you. The females of our lands are very beautiful but they have been brought up in a manner that was lost to the human world many, many years ago, thank the gods. All here condescend to him as he is the Prince, and as far as the Fae are concerned that is equal to your Lord God Almighty. But Laen does not want or need to be worshipped." He looked up at her and a smile that reached his eyes lit up his face. "You, my darling girl, have stood up to him, shouted at him and told him he's a complete and utter bastard and, frankly, I think he needed to hear it. I think he wanted to hear it, from someone other than me that is. He wanted someone to stop him turning into a monster. He just never expected it to be you."

"You're wrong." She shook her head. "It's true there is ... something between us but it certainly isn't love."

Corin laughed, though it wasn't an entirely happy sound. "My dear young woman, Laen has built his whole life upon a belief system that you are turning on its head. He believes the human race - the women in particular- are wicked, sly creatures that are the cause of all the evils in our land. Except now he sees that you are not like that in the slightest." Corin stood and walked over to her, taking her hands. "Give him a chance, Océane. You have said you trust me, so trust me in this. He is one of the few people in the world I truly love. He is a good and honourable man. He would be everything you could want him to be if you will only let him. Give him a chance to show you who he really is, for all of our sakes."

Océane shrugged. "If you say so." The thought of Laen having any romantic feelings for her was so ridiculous she could laugh. Oh she had no doubt he would take her to bed in a heartbeat but that was all and as for him being a good man ... Well after the way she had seen him turn on the person he called his closest friend she remained to be convinced.

"What will you do?" she asked.

He shrugged. "I think I shall keep to my room and lick my wounds for a little while and then ... And then I shall go home."

"Oh." Océane was struck by just how much she wanted him to stay. The thought of being here alone without Corin's cheerful presence was very depressing.

"My goodness that almost sounded heartfelt, my dear," he teased, squeezing her hands.

"It was, you idiot. I don't want you to go." She looked up at him, feeling the tears brimming in her eyes, and saw the flicker of hope in his before he looked away.

"Oh, Océane, you don't know how much I wish that

were true."

She laid her head on his shoulder. "It is true."

He tilted her head up and smiled at her and she was struck all over again by those golden eyes. "Yes, my love, but not enough," he said sadly. "May I ask a favour?" He looked at her and she raised her eyebrows as he appeared uncharacteristically unsure of himself.

"Of course," she said in surprise. "Anything."

"A kiss goodbye."

Océane opened her mouth to reply but before she could, his mouth had claimed hers, his strong arms sweeping her into an embrace as his lips stole every coherent thought along with the breath from her lungs as he kissed her with everything he had. Finally he released her with evident regret, though he looked satisfied at the results as her cheeks were flushed and she breathed heavily.

"Thank the gods!" He chuckled. "I was beginning to fear I had entirely lost my touch."

Océane shook her head, quite unable to process a sensible answer.

"Goodbye, my dear," he said, and brushed his lips against her forehead before turning away and leaving her alone.

Chapter 18

Océane didn't see aanyone for the whole of the next day except for a watchful maid with distrust in her eyes who brought her meals on a tray.

By the time she had finished lunch she was pacing and trying to devise an escape plan, which was obviously ludicrous as even if she could get out of the castle, she had no way to get back to the mortal realm. She had no idea where the gates were, let alone how to use them. Carla had been brought to her mind however, and now that the possibility of her own immediate demise seemed a bit less likely she had begun to worry for her friend in earnest. She would likely be out of her mind by now and would probably consider, quite rightly, the idea that Océane had been abducted or worse. There would be no other possible explanation for her complete disappearance with not so much as a text to explain. They had spoken practically every day of their lives since they'd met and such a thing was totally out of character. She could only imagine what effect this was having on her. Carla was far too sick already to have to deal with such stress.

She wondered how her last hospital appointment had gone and worried at a finger nail that was already bitten way past what was attractive. She'd had the uneasy feeling for some time that Carla was putting a brave face on things ... again. Now she feared what kind of news she may have received and knew that whatever it was, she was dealing with it all alone.

She had to get home, one way or another.

She began pacing again after pounding on the door of her room had brought no response from the guards other than an angry shout.

It was boredom that finally brought her to spying when she'd heard giggling coming from outside her bathroom window. She had taken yet another bath to try and while away the time and unwind a little, and she had left the window ajar afterwards to allow the steam to escape. The weather was cold and the rain fell in a fine unrelenting drizzle that made everything feel damp as thunder and lightning rumbled like an invisible predator on the horizon. Laen was clearly still in a temper and she hoped that Corin was all right. She could only imagine how he felt at having his best friend try so hard to kill him. Feeling the draft from the window swirling around her shoulders gave her the chills so she went to shut it. And as she did so, she heard it, a girlish laugh.

Looking down she saw a little girl of around six years old playing under cover of the terrace that ran around part of the courtyard. She had three wooden ponies and was pretending to gallop them around in a circle, splashing them in the puddles that gathered at edge of the terrace. She was an adorable child with long white blond hair, which ironically seemed to be the norm for dark Fae. Her rosy cheeks dimpled when she giggled, which was most of the time. Her dress was long, a light blue velvet and covered with a white pinafore. The hem of the pretty outfit was wet and muddy and she seemed oblivious to the fact that it was soaking in the puddle she was playing in. "I know what you need," the little girl declared to her horses, hands on hips. "A nice bed to sleep in. That will warm you up. I'll get you some lovely straw to make you cosy."

With that, she ran out into the rain and over to the building opposite the window and Océane's heart sank as she realised exactly what the child had in mind. There was a wooden ladder leant against the side of the building, leading up to an opening high up in the wall which was obviously where the straw was kept. The ladder was extremely tall and the rungs looked wet and slippery. Océane looked around frantically for someone to come and stop her before she fell. For such a little thing, however, she moved like lightening and was already on the fourth rung. Océane opened her mouth to shout at the girl and hope that the shock wouldn't make her fall off, but Laen appeared from nowhere and ran across the yard, plucking the child deftly from the ladder.

He put her down and stared at her severely as Océane watched with fear in her heart for the little girl's fate.

"Lise, how many times have you been told not to climb that ladder?" he demanded as Lise bit her lip and looked up at him with big doe eyes. Laen frowned. "Don't look at me like that, you know you shouldn't go up there!" he said, pointing up at the hay store. "You could have fallen and hurt yourself and ..."

Lise pouted and kicked her toe in the dirt, before looking up at him again through her lashes. It was obviously a well-calculated move and her target dissolved like an Alka Seltzer.

Laen stopped and shook his head. "Oh, you little wretch. You know full well I can't be cross with you."

She beamed at him and ran into his arms as he picked her up and swung her around, making her squeal with laughter. "Do it again, do it again, Lala!"

Lala?

Océane smothered her mouth to muffle the snort of laughter that escaped at hearing the almighty Prince of the Dark Fae addressed in such a way.

She watched in amusement as Laen knelt down so he was closer to the little girl's level. "Promise me you won't climb that ladder, and I'll do it again."

Lise looked at him, a tiny frown creasing her forehead as she appeared to consider her options. "I'll promise ..." she said carefully, "if you'll be my horsey."

Laen groaned. "Oh no, Lise. Not that, please!"

Lise folded her arms with a determined expression. "Horsey."

Océane swallowed a giggle as she saw Laen accept his fate with humility.

"Gods, I pity the man you marry, Lise," he said as Lise jumped up and down when she realised she'd won. Her tiny fingers grasped his big hand and she looked up at him adoringly.

"Can I marry you when I grow up, Lala?"

He sighed and the look he gave made Océane swallow. "Well I'm glad someone wants to," he said with a sad smile.

"Horsey now, please," Lise demanded, apparently determined not to be distracted from her purpose.

Laen folded his arms and gave her a stern look, though it was clearly all for show as the child could wrap him around her finger. "Do you promise then?"

"Yes, yes, promise," she said, jumping with impatience and sending her blonde hair bouncing on her shoulders.

"Come on then, you little minx, your steed awaits." Obediently he got to his hands and knees on the dirty cobbled floor beneath the terrace and bent his massive frame as low as he could so that Lise ccould climb on to his back.

Océane watched with a combination of amusement and wonder that the man she had seen in the same courtyard trying to kill his friend the day before could be so sweet to a little girl. He seemed not to care that the dirty hem of her frock was leaving muddy marks on the fine white linen of his shirt or that the cobbles were probably ruining his trousers, not to mention the fact it must be hurting his knees. Instead he allowed the child to order him around and submitted to her demands to *go faster, Lala* with patience and good humour until a horrified voice rang out across the court yard.

"Lise!"

A stocky man appeared and rushed towards them looking utterly mortified as he took in the scene.

"Papa, look at my horsey," Lise squealed in delight.

"Your Highness!" choked out the man in shock, obviously quite at a loss for words.

Laen sat up carefully, with one hand guiding Lise so she could slide down his back without falling off. "It's quite all right, Drew, she's no bother."

Lise ran over and took her father's hand. The poor man looked like he was about to suffer a cardiac arrest. He looked down at her and shook his head in what appeared to be a hopeless gesture. "How many times must I tell you that this man is your Prince?" he demanded. "He is *not* your plaything!"

"He's my horsey," she said, crossing her arms and pouting as her father swallowed and turned to Laen in despair.

"Just wait until she's seventeen," Laen said with a grin as Drew's panicked eyes widened in fright.

"Please, Sire," he begged. "It doesn't bear thinking about." He looked down at his daughter who was grinning at him and looking quite unrepentant, and his face softened. "Come along, you little devil, let's go and tell your mother what you've been up to this time."

Drew led the little girl away and with a puzzled expression and a strange feeling growing in her chest, Océane watched as Laen left the courtyard in the direction of the stables.

***

A little later Corin stood with his hand raised at the door of Laen's study and steeled himself before knocking and walking in. His friend, if he could still call him that, stood at the window once again, simply staring out over the landscape. He wondered if this would be the last time he stood here in Laen's study or if he would no longer be welcome, and he was overwhelmed by sadness. Not only was he not going to get the girl - he was losing his one and only true friend.

"You're still here then?" Laen observed, though he didn't turn around. His voice was even, neither angry nor remorseful and Corin swallowed, hoping they wouldn't part with so much left unsaid. He would rather Laen ranted and raged and threw him out than offered him indifference. That he could not bear.

"Apparently," he replied, his voice equally emotionless.

"I thought you would have been keen to get away now."

"I am, but I wasn't thrilled about leaving in this dreadful weather," he said, forcing a weary smile. "You know I can't abide riding in the rain."

"By all means borrow a carriage," Laen growled.

Corin sat down in one of the big leather arm chairs and closed his eyes. "My, my," he murmured. "You really are eager to be rid of me."

Laen didn't answer but continued to glower out of the window as the rain pattered against the glass a little heavier.

They remained in silence, and with the weight of things unsaid hanging between them so heavily Corin felt he could have sliced through it with his sword. He considered all the ways he could try to explain to Laen what had been going on but rejected each beginning in turn. It was not in his nature to be at a loss for words but Laen had been withdrawing further and further from him over the past months and finally he felt as though things were coming to a head. Maybe it was for the best, he wondered, maybe it was fate as the darkness that his dreams threatened grew closer still.

"She saved your life," Laen said.

Corin looked up as Laen's voice brought him back to the here and now. "Yes." He nodded. "Yes she did, and yours too, come to that. You know you would never have forgiven yourself."

Laen did not turn around.

"I wouldn't have killed you," he said, glancing over at Corin. "I could never ..." His shoulders slumped and he leaned heavily against the wall as if he was suddenly exhausted. "I mean ... it crossed my mind for a moment but ... I could never do that. Not to you. You must know that?"

Corin let out a breath and smiled. "I thought not but I admit ... I am very glad to hear you say it just the same."

He was silent again but Corin kept quiet, aware he was building up to something. You had to give Laen time to speak what was on his mind.

"You'll take her with you then?"

Corin sat up in his chair. "You would allow me to?" he asked in surprise.

"She would have sacrificed herself for the man she loves. That deserves some kind of reward doesn't it?" Laen shrugged but still kept looking out of the window, apparently unable to look his friend in the eyes. "Though I don't suppose it will be long before you tire of her. What will happen to her then?" he asked and Corin could hear the hurt and bitterness in his voice.

"Oh, Laen," Corin said, shaking his head. "I know this is all my fault but you really must listen to me." He got to his feet and crossed the room, laying his hand on Laen's enormous shoulder. "Nothing has passed between Océane and myself other than a kiss, and I took that, she did not offer it. She doesn't love me."

He felt Laen tense and sensed anger in his stance. "Don't be idiotic. Please give me a little credit," he growled, shrugging off Corin's hand. "She spent an entire afternoon alone with you and you expect me to believe that she is not in love with you and that you didn't lay a hand on her - again!"

"Yes, Laen I do, because it is the truth."

Laen did turn now, frowning at him. "What do you mean? Yesterday when you came back you said ..."

"No, Laen. I didn't say, I implied and you are always so damned ready to believe the worst of her and me!" he snapped, hearing the fire in the hearth blaze up the chimney as his own anger sparked.

The confusion in Laen's face was clear to see. "I nearly killed you yesterday and now you tell me you didn't ..." He stopped, too baffled to continue. "Why?" he demanded. "Why would you do that?"

"Because I was angry and ..." Corin hesitated and looked away from him for a moment not wanting to see the words spelled out for him before admitting the truth of the matter. "And because I was jealous."

"What in the name of the gods have you got to be jealous about?" Laen shouted in fury.

Corin turned and faced him, equally enraged. "Because she doesn't want me, she wants you, dammit!"

Laen opened his mouth to say something, and closed it again and Corin knew he still wouldn't believe it. He had spent too much of his life alone and unloved to accept someone could fall in love with him so readily, especially after the appalling way he had behaved. Frankly Corin was struggling to understand how it had happened himself and he knew it was true. As predicted, Laen shook his head. "That's ridiculous and you know it," he said, turning back to the window.

"No, my friend, it is the truth." Corin said, wondering how Laen could still be so completely blind as to what was right under his nose. "Much as it pains me to admit it, I am telling you the truth ... and believe me when I tell you it does hurt."

Laen turned to look at him and Corin stood under his gaze, hiding nothing and knowing that Laen must be able to see what was in his eyes as clearly as he could see the words flickering under his friend's skin. "Gods, Corin. You love her?"

Corin laughed, though it was not a happy sound. "Ironic, isn't it?"

"But ..."

Corin watched, amused despite everything as Laen floundered, completely bewildered at the turn of events and still clearly looking for a reason to prove Corin had lost his mind.

"But yesterday she saved you. She could have been killed!" he exclaimed. "And you mean to tell me she doesn't love you?"

"Oh, I think she is very fond of me and yes maybe she does love me but ... just as a friend." He snorted. "I had never thought to dislike that word quite so intensely." He looked at Laen through narrowed eyes. "I begin to feel that friendship is greatly over rated."

Laen looked at him and away again and shook his head, his thoughts clearly still in a tangle. Corin decided to give him a moment to process as whatever it was looked to be giving him a migraine, and walked to the desk to pour them both a large drink. For his part he felt ready to drink himself through Laen's considerable cellar and back out the other side.

"Maybe it's true that she is the kind of woman who would sacrifice everything for a friend," Laen mused. "She is ... different from anyone else I have ever met, so ... So full of fire," he said, the admiration clear in his voice. "But just because she doesn't love you, it doesn't follow that she wants *me*."

Corin stared into his now empty glass. "Do you want

her, Laen?" He looked up and saw the uncertainty in Laen's eyes, the fear of everything his admission would imply. He knew the question had been burning in his friend's mind for days and that it hadn't been until yesterday when he'd seen Corin lead Océane into the folly that he had really answered it with any truth.

"Yes."

Corin felt an ache in his chest at the answer which he knew was foolish. Nothing had changed. He had known it before Laen had. "Well then, what are you waiting for, you fool?"

Laen didn't answer and Corin put his glass down, stepping closer and grasping Laen by the shoulders. Through a heroic effort of will he did not yield to the urgent desire to give the pig-headed half-wit a damn good shake, and instead spoke with a patience he was far from feeling.

"You've not exactly treated her kindly, Laen. Yet there is something between you despite that. What do you think might happen if you showed her the truth, if you actually put your heart on the line and admitted how you truly felt?" He paused and did squeeze his shoulders this time, though there was about as much give as trying to crush a boulder. "What would happen if you showed her that you really are a good and kind man who could love her as she deserves, if you stopped treating her like the enemy when you know full well you were wrong about their kind?"

Laen frowned and looked back at him and Corin felt as though he was looking into his own eyes as he knew only too well that the idea of giving his heart over to someone else's care scared the big man just as much as it did himself. Gods, what a pair they were.

"And what if you're wrong?" Laen demanded.

Corin shrugged and let him go. "Maybe we need to get our hearts broken. For my own part, I can say it is a ... humbling experience."

Laen walked over to his desk and picked up the board

with the half-finished painting on. "And what of this ... The Dark Prince is Lost?"

"You could just ask her," Corin replied dryly, wondering how much more his patience could stand before he beat the idiot around the head with the first heavy object he could lay hands on.

"How can I be sure she would tell me the truth?"

Corin frowned. "I have spoken to her and I believe her story, every word of it. Laen, you have to begin to trust her if you are going to get anywhere but ..." He smiled as an idea began to form in his mind.

"What?"

His smile broadened as he heard the suspicion in Laen's voice. He went back to the desk and poured himself another drink and looked down into the deep black liquid, swirling it thoughtfully. "We could take her back to get the original."

"What do you mean?" Laen looked at him and frowned. He looked nervous. Corin downed the drink, enjoying the burn as the liquor made its way into his blood and helped himself to another. "Well, she's bound to have written it down somewhere, probably on a computer."

"On a ... what?"

Corin rolled his eyes. "Gods, Laen. You really must educate yourself about the human world; your ignorance is really most unbecoming."

Laen glowered at him and a rumble of thunder growled in the distance. "Damn it, Corin, just tell me what the hell is going on!"

"I was about to but I have to go and explain every single blasted word. It's like talking to a child!"

"Watch your mouth!"

Corin slammed his glass down on the desk as his patience departed. "Look, you big oaf, I've just handed you the woman I love on a plate, and I'm not at all sure you deserve her right now so you'll have to forgive me if my good manners are all used up!" Corin glared at him and waited to see whether he was about to get pounded again but Laen just took a deep breath.

"So," he said as Corin watched a little nerve leaping in his jaw. "What is your point?"

"My point is that she will have the original ideas written down and we should take her back home to get them," Corin said, pleased at the idea. He would have to go with them of course. Laen would never survive the human world without revealing the existence of the Fae nation as a whole but he hoped it would also give him a chance to make things right between them. Perhaps this time he really could try and help Laen not to make a complete pig's ear of winning the woman he had clearly lost his heart to, if only he would admit it. The gods knew he had spent much of their younger years educating him on the art of seducing a woman. Though despite his best efforts Laen's technique still seemed to rely heavily on brooding in a dark corner, but he had to concede it had not harmed his success rate.

This time however he felt he needed to handle things with a little more finesse. Besides ... an adventure might be just what they all needed.

Chapter 19

Laen ushered the guards from their sentry duty outside of Océane's doors and barked at them to find something more useful to do. He then stood in the spot they'd vacated and wondered if it might be better if he came back later. Because she might be ... sleeping. Yes, she might be asleep - despite the fact it was well into the morning. Or maybe she was busy. He huffed in exasperation with himself, pacing up and down for a moment until he finally admitted that she was neither busy nor sleeping but probably damned angry with him and liable to bite his head off the minute he stepped in the room.

He raised his hand, which hovered over the heavy oak door, and then he cursed and walked away back down the hallway. He made it about thirty feet before grinding to a halt, cursing some more and retracing his steps.

His hand rose to the door again. He could do this.

The knock seemed incredibly loud in the quiet corridor and he winced and then clenched his knuckles as he waited, and no reply came. He gritted his teeth and was about to leave when a slightly puzzled voice called out.

"Come in?"

He realised that nobody had ever knocked on the door before ... except maybe Corin as she was a prisoner and had not been allowed the right to privacy. He sighed as another layer of guilt added to the weighty pile he already felt smothering him. He told himself to man up and he opened the door.

She looked startled as well she might as she saw him come in, and he wondered how he could ever have made such an unflattering comparison about her eyes. The deep chocolate depths of them widened in surprise. His heart gave a lurch as they fixed on him and he prayed to the gods that he wasn't about to mess everything up. He hesitated in the doorway like a fool, his hand still on the handle like he wasn't sure if he was actually going to come in or turn and run away like the pathetic excuse for a man he knew he really was. Making his decision, he turned suddenly and pushed it shut, rather more firmly than he had intended and she jumped out of her skin as it slammed.

Damn.

Her eyes never left him and as he returned to meet her gaze he felt his wits and his tongue tie themselves in a pretty bow. It seemed the only way he could interact with her was if he was being an utter bastard and scaring her half to death. It was entirely her own fault however for looking so ... So ... Damn. She had chosen a red dress today. No, he amended, not red, plum. The deep red of a ripe plum, and gods did he want to sink his teeth into that tender flesh. He swallowed and shifted his weight from foot to foot.

Think boring thoughts, think boring thoughts ...

He looked up to see her still watching him, curiosity burning in her eyes as her eyebrows lifted enquiringly.

"May I ..." He discovered his voice sounded hoarse so

he cleared his throat a little too loudly and tried again. "May I speak with you for a moment?"

She frowned at him and shrugged. "Prisoner ... remember?" she said, pointing at herself with a raised eyebrow.

"I was trying to be polite," Laen muttered, thinking that he must be out of his mind to want this woman so very badly. He'd barely been in the room two seconds and he was already sweating and vexed.

"First time for everything," Océane replied with a sweet smile.

He ignored her sarcasm, because he had to agree with her. Instead his eyes travelled over that dress again. The front was held together by laces that pulled the material firmly across her breasts. The soft creamy swell visible above the low neckline was suddenly the only thing he could focus on. He tried to look away but his eyes seemed to be glued in position and he wondered what she would do if he crossed the room and ran his tongue over the delicious mounds. He could consider nothing else more worthy of his attention in the whole of the kingdom.

Focus, man, for the love of the gods!

He tore his eyes away with a tremendous effort of will, only for them to drift immediately back as he was distracted by the thought of how the dress would fall to the ground if he simply gave those laces a tug.

That elegant eyebrow of hers arched once more. "Was there something you wanted?"

Her sarcastic tone implied that she knew full well what it was he wanted and he hurriedly cleared his throat again. "We are taking you back to your home."

She looked back at him in astonishment. For a moment her face split into a wide smile, but it fell abruptly and for just a moment he thought he saw regret in her eyes. "You ... You're really going to let me go?"

No! He shouted internally. *I will never let you go.* He felt his chest tighten just at the thought of it and shook his head. "I did not say that," he replied, rather more severely than he had intended to. "I said we were taking you home. I never said we would let you remain there."

"Oh."

He stared in surprise, as she sounded relieved, but then she added "you bastard" onto the expression for good measure. Just in case he was in any doubt.

He grimaced. "Nonetheless, we will be leaving shortly. I will get someone to bring you your ... clothes." He said the word with distaste. The thought of seeing her in those ugly rags again did not please him. The idea of taking her back to the human world was even worse. From what he had seen it was filthy and grey and seething with danger. How had she lived there ... all alone? The tightness in his chest seemed to reach his throat as he considered the idea of her returning there. Who would protect her? Who would see that she was safe and warm and ...

"Well?" Océane demanded.

He jumped as he realised she had addressed him. "I ... What did you say?"

She frowned at him like he was a lunatic.

"I asked why you were taking me home." Those big brown eyes focused on him and he had the strangest feeling she could see right through him, through the menacing face he showed the rest of the world to keep them away, to make them leave him alone. Even stranger was the fact that he wanted her to, wanted her to know everything about him, good and bad. He said none of that of course, because he was a coward. That was the truth of the matter. He wanted to kneel at her feet and beg for forgiveness but even if he could get the words out he wasn't sure he could bear the idea she might never. She was far too smart to forgive a man who had abducted and brutalised her. Why the hell would she? Shame burned so fiercely that he could hardly breathe.

"Well?" she pressed.

He forced himself to answer the question. "Because I

want you to show me the rest of the story."

"Oh." She looked uncomfortable and his heart grew heavier still as he saw a blush stain her cheeks. She didn't want him to see it. What had she written? *The Dark Prince is lost* ... She must have written some bloodthirsty ending for him. The villain should always have his comeuppance after all so that the hero could carry the girl off into the sunset.

"I take it you do have it written down on a ... computer?" he asked, hoping suddenly that she hadn't, that there was no record of it and he would never need to know what she had planned for him.

Océane nodded and Laen sighed. Well then, finally he would get to the truth of the matter and when he discovered the ending ... When he discovered the ending ... "Very well," he said, turning to leave.

"Um, Sire ... Er, Your Highness?"

He turned back with a frown. It always sounded so sarcastic when she said it. "Yes."

"Why didn't you just ... you know." She waggled her fingers in the air by her forehead. "Use your superpowers like Aleish did if you wanted to know so much?"

He looked at her in horror. "Because that would have been a gross invasion of your privacy, such things are strictly forbidden by Fae law!"

She looked surprised. "Even for prisoners?"

He raked his hands through his hair, before stuffing them into his trouser pockets. "Well, no, actually, but first of all ... I cannot do that," he admitted. "It is Aleish's gift. My talents lie ... elsewhere." *Yes, in fighting and killing and waging wars and abducting helpless women.* "I hoped that you would eventually tell me the truth and in any case I do not approve of such methods." He saw her dumbstruck expression and continued. "It is usually necessary to sift through many ... private thoughts before finding anything useful and I find it ... distasteful."

She took a step closer and he could see she looked puzzled. He guessed that she had believed there were no limits to his brutality. She leaned on the bedpost and he felt as though he was standing in a spotlight as her gaze never left his face.

"You threatened to do a lot of things against my will," she said with a soft voice, though her eyes were fierce, burning into his soul. "Wouldn't that have been a gross invasion of my privacy ... or do you not find things of that kind *distasteful?*"

He closed his eyes, too ashamed to look at her.

"Océane," he began, wondering how on earth he could ever make this right when there was nothing he could do to change what had happened. There was nothing that would ever wipe out the stain on his honour that he had put there through his own stupidity. "Océane, I have no right to expect anything from you. I know what you must think of me and I do not blame you or dare hope to change that but ... But please believe me when I tell you, I would never have done such a thing. How I behaved was ... vile and unforgivable and I can hardly bring myself to remember it. I can only tell you that I hoped to frighten you into telling me the truth." He took a step closer and held his hands out before dropping them uselessly and averting his gaze once more. "I know that is not exactly a good thing either but ... in the circumstances I did not know how else to find out what it all meant. I know that in no way excuses my actions though and ... I'm ..." *Sorry*, he screamed internally, *I am so sorry, please forgive me!* The words burned on his tongue and he wanted so badly to say them but his voice failed him and they sat in his throat, so heavy that he couldn't swallow. He couldn't bring himself to look at her again, too afraid to see the disgust in her eyes at his pitiful attempt to redeem himself. Instead he turned away and walked back to the door.

"Wait!" she called and his heart leapt as he stopped beside the door. "You said we are taking me home. Who's we?"

Laen didn't turn around. "Myself and ... Corin."

"Oh!" she said, and he could hear the relief in her voice. "OK, great."

He nodded and walked out the door, shutting it carefully behind him even though he wanted nothing more than to smash it to bits. He took a breath and reined in his anger. This was his own fault. It was all his own doing. He had no right to blame Corin when he was obviously the one she wanted, and why not? What would any sane woman do, choose the man who had beaten and abused her or the one who had done nothing but try to protect her and make her feel safe? Corin had rocks in his head. Falling in love had clearly addled his brain if he couldn't see that Océane wanted him.

He walked back along the corridors feeling as though the miserable grey clouds outside were wrapped tightly around him, that he was dissolving into them until nothing was left but a dirty black cloud that lingered in the background, sucking the life and the goodness from everything it touched.

***

Corin looked up as the door to Laen's office opened and his heart sank as the man himself came in. He did not bear the demeanour of someone who'd had a happy morning.

"I am guessing it didn't go well?"

Laen shrugged and strode past him, taking up his usual position by the window with his back to Corin. "What did you expect?"

"Devils and whores, Laen, I expected you to make an effort," Corin exclaimed, exasperated. Gods! Did he have to do everything himself?

"I did!" Laen shouted and then sighed, his great shoulders slumping as he turned to him. "I tried, I swear it, Corin. I tried to explain - I did explain but ... I could not say it. I ..."

THE DARK PRINCE

Corin's annoyance melted away as he walked over to him. He tried hard to keep the sympathy from his eyes as he knew it would only make Laen angry, but his heart broke for his friend as he saw the despair in his eyes. Laen simply could not apologise; he'd had the ability beaten from him when he was a very small boy. Dark Fae warriors underwent a very particular training and were never allowed feelings of regret or sympathy, and the King had gone to great lengths to ensure Laen received the same treatment.

He laid his hand on his friend's arm for a moment. "You don't always have to say *I'm sorry* to have your meaning understood, Laen."

Laen's black eyes were full of regret as he spoke. "But she deserves it. She deserves to have my head on a damn platter! The least I could do ... The very least ..." He cursed and folded his arms, looking steadfastly out of the window.

"The least you could do was try and explain, and you have done so. Give her time to think over what you have said. It is simply the first step, Laen. You have given her little reason to trust you and now you must take some time to earn that trust. Have a bit of faith, man!" Corin slapped his back and smiled at him as Laen shook his head.

"Why are you even doing this?" he demanded.

Corin shrugged. "You are my friend. I want you to be happy. I want you both happy."

Laen frowned, his expression gruff. "I do not deserve you do I? I never have."

"No," Corin said with a heavy sigh. "You must have been horribly wicked in a previous existence."

There was a snort of laughter. "That is usually my line," Laen replied as Corin grinned at him.

"I know."

Laen's amused expression changed to incredulity as he finally took in the way Corin had dressed today.

"What in the name of the gods are you wearing?' he demanded.

Corin's grin widened. "We need to pass as human males, so when in Rome ..."

A puzzled expression filled Laen's eyes. "Rome? I thought we were going back to Paris?"

"Oh, really... Laen, it's an expression. I just mean we need to blend in. Here put this on, it's all I have that may fit you."

He threw him a black T-shirt. Hopefully with Laen's usual attire of leather trousers and boots it should make him look reasonably normal. Reasonably. Corin was dressed as usual for one of his trips through the gates though he could understand why it appeared strange to Laen's eyes. He wore fitted black jeans, a T-shirt, boots and a black leather jacket. If he said so himself, it rather suited him.

Laen gave him a look but said nothing as he undid his shirt. Corin was well aware Laen knew he stored clothes and things he needed for his trips through the gates here in the room that was kept for him. The gates in Alfheim were actually much farther away from his home than crossing the border into Laen's terrain so he generally came here instead. He usually spent a few nights with his friend before heading off to the human world to escape from his responsibilities and his ties to the land when things got too much. The visits had become increasingly frequent. Laen had turned a blind eye for the sake of a quiet life for many years but recently it had become a source of tension between them. He hoped now that this would cease as he had a feeling his visits may be getting longer.

Laen pulled on the T-shirt and grimaced. "It is too small."

Corin covered his mouth with his hand to hide his smile and frowned critically, looking him up and down. He stifled a snort of amusement as Laen held his arms out in disbelief. "Well, yes and no," he said, trying hard not to laugh. "It is rather tight I grant you, but that is how they are worn."

"You have got to be joking."

Corin had to concede that the black muscle shirt did look rather like it had been sprayed on as it showcased an impressive six pack and displayed arms that looked like they could rip up ancient oak trees without breaking a sweat. "No, I'm not joking I assure you," Corin replied with a grave tone. "But do us all a favour and keep your coat on or ... we may be trampled in the stampede." Laen's blank expression and complete failure to understand the joke tipped him over the edge and he roared with laughter, at which point the big man blushed as the penny dropped. Corin laughed harder. "Oh, gods, Laen, please stop it. You are too funny."

"Idiot." Laen grumbled as he pulled his big leather coat on. It almost reached his ankles. Along with his pale skin and black attire he now looked like a Goth on steroids. "Come on, let us go and see if the horses are ready, if you have quite finished," Laen said.

Corin cleared his throat and nodded, wiping his eyes as his laughter subsided. He followed Laen out of the door and took the familiar route to the stables. But as they went, his thoughts took a more solemn turn. He had spent every moment since he had come up with this scheme trying to convince himself that he was doing it for the right reasons, which he was. He had told Laen the truth and he did want them both to be happy, that was why he was doing this. It had absolutely nothing to do with the fact that he also wanted a little more time with Océane, none at all. He knew he couldn't have her but ... he reasoned that if he was to let them go alone, Laen would only mess it up due to his ignorance of the human world. Besides, it was a good chance for them to give Laen a crash course in the better features of the human race. Not only that, but if he was also hoping to be with her for a little longer, well, that would be nothing short of masochism, which would be stupid ... and he was not stupid, he hoped.

Chapter 20

Océane pulled her jumper on with a surprising amount of regret. She had gotten used to the way the dresses felt swishing around her ankles and she had to admit to enjoying the admiring glances she received from Corin and ... She sat down on the bed, so heavily the springs creaked. Her skin prickled with heat that spread low in her belly as she remembered the way Laen had watched her when he had come in earlier. He had looked at her like he was starving and she was his only source of nourishment, like he would do anything ... just for a taste of her.

She had been just moments away from crossing the room and throwing herself at him when he had left inexplicably. She knew she should be relieved that he had saved her from doing something so rash and dangerous and completely out of character but she just felt cheated and ... bloody frustrated. Dammit, why did her wits always desert her when this man was around? It was the perfect opportunity to give him a good dressing down and she had wasted it.

Speaking of dressing down, however, she hadn't been able help looking at the leather trousers he always seemed to wear and noticing how well they clung to his muscular legs. Groaning, she lay back on the bed and told herself to behave. Lust was the path to nothing good. Instead she considered the explanation he'd given of his behaviour and she found she wanted to believe him. She had felt he had been sincere, only... he had never looked her in the eyes when he spoke. She picked at the bed covers with nervous fingers and wondered what would happen when they got to Paris. What would he think when he read the ending of the story?

There was a knock at the door and her heart pounded as she wondered if he had returned for her.

"Come in," she called. The door opened and she felt her face split into a grin. "Corin!" she leapt off the bed and ran to give him a hug. "Oh, I'm so glad you stayed." To her surprise he gave her just a brief embrace and stepped quickly away from her but he looked pleased by her reaction.

"As am I, darling. So are you ready for our trip?"

She nodded and found her mouth was dry as she looked him over. Corin dressed for the Fae world was enough to give any girl palpitations but now ... He looked like every woman's erotic fantasy. He raised his eyebrows at her and she grinned back at him before giving him a slow wolf whistle.

"You have no idea how appropriate that is, darling." He chuckled.

"Oh?"

He stepped closer to her, golden eyes glittering with amusement and bent to whisper in her ear. "In our world ... they call us the wolves."

"Do I want to know why?" she asked him with a quirk of her eyebrow.

A wicked smile played over that gorgeous mouth as he

replied. "Because we eat up all the pretty little lambs."

She laughed, shaking her head. "Oh, I just bet you do."

He opened the door and gestured for her to go through. "Just wait until you see Laen."

She paused as a thousand butterflies seemed to burst free of their cocoons in her stomach. "Oh?" she said, hearing that her voice was a little shaky.

There was a knowing look in Corin's eyes as he tilted his head, considering her. "And how did you get along with him this morning, when he came to apologise?"

She hid a blush by walking through the door and out into the corridor. "I don't know." She shrugged. "OK, I guess." She stopped and turned to face him. "Did you make him come or did he mean it?" she demanded. "I mean ... he sounded sincere but ..." Sighing, she shook her head. "I don't know. He's impossible to read."

Corin took her hand and tucked it comfortably in the crook of his arm. "He really isn't, darling, not once you know him." He was quiet for a moment as they walked the corridor. "You must understand, Océane, Laen has had a hard life with very little in the way of love or affection. It ... It has affected his ability to show his feelings, but that does not mean he doesn't have them." He looked down at her and gave a smile that was full of warmth but that seemed to be rather wistful. "He has feelings for you, my dear, I promise you. The trouble is that he does not know what to do with them." Océane snorted as she remembered the desire in Laen's eyes and Corin chuckled. "I was speaking of feelings of a romantic nature. I can assure you he would not be at a loss for anything else."

Océane blushed to her toes and wondered how on earth he always knew what she was thinking. She glared at him suspiciously. "Are you sure you can't do the same freaky mind reading stuff as Aleish?"

He laughed again and she could not help but smile at him despite her annoyance. "No, darling, I can't. I promise. Mind reading is not one of my talents. I am, however, extremely observant and very good at reading people. The look in your eyes and the colour in your cheeks was quite enough to guide me as to your thoughts, and knowing Laen as I do ... I just joined the dots."

They walked out of the castle into the same courtyard that her bedroom looked out on and she glanced up at the little balcony, wondering if she would ever see it again. Stupidly she realised that she wanted to, very much. As she looked around she noticed that the thunder and lightning had stopped and, in fact, the skies had lightened. She wondered with a sigh if the idea of tormenting her by putting her on a bloody horse again was cheering Laen up.

A couple of hours had passed and frankly Océane had needed the time to collect her scrambled thoughts after seeing Laen. She found it hard to look at him at all. He had stowed his long leather coat behind him and the black T-shirt he was wearing clung to his chest, lovingly accentuating toned abs and ... biceps that made her heart pound. Covertly she watched them flex as he easily managed the brute of a horse he rode and she felt her mouth go dry as she remembered how they had felt around her waist. She wondered if she'd bump into anyone she knew when they got back and sincerely hoped she did. She had every intention of grabbing both men by the arm and saying, 'Yep, they're with me!'

She glanced over at Corin and tried to catch his eye but he carried on looking straight ahead. She watched him carefully. He'd been unusually quiet since they'd left and she hoped he was OK. She realised now that she had hurt him and wondered once again why on earth she didn't want him instead of Laen. He had been so very kind. She hoped he would find someone soon. She had the feeling that he was dreadfully lonely but some sixth sense told her it was more complicated than that. Looking away she realised Laen was surveying her as she watched Corin and she thought he seemed a bit off as well. After his apology this morning and what Corin had said, she had hoped maybe she would find a change in him but he seemed as moody and unreadable as ever. At least it wasn't the angry 'I hate you, human scum' kind of vibe that she had come to expect.

"Is it much farther?" she asked for the fifth time, in the hope of making conversation. The silence was doing her head in.

Laen replied without turning around. "Not much farther, no."

"And so we just go to my flat and come back again?" she pressed.

"Yes."

Bloody hell, it was like pulling teeth. They were not just going to her flat and coming back though, she would make sure of that, she thought with a smile. They rode on in silence and Océane watched the scenery change with interest and remembered the day she had arrived in this strange world, when everything she knew had changed. Dark Wood glowered in the distance and she saw Corin look towards it. His expression gave her the feeling that he knew only too well what dwelt there and she wondered what it was in the darkness of the trees that troubled him so.

The sun was going down, colouring an already sombre sky in shades of shocking pink and lurid purple when the men stopped the horses in the middle of a field. She looked around in surprise. They were in a meadow with hedgerows on two sides and woodland on the others but they appeared to be in the middle of nowhere. "Why have we stopped?"

"We're here," answered Laen.

"Where?" Océane looked around her in confusion. Other than the trees and bushes, they were standing in a sea of long meadow grass. She could see a mountain range in the far distance, the snow-covered peaks drifting in and out of sight as the pink-tinged clouds drifted past like candy floss, but there was nothing in the way of a gateway as she had expected. Laen stepped over to her and to her immense surprise offered to help her off her horse. She shook her head nervously and slithered to the floor in an ungainly heap. She was pleased he was being thoughtful but the idea of his hands on her waist made her breathless and she didn't want to react like that in front of Corin. The thought just made her too uncomfortable.

Laen turned away as a man appeared out of the tree line. He bowed low to Laen and Corin as they handed him payment. The man then took the horses and disappeared back into the trees.

"Now what?" she asked, looking around and feeling increasingly perplexed.

Corin smiled at her. "Watch."

Laen walked to the middle of the field and held his hand out. For a few seconds nothing happened and then it seemed to Océane that the world in which they were standing had a skin over it. Around Laen's hand that skin began to wrinkle and pull back and through the hole she could see Paris, cars, noise, people rushing in all directions and not one of them taking a blind bit of notice of the hole in their world.

Once it was big enough, Laen stepped through, followed by Corin who held his hand out.

"Come then, my dear. Adventure awaits," he said with a smile, though Océane thought the devilish twinkle that was usually in his eyes was missing and it made her sad. She took his hand and followed him through. There was a rush of cold air and a hard prickling sensation as she stepped into the gash between realms, a sweet almost sickly smell rising up around her until both feet were securely placed on the Parisian pavement. There was a pull on her skin and the gate shut like an elastic band snapping back to shape.

Her first thought was, *damn it's bloody freezing!* It was clearly still February and Laen hadn't bothered to pick her coat up when he had abducted her. At least she wasn't just wearing a T-shirt though, she thought in amusement as she could see goose bumps up Laen's arms. She was suddenly struck with the strong desire to rub her hands up and down them to warm him up and she took a hasty step back just in case the feeling overcame her good sense. She couldn't help but watch as he pulled the heavy leather coat back on, surreptitiously eyeing those shoulders and arm muscles as he moved.

"Why can't they see us?" she asked, dragging her reluctant eyes from the floor show.

"Because we do not wish them to." Corin smiled and Océane felt goose-flesh creep up her own arms as she wondered what other tricks they could do. Probably best not to ask.

"You know where you are?" Laen demanded and Océane rolled her eyes.

"Of course I know where we are!"

"Very well then, which way to your home?"

Océane looked up at those black eyes that watched her and wondered how he was going to react. She stepped a little closer to Corin just to be on the safe side. "We're not going there."

"What?" they said simultaneously.

"Océane ..." Corin said, looking worried, "you do need to do this."

She glanced at Laen, whose face was blank, totally impassive, and she bit her lip. Taking a deep breath she thought of Carla and put her chin up. "I'll take you. I promise I will, but not yet. There's something I have to do ... Someone I need to see." She thought she saw a flicker of emotion in Laen's face at that but it was gone too fast to be sure. She hurried on, the words tumbling over each other in her rush to explain. "It's my friend. You see she's very sick and I need to go and see her. She'll be so terribly afraid for me disappearing like that with no word and I think the stress of worrying for me will make her worse. We've been friends forever and I've never left without explaining where I was going, please ..." She paused and took a step towards Laen. "Please. I need to see her." He was watching her with curiosity and she stood still, waiting for him to yell at her, but he said nothing. To her surprise and relief his face softened and he nodded his consent. She beamed at him, delighted.

"Oh, thank you!"

***

Laen felt as though she was holding his heart in her hand and squeezing it tight as she smiled at him. Firstly, she had never smiled at him before, at least not a proper smile, and it was a new and instantly addictive experience. He needed her to do it again. Secondly, the thought warmed him that she had risked his anger to see a sick friend. He now wanted with all his heart to believe that Corin was right, that the human race was really no different from their own. Years of blind hatred were not easily overcome though, and he needed evidence of that before he could truly believe it.

They followed in her wake as she headed into the crowds and they walked through the busy night time streets of Paris. Laen looked around him in interest though his hand was clasped tightly around the handle of a dagger which was stashed in the deep pockets of his coat. People hurried past them on all sides, heads down and bodies wrapped up in thick layers of clothing. At one point Océane reached back and took both of their hands, towing them across a busy street.

"You have to move or they'll run you down, no matter if the light's red," she said, her eyes glittering with laughter at Laen's shocked expression. Car horns blared and drivers yelled. The sounds of sirens drifted on the icy winter night as music slid from the shop doorways along with the smell of cooking. Sitting outside the cafés under heat lamps and drinking tiny cups of coffee or cloudy glasses of Pastis,

Parisians talked animatedly about their days. He paused for a moment in front of a shop where the mannequins had horse's heads and garish sparkly clothing, and Océane grinned at him. He found himself smiling back even though he knew he looked shocked. He was shocked. The last time he had visited, he had been totally focused on the job at hand and could not afford to be distracted. It had also been daytime, which he had found enough of an assault on his senses. Paris in the daytime was indeed a jarring contrast to his own world but it seemed to come alive at night. Once again he felt fear crawling down his spine at the idea of releasing her - as he knew he must - and allowing her to return to this place alone. He glared at any man who dared get within ten foot of her and one fool who had the stupidity to jostle her in passing looked like he would be in need of a speedy change of underwear when he walked smack into Laen's chest as he intercepted him. "Watch your step, damn you," he had growled with such menace the poor bastard had turned a sickly shade of green.

Océane hurried over and pulled him away with assurances that she was fine but it did nothing to ease the tension thrumming through his blood. He didn't want her back here. It was too dangerous. She should stay in his lands where it was safe, where he could protect her.

They walked on and Laen stopped to look at a large bronze sculpture of a centaur. "You have those here?" he asked in surprise and Océane laughed.

"Only in books."

He let out a breath, relieved, and then caught her looking at him. He shrugged and smiled a little. "I did not get much time to look ... the last time." He trailed off, wishing he hadn't reminded her of what he had done the last time he was here.

Before Océane could respond, a tiny bundle of clothing rushed with fierce determination across the street and grabbed her by the arm. "Océane?"

Laen stepped forward, all protective instincts on alert but Corin grabbed hold of him, shaking his head. They looked at each other and then down at the woman curiously, wrinkling their noses. She appeared to have newspaper stuck down her coat and she smelled ... strongly. She was also giving Océane a severe telling off about something.

"Worried sick, we were. Fancy going off and not telling anybody, I'm surprised at you. You best get yourself round and tell Pierre you're still in one piece and not decorating the streets of Paris in black bin liners." The woman huffed crossly, looked Corin and Laen over, apparently finding them wanting as she rolled her eyes. She muttered darkly about men and finally stalked off.

"I will, right away," Océane promised to the retreating figure.

"Make sure you do," she said over her shoulder before disappearing back into the crowd.

Océane looked at Laen nervously and he frowned at her.

"Um," she began, looking anxious. "I need to make a detour ... I have to ..."

"Who is Pierre?" Laen demanded, ignoring the fact that Corin was giving him a pointed expression and shaking his head.

"Oh, well ... He's a friend ..."

"A friend from where?"

"Er ... You see I volunteer one night a week ..."

"Volunteer for what?" he barked, knowing full well this was not the way to gain her trust. But he felt his control spiralling as she fell further back into her own world and away from him.

Corin sighed. "Laen, if you let her finish a sentence I feel sure she will explain."

Laen narrowed his eyes at Corin, hating the fact he knew he was right, and he gritted his teeth. "Very well, explain."

"At a soup kitchen, I volunteer one night a week. Pierre, that's the guy who runs it, he's been worried about me ... Disappearing like that ... I just need to call in and tell him I'm OK."

His fists clenched tighter around the dagger once again as he was overwhelmed with the desire to demand what in the fires of Tartarus Pierre meant to her. But his jaw ached he had it clamped so tightly shut, not trusting himself to speak in case he ended up interrogating her all over again. After all she must have had a life before she came here and innocent or not that didn't mean she hadn't got someone she cared about. Visions of Pierre being some gorgeous human lothario danced in his mind, driving him insane. By the time they reached the soup kitchen he was wound so tightly that people instinctively dived out of his way, such was the air of violence he brought with him.

The kitchen was busy, as it always was on a cold night. It was one large room filled with tables and chairs with a serving counter set up at the end where dozens of people lined up to get a hot meal and a cup of coffee.

"What is this place?" Laen asked.

"A charity ..." Océane looked at his blank expression. "A place where the homeless can get out of the cold for a bit, have something to eat for free."

"These people have no homes?" he demanded, looking around at the shabby huddled figures, bent with total concentration over their plates.

Océane shook her head.

"Why not?"

She shrugged. "Too many reasons to tell. Some have run away from home, lost jobs, loved ones ... been abused. People donate money to keep this place running and the volunteers come, for free, to cook and serve the food."

He looked into her eyes and found he needed the warmth in them. He wanted to keep looking at her the way he would stare at the hearth on a cold night, drawing comfort from the flames. "Why? Why would you come here?"

She hesitated and he felt she was considering whether or not to tell him the truth.

"I would come here when I was feeling bad. Some days I didn't want to get out of bed, it didn't seem worth it. You know?" she asked and he nodded, stepping a little closer to the warmth she radiated. Yes he knew. She shrugged and it was such a hopeless gesture that he felt it as a physical pain, all the sharper for the clarity of his understanding. She folded her arms around herself and instinctively he knew how small she felt here in this bustling world full of people, how insignificant.

"There just didn't seem to be any point in it, in anything. The idea of getting up and doing something with my life seemed like the efforts of a grain of sand in trying to change the face of a desert." She looked back, gesturing to the queue and he drew his eyes unwillingly from the safety of her gentle expression to the press of bodies crammed into the room behind them. All classes and races, ages and religions brought to the same destination by a myriad of reasons, fate scattering them together like missing puzzle pieces, displaced, lost, forgotten, accidentally slipping through the fingers of a careless hand. "Those were the days I came here," she said. "Strangely this place was the mirage that got me out of bed and it became my oasis. Not because it was a pretty lie but because the ugly truth gave me clarity. I had no right to pity myself so much." He looked back at her and felt such a surge of empathy and affection it was all he could do to stop himself from reaching out and pulling her into his arms. Anything to keep her safe, to save her from such emptiness.

"It helped?" he asked, this time trying to moderate his voice to make it an enquiry, not a demand.

"Yes." She nodded. "Yes, it helped."

"Océane!" A man pushed his way through the line and pulled her into an embrace. "Where have you been?"

"I'm so sorry, Pierre, I ... Well, it's a long story."

Laen looked at Pierre and to his relief found he was an older man, tall and wiry with a short beard. He knew, without being conceited, that this man was no match for him, but nonetheless, he strongly disliked the way he had so casually put his arms around Océane. Pierre stood now with one arm across her shoulders looking at both Laen and Corin with undisguised suspicion. "Is it really?" he asked. "I've got time."

***

Océane glanced at Laen in alarm as he looked very much like he wanted to squash Pierre like a bug. On the one hand she was rather pleased by the proprietary look in his eyes as he was clearly jealous. On the other hand he was positively vibrating with tension and clearly looking for a means of venting it and she would rather Pierre left with all his limbs intact and in the appropriate places. She searched her mind for a plausible explanation but came up empty. "Ummm ..."

She was well aware that with every second she failed to explain herself, Pierre was getting more suspicious and was now glaring at the two men and Laen really wasn't helping. Corin had pulled a baseball cap from his jacket pocket before they came in and made Laen wear it to try and disguise the writing on his face. He had also instructed him to stay in the shadows. Now, though, he was doing exactly as Corin had instructed, he just exuded hostility and definitely looked like someone you would not wish to meet in a dark alley.

"I think maybe we should introduce ourselves." Corin stepped forward in front of Laen and held out his hand to Pierre, who took it reluctantly. He offered the man his most charming smile, which only made him frown harder. "I am Corin Albrecht and this..." He gestured briefly to the glowering figure at his back. "Is my friend, Laen. If perhaps you would allow me to explain?"

"Oh, God, yes please explain, Corin ... You're so much better at it." Océane looked at him with gratitude.

"You see we are old friends of Océane's from out of town and I'm afraid we turned up unannounced, very ill-mannered I know, but we wanted to surprise her and ... Well I'm ashamed to say we have rather monopolised her time while she showed us ..." He waved his hand to encompass their surroundings. "The ... er highlights of Paris."

Pierre frowned harder, looking unconvinced, and turned to Océane. "Is that right?"

"Oh yes, Pierre, and I'm so sorry I didn't let you know but I lost my mobile and ... And ..." Océane blushed as she stumbled over the lie but Pierre seemed to accept the story and shrugged.

"That's OK, no need to apologise, just as long as you're all right."

It suddenly occurred to Océane to wonder why on earth she was reassuring him. Surely she should be running around screaming her head off that the gorgeous nutter in the hat had abducted her and was holding her prisoner. They would surely call the police and rescue her and she would never go back to the Fae Lands or see Laen or Corin again and her life would return to normal.

"Yes, honestly. I'm perfectly fine, fit as a fiddle, never better!" she replied with her brightest, most reassuring smile.

She said goodbye to Pierre and turned to see Corin and Laen with identical expressions on their faces, and knew that they were wondering exactly the same thing.

Chapter 21

Back on the streets of Paris, Océane wondered if she had finally lost her mind. Perhaps it really was Stockholm syndrome after all, she mused, casting a sly look at Laen. Bloody hell, but he was gorgeous. It was just that she felt like she wanted to give him a chance. Corin had said she should and he had known Laen since they were children. She knew Corin was a little in love with her and she didn't think he would suggest such a thing if he didn't sincerely believe it. She decided she would give him the benefit of the doubt if for no other reason than that she desperately wanted to. But if he showed even a glimpse of his previous behaviour she would be off and running through the streets of Paris.

"I'm freezing!" She shivered, trying to stop her teeth from chattering.

"Would you like my jacket?" Corin asked, though in truth he didn't look much warmer than her.

Océane shook her head. "No, come on. Let's go and warm up." She darted into the next café on their path before either of them could reply, and Laen and Corin were obliged to follow her inside. It was blissfully warm and packed with people who'd obviously had the same idea. The room was filled with the low chatter of conversation and music playing, the scent of fresh coffee and burning dust from the overworked heating system on the air. Threading their way through the crowded room, they found a free table crammed in the corner and ordered coffees.

Océane watched in amusement as Laen tried to fold his huge body up and tuck his knees under the tiny table with little success. Corin grabbed at the wine list, which made a bid for freedom when Laen's knee bashed the table top and catapulted it in his direction. He rolled his eyes at Laen. Océane smothered a giggle as the big man blushed before rediscovering his usual *'don't speak to me if you want to keep breathing'* expression. As she looked up she saw that every female in the room and a few of the men were looking in their direction as though they had just seen exactly what they wanted from the menu. She gave them the evil eye and they looked away fast, probably wondering how in hell someone like her had ended up in the company of two earth-bound gods.

They made their orders and she hid a smile as the waiter made doe eyes at Corin. She looked at Corin to see how he reacted and smiled as he seemed unperturbed and winked back at her with a grin. As they waited for him to return with their orders she felt tense and clenched her fists to stop herself from biting her nails. She needed to do something as the awkward silence that now hung over them was appalling. Once the coffees arrived it became even worse as they all sipped quietly and she could do nothing but stare at Laen's big hand as it gently cradled the tiny coffee cup.

To her surprise, Corin broke the tension by declaring he had just seen someone he knew. Taking his coffee in hand he got up and disappeared around the corner. She watched every head turn as he passed before she stared down at her cup, blushing. It had obviously been a blatant lie and they both knew he was giving them time to be alone together. With nervous fingers she tore open the packet containing the small chocolate that had come with the coffee with such haste that it flew from the wrapping and across the table. Laen's hand reached out so fast that she didn't have time to register the fact before he handed the chocolate back to her.

"It's OK." She shrugged. "You have it."

She looked away from those disturbing black eyes and back down to her coffee only to see him put his own unopened packet on the saucer of her cup. She looked up at him and gave a nervous smile. "Thanks."

"Try not to juggle it," he said, his voice gruff but with an amused look in his eyes.

She picked up the little packet and handed it back to him. "Perhaps you should do it. I seem to be all fingers and thumbs."

Obediently he opened the packet with care and handed it back to her. She retrieved the little chocolate from its plastic cover and popped it into her mouth. "Try yours," she said, gesturing at the one she had thrown at him only to realise his gaze was focused on her mouth, his expression one of such hunger that she didn't think one little chocolate was going to help much. She chewed self-consciously and wondered what the hell to do next.

***

Laen had watched his best friend retreating with a mixture of gratitude and horror as he couldn't think of a single, damn thing to say to the woman opposite him. There was so much he wanted to say... needed to say but he just didn't know how to begin. He had never been good at talking about emotions, and would frankly rather stick pins in his eyes. He knew this irritated the hell out of Corin, who didn't find it a problem at all and was forever trying to get him to open up - with little success. It was usually Corin who mediated for him when such intervention was required with a woman. To be fair this wasn't often as his affairs rarely lasted for more than a night. He didn't like emotional entanglements and would swiftly disengage from any potential for tearful goodbyes. Corin strongly disapproved of the way he treated his lovers and often stepped in to pick up the pieces. At one point he had been forced to observe that Laen's women all suffered from whiplash, he sprang from their beds so fast. Not that Laen cared. He didn't care if they hated him and in fact preferred it to the idea that they might be wasting their love on him. This time, however, he discovered he cared very much and he was aware that, so far, he'd made an unholy mess of it.

He had spent the last half an hour wondering why Océane had been quite so quick to reassure Pierre that she was all right. It would have been the perfect time for her to sound the alarm but she hadn't even tried. What's more, for some reason he hadn't been concerned that she would. He trusted her, he realised with a jolt. He looked across the table and her dark eyes held his for a moment until she blushed and looked away. How he had found himself in his current position, he simply couldn't fathom. Océane was supposed to be his prisoner but somehow she was leading him by the nose around Paris and what's more, he didn't mind in the least. Somehow he had to make it clear that he wasn't an ogre ... or at least that he wouldn't be to her, not if she wanted him. For her he would happily curl up in a ball and purr like a kitten if she wanted. He tried to bring to mind all of the sage advice Corin had given him over the years about flirting with women, and couldn't remember a word. Feeling increasingly uptight as the opportunity that Corin had given him began to slip away, he told himself sternly to man up. He cleared his throat and Océane looked up at him expectantly. Damn.

"Does ... your friend live close to here?" he asked, hoping this was a way to get her talking. He breathed a sigh of relief as Océane lit up and snatched at the conversation with enthusiasm.

"Yes, about ten minutes away." She nodded and then looked anxious as though she was wishing it was farther so she could talk about it more.

Laen fumbled around for his next line as he systematically shredded the plastic cover of the chocolate he had handed her. "You said she was sick, what ails her?"

Océane bit her lip, cradling her empty coffee cup between her hands. "Cancer," she said, her voice barely more than a whisper. "She was diagnosed a long while ago. We've been friends since we were children. We don't have any family, so it's always been her and me against the world," she said with a smile.

Like him and Corin, he thought with a frown, though Corin's family were not in any way as cold and cruel as Laen's. Corin's Mother, the Queen of Alfheim, had her own special way of tying him up in emotional knots with her games at court. From whoring him out to those she needed influencing and brought on side, to locking him in the dungeons if he spoke out against her. She was as manipulative as she was beautiful. Their circumstances and their positions as crown Princes within the land's most powerful families had given them common ground when they were actually polar opposites. Their friendship had not always been an easy one but they had always found a way through or, at least, Corin had always been generous enough to forgive whatever it was Laen had done. He didn't deserve it on the whole but besides his sister Aleish, Corin had been the only person who had ever given a damn if he lived or died. Corin would lay down his life for him in a heartbeat and Laen would not hesitate to do the same.

"He's a good friend to you, isn't he?" She gestured in the direction that Corin had left in and Laen nodded.

"Better than I deserve. To be honest I ..." He stopped and shook his head. "I cannot understand why he bothers."

"I think that about Carla. She's such a lovely girl. She's always cheerful even when I'm being a bitch. I'm afraid

I've got a terrible temper," she admitted and he smiled inwardly as he remembered how she had raged at him. She paused and his heart broke as her eyes filled with tears. "She doesn't deserve the life she's been given. She doesn't deserve to be so sick. It isn't fair." She stopped as her voice broke and looked away as she brushed away a tear.

Oh, nice work, Laen, he thought to himself savagely. You finally open your wretched mouth and now she's crying! Feeling like a brute, he reached over the little table and took her hand, giving it a gentle squeeze.

"I am so sorry."

Her head shot up as she looked at his big hand covering hers and her shock was palpable. He felt his heart sink into his boots at her reaction and was about to withdraw his hand when she looked up at him. His breath caught in his throat. Her beautiful eyes were so warm and glittering with tears, and then on top of that she did the most wonderful thing. She smiled at him again. Totally lost and bewildered by the fact that she hadn't withdrawn her hand the minute he touched it, he brought his other hand to the table and held hers within them both.

***

Océane stared at their clasped hands in disbelief. Laen was holding her hand! She somehow resisted the urge to squeal but almost lost it and giggled. She bit her lip savagely to contain herself and sat utterly motionless in the hope she wouldn't spook him. It would appear that he was far from being spooked however when he slowly but insistently rubbed his thumb over her palm in a circular motion. The sensation was all at once soothing and disturbing and somehow became so physically intimate she thought she might actually spontaneously combust.

"Do you miss your home?" he asked.

She looked up from their hands in confusion and had to focus hard on the question before she could answer as his touch was so incredibly distracting.

"Yes, of course ..." she began automatically and then stopped. "Yes and ... no."

"Oh?"

She couldn't miss the hopeful tone of his voice and she smiled a little as she replied. "This whole experience has been ... terribly frightening."

"I know," he butted in, his hands tightening on hers. "I shouldn't have ... I should never have treated you like that!" She was taken aback by the self-loathing in his voice but she wasn't about to disagree.

"No. You shouldn't," she said and was quite pleased that she'd sounded so severe as the thumb stroking her palm was doing things to her insides. To her disappointment he began to withdraw his hand, obviously thinking she was angry with him. She held on to it though and wouldn't let it go. The look on his face made her pause. He seemed so relieved and the smile that followed made her heart do a little somersault in her chest. "Anyway, that aside, your kingdom ..."

He shook his head. "I am not king yet."

"Well, whatever it is, your land ... It's so beautiful. I'm envious. Paris is an amazing place, great for my work. There are museums and galleries everywhere you turn but ... I've always wanted to live in the country. The city smothers me, it's so big and busy and ... lonely," she admitted.

"You are lonely?" His voice was gruff but his eyes, usually so fierce and intimidating, were filled with concern. She swallowed, her heart pounding in frantic excitement.

"Yes, I am." She looked back at him and willed him to say what it was he was thinking so that she needn't keep guessing, but he said nothing. Instead he just brought her hand to his mouth and kissed it gently. It was the barest touch, but Océane still felt his lips burning against her skin even when they were no longer touching her. The feel of them seared like a brand and she felt a ripple of desire flood through her veins and pool in a central point that she had to try very, very hard to ignore. Her breathing hitched despite herself and she looked determinedly at the dregs of her coffee, quite unable to look up and meet his eyes, which she knew were studying her every move. She licked her lips nervously as he lifted her hand once again, turning it this time to plant a soft kiss against her palm. This time she did look up and the smile he gave her made her heart leap in her chest.

She watched in approval as he moved his chair as close as he could get, and she leaned into him, feeling the heat of his big body warming her even through his leather jacket. Her head naturally fell to rest against his shoulder and for a moment she felt like she had found the most comfortable spot in the entire universe; a safe haven in a world that had not treated either of them kindly. She dared to look up at him and found it hard to breathe as she caught the tender look in those black eyes. Moving instinctively she raised her head, hoping that maybe ... maybe he would kiss her, but at that moment Corin returned to the table, putting a hand on Laen's arm. "I suggest we get a move on," he said with a hesitant smile.

Océane straightened up quickly and tried to remove her hand from Laen's before Corin could see but he had taken them both by surprise. He smiled at them in his usual manner but Océane had caught the look on his face as he saw them together and her heart twisted with guilt. Oh, why couldn't she have just fallen in love with Corin, it would have made things so much simpler. Not that she was falling for Laen, she assured herself, she just, she just ... Well, she was just curious about him. Yes, that was it ... curious. A little voice snickered in the back of her head and she told it firmly to keep its opinions to itself.

"Actually," she said to Laen, deciding she was going to test him and see if he really could be trustworthy. "My flat is closer to here than Carla's. If you promise I can still go and see her, we could go and get the story first."

Laen smiled at her. "Yes, of course."

Oh. She tore her eyes away from his mouth with effort. It really was a devastating smile and all the more so for being rare.

Corin paid for their drinks and she led them out of the café and back onto the icy pavement as they followed her home through streets with too many forgotten corners and past the jagged-toothed windows of forsaken buildings. The closer they got, the more colourful the walls became, illustrated with spray-painted markings announcing the possession of place or person like dogs pissing on a lamp post. Somehow the swirls of garish colour only made the place duller still.

Eventually they stood outside her building. It was a massive block of flats that made Océane feel smaller than ever stood in the landscape of her own life and as usual the lift was broken. They had to climb seven flights of stairs up to her floor. She took the all too familiar path and with each footfall her body felt heavier, colder. As always she felt like the cold grey concrete beneath her feet was sucking the life from her soul, like the longer she stayed the more the colour and vitality leached from her life and she walked her days like a faded old film. Her movements were captured faithfully but the colour was reproduced in black and white. Before the men at her side had arrived she had existed in the brightly coloured world that lived in her head, her real life a shadow compared to the vivid beauty of what lay in her imagination. The glittering lights on the horizon sparkled, sharp and cold and only illuminated everything she already knew.

She had spent as much time as possible hidden in galleries and museums, cloistered securely from the real world, surrounded by the beauty that she could not afford or was unable to bring to her own life. She had stayed here because she had begun here, not because she wanted to. Not because she belonged here. She didn't know why exactly, as Paris was a vibrant place, a whirlwind of creativity that should have fed her artistic nature, but she had never felt that she belonged and the excitement and exuberance of city life had changed with time and experience to an underlying fear of danger and isolation. The noise and the dirt and the bustle just segregated her more the longer she stayed. Now the sensation gripped her anew and she found herself totally out of place. Surely she didn't belong here? She didn't want to belong here! The thought made panic rise in her chest as the smell of refuse and urine assaulted her nostrils. The leavings of the human world flitted around her feet, chocolate wrappers and empty larger cans scattering on the wind along with the contaminated leftovers of the druggies who found an escape from their own monochrome world into a neon landscape of chemical devising.

With tears in her eyes she found herself longing for the sweet untainted air of the Fae Lands but it was so utterly foolish that she gave herself a mental shake. This ugly grey reality was her home and no amount of daydreaming about being whisked to her happily ever after by a handsome Prince was going to change that. Laen would read the story, realise he had made a mistake, and let her go. And she would never see either of those impossibly handsome Princes or their beautiful world again. She almost laughed out loud at her own stupidity. One of her teachers had told her once as a child that she should grow up and stop believing in Fairy tales. It would appear she still hadn't managed it.

By the time they reached her door she had composed herself again and dug her key out of her jeans pocket. She hesitated with the key still in her hand and looked around at them. They were the ones out of place here, not her. This was her life, her reality, where she belonged and she wished that she didn't have to suffer the humiliation of showing it to them, but she guessed there was no choice. With a sigh of regret she unlocked the door and stepped inside. She glanced at Laen to gauge his reaction, and looked away when she saw that he was very clearly shocked. She could only imagine what a Prince must think of her, living like this. She had done her best with the place with her meagre income but now she saw it through his eyes, the shabby brown chair with the stuffing hanging out, washing hanging over the back of the doors and the disgusting orange carpet she couldn't afford to replace. It was all mean and pitiful and that was without adding the strong smell of damp from the leaking pipe in the bathroom.

***

Laen stood in Océane's flat, imagining her here all alone, and had to stop himself as the pain in his chest threatened to overwhelm him. He simply couldn't believe that anyone could live like this. But Océane ... His Océane had been forced to. He took a breath and nearly choked on the stale air. He turned around and knocked into the kitchen cabinet, sending a landslide of crockery tumbling back into the sink. Cursing himself for being so clumsy, he stepped back and almost sat down as he backed into the tiny kitchen table. There was barely enough room to swing an undernourished mouse, let alone a cat. One small room served as a kitchen, living and dining room with a door that led to an even smaller bedroom and a bathroom so tiny he couldn't have turned around in it. Yet every available surface was crammed with plants, some of which looked wilted and thirsty. Océane sprang into action, grabbing a chipped mug with a discoloured picture of Monet's garden on, filling and refilling it with water and dashing around while Laen looked on with the painful ache in his chest growing stronger. He hated the idea of her stuck in this tiny room, longing for green fields and trees and compensating with as many plants as could possibly fit. It made him want to sweep her back to his land and promise her that every single inch of it down to the very last blade of grass was all hers if she would only take it from him.

The feeling shocked him so much that he couldn't speak.

THE DARK PRINCE

She finished her watering and put the mug down as he watched her wringing her hands uncomfortably, looking at them both with big frightened eyes. He didn't want her to look at him like that, not again, and he struggled to find a way to tell her that it was all right, that he wouldn't let her live like this for a moment longer, but he couldn't fathom how to begin. Instead he just stood there like a fool until Corin spoke.

"The story?" he prompted gently and she nodded and pulled a laptop out from under the chair. With a complicated arrangement that required careful balancing of various boxes connected by leads, she managed to set up the laptop and printer and out came the story. Laen watched the proceedings as his brain turned and came up with absolutely nothing of help past the fact that he was in love with her and there wasn't a damn thing he could do about it.

Once the story was printed she got a plastic folder and put the pages inside, holding it out to Laen with defiance in her eyes. Her chin was up as she looked at him, as though she was daring him to find fault with it. "There."

Laen looked at her, surprised by her manner and tone of voice. He felt she was cross with him suddenly and he wanted more than anything to tell her it didn't matter. He didn't want to read it any more. He really didn't. If she had written him a gruesome death or assassination, then he didn't want to know.

He didn't think his heart could stand it.

The story, however, was the reason they were here and he couldn't say anything now. When they got back to his home he would give it back to her, unread, and perhaps then she would understand what he was trying to say. He could only hope so as he seemed to be quite unable to find the words himself. It would be all right, he assured himself. He just had to get her back to his home and everything would be all right.

He watched as Océane grabbed a coat from her wardrobe and turned out the lights, and they headed back outside.

Chapter 22

Océane stood outside the door to Carla's flat wondering how on earth she was going to explain not only her absence but also the two men standing behind her. Carla may be sick but it hadn't affected her brain and she was going to want answers. She turned to Laen and Corin, who were looking at her quizzically, wondering what she was waiting for.

"I don't know what to say to her," she admitted, clutching her arms around her body. She had never felt so cold in all her life.

"Don't worry, my dear," Corin said with a reassuring smile. "Just use the excuse we gave Pierre and we will back you up, won't we?" He turned to Laen who nodded but said nothing and Océane wondered if he was counting the moments until he could get out of this filthy place. He hadn't spoken a word to her since he had seen her flat and she figured he had worked out the fact that she was so far beneath him she may as well be an amoeba. She wondered what his family would say if he brought someone like her home. They'd probably chop off his head for sullying the bloodline. He probably felt that way himself anyway. He certainly had when she'd first arrived.

"OK." She turned back to the door and took a deep breath before knocking. She didn't like lying to her friend but if she told her the truth she'd have her carted off to the funny farm.

She heard the keening wail of a police car a few streets away as she shuffled about on the door step while the dazzling lights of Paris turned the night sky a pale purple. It was as though the jet sky had faded from misuse, and the sickly violet was what they were left with in place of the deep star-studded black she had seen in the other world. She shoved the longing for it away and instead focused on the soft footfalls she heard approaching the door. There was the noise of various bolts and locks being turned and slid back and Océane's heart froze when the door was finally opened not by Carla but by a nurse.

"Oh, my God. Is she OK, what's happened?"

"I'm guessing you're Océane?" the nurse queried and Océane nodded, frantic to know what was going on. The nurse extended her hand and Océane took it. "I'm Charlène. I've been looking after her. Please come in." She let them in the flat, which was almost identical to Océane's even down to the smell of damp that clung to the walls and the hideous wallpaper that both she and Carla despised. She gestured for them to take a seat and then carefully closed the door to the bedroom. Océane watched her, hardly daring to breathe as she turned back around and instinctively knew she was going to be hearing bad news. She felt a lump appear in her throat and suddenly felt sorry for the nurse having to be the one who broke it to her. She was a young black woman, tall and slender and she had the most beautiful hair. It was very long and tied back into hundreds of tiny, delicate plaits. Perhaps it was a strange thing to notice when she knew what was coming. Carla would have admired it and commented on it by now for sure, she thought, and swallowed hard as the nurse sat herself down, her eyes soft and full of sympathy.

"Is she OK?" Océane asked, hoping anyway for an answer she knew she wouldn't hear.

The nurse reached forward and touched her hand. "I'm so very sorry but it appears that the cancer was far more advanced than anyone had realised."

Océane felt her eyes fill and shook her head. "No, no, no. Oh, no ..." She put her head in her hands and after a moment felt the armchair she sat in creak as someone sat beside her and placed a comforting arm on her back. "Why isn't she in hospital?" she said, her voice thick as she tried to hold back her tears.

"She was. She was taken straight in after the results came back but there was nothing they could do so she discharged herself." Charlène smiled and it was a warm and genuine smile. "I have never, in all my days, known a more stubborn woman than the one in that bed." She shook her head, the admiration for Carla clear in her eyes. "She wanted to come home and so home she came. Gave those doctors what for, I can tell you."

Océane nodded and tried to smile. That certainly described the girl she knew. She looked up to see Laen standing in the corner of the room. His shoulders were hunched over, his arms folded and he was staring at the floor, not meeting her eyes. Océane swallowed as she turned to find Corin sitting beside her and reached up and found his hand. He squeezed it gently, giving her courage. "Can I see her?" she asked the nurse.

"You better had, she's talked of nothing but you since I've been here," Charlène said, getting up and smoothing down her uniform, which was rumpled no doubt from trying to catnap in the uncomfortable chair. "She's had the police around you know."

"Oh no." She put her hand to her mouth and stifled a sob as the guilt welled up and threatened to overwhelm her. They had always been there for each other. They had met in the orphanage when they were eight years old and they had been each other's family ever since. There was nothing they hadn't seen each other through, no secret they hadn't shared, and now as Carla was dying ... She sobbed silently, drawing in great heaving breaths that filled her lungs but didn't seem to give her any oxygen. In her misery she thought she heard Corin speak to Laen sharply but Laen didn't come. It was Corin who crouched at her feet and pulled her into an embrace, his hand stroking her hair and murmuring soft words she could not take in but were nonetheless comforting.

She heard the nurse speaking to him, her voice hushed. "How about I take a walk for ten minutes and give you some privacy?"

"You are very kind, thank you," Corin replied, and there was a blast of cold air as she opened and shut the front door and left the three of them alone. "What do you want to do, Océane? Are you ready to see her now?"

She nodded, too numb to speak and Corin helped her to her feet. "Would you like us to stay or should we leave you alone?"

She shook her head vigorously as panic rose in her chest and she clasped his hand tight. He returned the pressure with a sad smile. "Whatever you need, darling." She didn't look at Laen. He had obviously made his choice, and whatever it was it clearly didn't include her. He didn't care for her, that was obvious enough or it would be him holding her hand, trying to comfort her. She had Carla to worry about now, nothing else mattered. Her own heartache would have to wait.

"We'll give you a few moments before we come in, shall we?" Corin asked. "We don't want to frighten her," he said with a wry smile and gestured at Laen. She nodded and walked to the bedroom door, and took a breath of air that seemed thick with the redolent smell of sickness before walking in as quietly as she could. Carla was lying down, propped up on pillows with her eyes shut, and

Océane gasped at the change she saw. She had always been skinny and the chemo had been taking its toll but now her face seemed to have sunk in on itself. The last time they had spoken about her illness Carla had indicated that the treatment had been successful. Now as she looked at the frail girl in front of her, she wondered just how truthful she had been. Had she known all this time and kept it to herself?

The wig that she had taken to wearing to hide the effects of the chemo was gone and her head was bare. It made her seem vulnerable, as delicate as the finest bone china that would shatter if handled too roughly. Her pretty blonde hair had been her pride and joy and Océane had held her on the only occasion that she had given in and wept for the loss of it. It had been the one and only time, and then Carla had accepted it with resolution and made much of the variety of wigs and scarves that she had found. She had laughed with Océane as she had tried on the more outrageous styles and joked that she had always wanted to be a redhead ... No hair, just a red head.

Océane swallowed down her own grief as she remembered. Carla was the bravest person she had ever known and she owed it to her to be brave too. She swallowed a sob and knelt beside the bed, taking her hand and feeling the shock of how bony and frail it was. The skin was dry and fragile as old newspaper. She took a breath as her friend's eyelids flickered and she came to.

"Océane?" Carla's bright blue eyes seemed to have lost their colour somehow, but the sharpness remained nonetheless.

"Hi."

"Where have you been?" Her voice was weak and raspy but the despair came through loud and clear. "I've been so frightened. I thought ... I thought you'd been abducted, murdered!" The delicate hand Océane was holding suddenly grasped hers so tightly it hurt. "Where were you?" she demanded. The anger and fear in her voice was more than Océane could bear and she dissolved into floods of tears that ran down her face unchecked, preventing any kind of explanation as she could barely breathe much less speak.

"I'm so ... so sorry," she mumbled through the storm of her tears and then there was a soft knock on the door, which opened a crack.

"Océane?"

Carla frowned at the soft male voice behind her bedroom door. "Who's that?"

Océane sniffed and wiped her eyes and wondered how she would ever be able to explain. How would Carla ever forgive her for this? "Oh, well ..." she stuttered as the tears continued to fall. "Actually they're ... friends of mine." The door opened some more and Carla's eyes widened when she saw Laen and Corin.

"Since when?"

Océane wiped her face on her sleeve. "Ummm ..." she began.

"Get in here!" Carla demanded of the two men who obediently stepped a little way into the cramped bedroom. Carla reached out a skinny arm and turned on the bedside lamp with a snap. If it had been in any other circumstance Océane would have laughed at the expression on Carla's face as the dim light caught Corin's gold eyes and shone on the white blond of Laen's hair. Her eyes travelled over the men at the foot of her bed and for a just a moment she was utterly speechless. It didn't last. "Holy mother of God," she said in wonder. "Where did you find them ... Hunks R Us?"

Océane sniffed as her lip trembled. "It's a long story."

Carla snorted. "You'd better hurry it up then."

Océane looked at her friend and felt hot tears sliding down her face. "Oh, Carla." She buried her head in her hands, quite unable to look her in the face. She sobbed quietly as Carla sat in silence and it wasn't until she heard male voices that she looked up.

"Laen, no, don't," Corin said, his hand grasping Laen's arm but Laen turned his head, his black eyes wide as they fell on Carla. He turned hurriedly away.

"I ... I cannot." He wrenched his arm from Corin's grasp and pushed his way past him and they heard the sound of the front door slamming shut.

Océane gasped, looking at the door he had rushed through in horror. How could he? Even if he didn't care for her at all ... how could he leave like that? She'd seen the expression of disgust on his face when he'd looked at Carla and fury welled up inside her. So much for giving him a chance. He truly must be disgusted by the human race if he could find no pity or compassion for her friend, her dearest friend who had been dying alone - because of him!

She pulled herself together. She had no time to waste on him now. There would be time enough for her own grief. She took a deep breath, gritting her teeth, and looked up to see Carla watching her.

"So that's it," she said, her faded blue eyes shining with hurt and reproach. "You found yourself a man and decided you didn't have time for me?"

"No!" Océane clutched at her hand. "No, Carla, I swear to you that wasn't it."

Carla struggled to sit up in bed, her movements jerky and full of anger. "How was it then?" she demanded before dissolving into a fit of coughing, clutching at her frail chest and gasping for air. She gestured with desperation for the oxygen that was set up beside the bed and Océane went to grab for it, her fingers clumsy with panic as Corin came forward and put his hands on Océane's shoulders. With a calm smile he manoeuvred her out of the way and sat on the bed beside Carla and took her hand.

Suddenly the coughing stopped as quickly as it had begun and Carla began to breathe easily, her chest rising and falling as she fell back against the pillows. Her friend's gaze focused once again and moved gradually from the strong hand that was holding onto her so very gently and up to stare at Corin's golden eyes with awe. Océane took a breath of wonder as she looked on and Carla's face relaxed, her eyes brightening visibly.

Carla sighed and brought her other hand closer to him, resting it over the one holding hers as a breath of laughter escaped her lips. "What are you?" she whispered. "What is that light? Are ... Are you an angel?"

Corin laughed softly. "No, my dear, very far from it, I'm afraid."

She sat up, inching forwards like she was moving towards the heat of a fire. "But ... But there's a light around you, like you're lit up from the inside. I can see it."

"It's magic, Carla. I'm no angel I promise you. I am Fae, not an angel and not human. Not of your world."

She blinked at him but seemed to accept his words without difficulty. "Do your people all shine like this?"

Corin seemed to hesitate for a moment and his eyes drifted to Océane before he shook his head. "No," he said. "No, they have magic but ... they do not shine with it."

Carla smiled, as though she had known the answer all along. "No. You're special aren't you?"

Corin didn't answer, his face passive and this time Carla squeezed his hand. "Sucks huh? Being special?"

He snorted with amusement and nodded. "Yes, in truth it really does suck."

She sighed and lay back on the pillows, looking at him with a contented smile and keeping a tight hold on his hand. "Can everyone see that?" She gestured vaguely to the light that she seemed to be able to see around him and Corin shook his head.

"No. Usually I ... Well, I hide it from my kind. It would cause problems. Too many questions. I have freed it to ease your pain."

Carla nodded as though she understood completely and then tilted her head, her expression curious. "Is that why can I see it?" she asked.

"No. Humans cannot usually see it unless they have the gift of sight which is very rare."

She smiled, intrigued. "You mean they can see your kind, your magic?"

He nodded and a small frown furrowed her forehead. "I can't though ... I don't have the sight so ... why?"

Corin lifted her hand very gently and kissed her fingers. "You know why," he replied and a forlorn smile flickered over her mouth as she nodded.

"Because I'm dying."

Océane covered her mouth with her hand and tried hard not to break down as Corin covered Carla's hand between both of his. The smile he returned was sad and lovely. Carla seemed peaceful now though and lifted her arm, touching his face with reverent fingers. "So beautiful."

"Thank you," he said and Océane could see tears glittering in his eyes too.

"Am I going to die now?" she asked, just as calmly as though she was asking if it was time for dinner.

He shook his head. "No, not yet. You will see Océane once more, I promise." He moved forward a little, getting closer to her. "There is no need to be afraid, Carla." Reaching out he stroked her cheek with his hand and she closed her eyes, leaning into it like a cat moving towards a caress.

"No," she agreed. "I'm not afraid ... Not now."

"And now you must get some rest. Océane will come back in the morning and you will feel strong enough to talk to her. Then she will explain everything to you."

"Will you come too?" she demanded, clutching at his hand. "Please?"

"Yes. Yes, of course I'll come too. Sweet dreams now, my dear." He leaned forward and kissed her cheek and Océane watched with tears streaming silently down her face as Carla closed her eyes and drifted into sleep with a smile on her lips.

Océane stood sobbing uncontrollably and Corin got up, pulling her against him.

"Don't worry, my love, now she has seen the truth of us, she will believe you when you tell her what really happened. She will understand that it wasn't your fault."

Océane nodded, so grateful to him that she couldn't find the words, would never be able to find words enough for the kindness he had shown. "Thank you," was all she could manage through her tears as she clung to him, though it seemed a paltry response for what he had done.

They heard the nurse letting herself back into the flat and Corin took her by the hand and led her out of the bedroom. The nurse went in to check on Carla and exclaimed as she came out. "My goodness, your visit must have done her good. I've never seen her sleep so peacefully."

Océane didn't reply. She was too numb. She simply stood clutching at Corin's hand. She felt adrift, like if she let go she would simply disappear, fade away into the dull, grey reality and exist as nothing more than a shadow. Carla was dying. Her best friend, her only friend, would soon be gone and Corin and Laen would return to their world and leave her here and she would be utterly alone. Sorrow and fear and anger wrapped her in their smothering embrace until she could hardly draw breath. The future suddenly looked cold and dark, a bleak reality she didn't know if she was brave enough to face. It just wasn't fair.

It wasn't fair.

Chapter 23

Laen had stumbled from the confines of Carla's flat with his chest heaving. Once out on the balcony he doubled over, retching and breathing hard, quite unable to rid himself of the smell of sickness and death that had hung over the frail creature in the bed. He hadn't needed to look at Corin to confirm what he knew. He may not have Corin's talent for healing but even he could see her life was fading. She had very little time left. She was too far gone for Corin to help her now other than to ease her pain. If he had seen her earlier maybe he could have cured her but not now. Now it was far too late. It was only the strength of her will keeping her here.

Carla was not ready to die.

Trapped in Carla's suffocating living space, Laen had been locked in his own personal hell. Looking at the dying woman in the bed had transported his mind back to a time that he had shut firmly out of his head many, many years ago. The sorrow that he had kept buried deep in a dark place for so long had threatened to overwhelm him as the stench of death clung to the back of his throat.

Once again he was six years old and watching his mother try to hang on to life with desperation in her eyes. It was the same desperation he could now see in Carla. Try as he might he could not stop his memories now, as though the barrier had been lifted and everything he had shut out over the years pressed down on him, the weight of sorrow squeezing the air from his lungs, crushing him with the agony of being left alone and unloved. He saw himself sitting on the mattress, remembered clearly the pretty yellow material of the bed covers, patterned with birds and butterflies flying joyfully against a sunny background. He remembered that same smell laced with his mother's perfume as he clung to her hand, crying and crying and begging her not to leave him alone. He would be a good boy. He wouldn't make his father angry again, if she would only stay with him. But she didn't stay. The staff had been forced to physically prize him away from his Mother's body and he had been taken to his room. He fought and kicked and screamed and tried to escape, tried to return to her and so they had locked him in - all alone.

Just the memory of his imprisonment and the terrifying isolation filled him with the urge to flee, to escape. To run and keep running until such emotion was locked away again. This was why no one got close. This was why it wasn't safe. Losing them hurt too much. And now he was going to discover that all over again. He ran back along the balcony that fronted the rows of flats, row after row of identical boxes stacked one on top of the other, and felt like the air was being used up. He wanted to run back home and feel the space and the breeze around him, to ride for a whole day without seeing another living soul if he wanted to. He got to the top of the stairs and stopped with his hand on the rail. Coward, a voice sneered in his head. You damn coward.

He wiped his eyes with an angry movement. He didn't cry. Not ever. He wasn't about to begin now, especially when he had no right to. It was Océane who was suffering. Yes Carla too, but her pain would soon be at an end. It would be Océane who bore the loss of her best friend, she who would be left all alone. He tried to imagine himself in her position, how he would feel if Corin was gone, if his only anchor to sanity left him alone. He leaned back against the wall and clutched at his head as he realised how badly he had let her down. He had fought to keep the feelings under control but he didn't want Océane to lose the person she loved as he had lost his mother, and he felt such terrible guilt for having kept them apart for the last weeks of her life. He couldn't bear it, couldn't face the memories that had begun to unravel before his eyes, a parade of misery that had begun with the loss of his mother and had plunged him into a nightmare of physical and mental abuse at the hands of his Father.

His knees gave out and he slid down the wall as his hand went to his coat pocket and grasped the dagger, but it brought no comfort. This was no enemy that could be defeated. If Océane had needed him to protect her from a foe, slay a monster, wage a war, any of this he could and would have done in a heartbeat. But to stay in that room and be her strength when she had needed him ... He had not been strong enough or brave enough for that. He had failed her and he knew she would never forgive him. He put his head in his hands. He didn't deserve her.

Eventually he dragged his mind from the past, from the pictures he had shut away and refused to look at. Though they were not faded and dusty as he had hoped they may become over time. They were just as fresh and garish and brazen in their agony as they had been when they had happened. Perfectly preserved. He tried to push them back to the place they had laid in the dark all these years but he knew they would not be content to stay there any longer. For now, though, he did the best he could and focused on someone else's sorrow. Somehow he got his reluctant limbs moving again, forced his unwilling feet to move back to the door that he had run from like the gutless bastard his father had always said he was. He stood outside and could hear nothing but the blood rushing in his ears. He had to face her, had to at least look her in the eyes. It took everything he had to put his hand on the door and push it open.

Stepping inside he found the nurse coming out of the bedroom while Océane stood red-eyed and motionless as though she had been turned to stone until she saw him. He braced himself for her hatred but the force of it still shocked him. The knowledge that he had destroyed what little chance he may have had to be loved by her froze his heart and he accepted that it would stay that way. There was nothing in this world or his that could thaw it when he saw the way she looked at him, when he saw how she clung to Corin's hand.

"Get out!" she said, her face impassive, her voice cold but anger burning in her eyes.

The nurse looked up in alarm and Corin cleared his throat, letting go of Océane's hand and steering her forwards with a hand at her back instead. "Thank you so much for everything you're doing for Carla. I can't tell you what it means to us to know she is being so well looked after."

Laen watched Corin smile at the nurse who stuttered and looked flustered under the warm glow of his praise. "We will come back and see her in the morning. Come, my friends, it's time we departed." He escorted them outside and they walked down and around the stairs and on to the street in silence as Laen waited for what he knew was coming.

"You bastard!" Océane shoved Laen with everything she had. "We really are less than nothing to you, aren't we?" She sneered. "How could you leave like that ... She's dying and you couldn't spare a little pity ... a few words with her? Dear God, I have never hated anyone in my life but I swear I hate you ... I hate you!" She screamed the last words at him as tears fell unchecked and he felt his heart break as she confirmed what he had known was true. Sadly it did not make the shock of it any less.

"Océane!" Corin stepped forward and put his hand on her shoulder, making her look up at him. "You don't understand. I don't think you're being entirely fair, you must let him explain. Laen ..."

"No." Laen shook his head. "It is far less than I deserve. I wish I could make amends, Océane. I wish for more than you will ever know. I do not believe I can ever make it up to you but ... you are free to go. And do not worry. You are not going to see me again."

He saw Corin look at him in astonishment but he knew it was useless. Corin had been wrong from the start. Maybe she had been foolish enough to consider him for those few brief moments in the café when he had begun to hope but ...

Corin walked over to him, grabbing his arm and towing him away from Océane so they could speak privately. "Laen, don't be a damn fool! Don't give up. For the love of the gods, talk to her. Explain yourself!"

Laen looked at him, knowing he could not hide his emotions. Sometimes he had thought that Corin knew his mind better than he did and there was no possible way of hiding the misery he felt now. The pain was clear in his eyes, it had to be as it was the only thing he could register. "Corin, even now can you not see how wrong you were?"

"I'm not wrong about her dammit." Corin cursed, exasperated, and punched him in the shoulder hard enough to make him stumble. "But maybe I was wrong about you. If you are too spineless to fight for her maybe you don't deserve her!"

Laen looked at him, his black eyes dead and cold. "And finally you understand," he said, the words hard and bitter in his mouth. "Gods, man. Why on earth would anyone choose me over you?" He snorted at the absurdity of it and shook his head. Walking away from Corin, he turned to Océane. She stared up at him. "Corin loves you, Océane, he is a good man." He paused and smiled at her. "You will find none better. He will take good care of you." He turned and nodded at Corin, ignoring his incredulous expression, and melted into the darkness.

"Laen!" Corin shouted furiously into the night.

***

Océane watched him go and felt nothing. She could feel nothing. She was so cold. A frozen shard had pierced her soul and now its icy touch leached into every fibre of her body. Her blood had become slush that ate away any warmth and her heart must be struggling to pump it around as with each laboured thud the detachment increased and the cold seemed to bite deeper - until she felt she would never be warm again.

"Gods, Laen." She turned at the sound of Corin's voice. He had sat down on a low wall that bordered the estate and put his head in his hands.

"Don't bother," she said in disgust. How could she have ever believed in him? She stood shivering and miserable and her eyes lingered on Corin as fear flickered down her spine like the feathery touch of hoarfrost on a barren landscape. She wondered if he would leave her alone too now that Laen had gone. She watched him as he stared at the floor, his long fingers tangled in his hair as though he would pull it out in frustration. He had clearly been furious with his friend for behaving as he had but now he just seemed defeated. His shoulders hunched against the bitter wind that blew the detritus of fast food packets scattering around his feet. He was as cold as she was, and she felt angry all over again at what Laen had done but on his behalf this time. Corin loved her but he had pushed his feelings aside for his friend. He was noble and generous and kind, everything that Laen was not and she felt a sudden surge of love and affection for him. She was glad, she decided, glad that Laen had shown his true colours. Better that she had been forced to see the truth now before she had messed everything up and made the wrong choice.

"W--what will you do now?" she asked.

He got to his feet and she stood close to him as he looked down at her. His beautiful eyes were full of sorrow but he smiled at her and kissed her forehead. "Well, let's start by taking you back to your home, shall we? Before we both freeze to death." He took hold of her hand and she clung to it like it would keep her safe.

"You won't leave?" she begged, hating how pitiful she sounded, how needy, but she was afraid to be left alone. She didn't want to be alone.

Corin reached out and stroked her cheek gently and with such tenderness she was afraid she would break down and cry again. "No, my love. I won't leave."

Chapter 24

They walked back towards Océane's apartment, neither one of them able to speak but their hands linked together; a tiny spark of heat in a night that seemed intent on slaying any warmth in its bitter embrace.

Stood in front of her door once again, she fumbled with the key in her numb fingers and it clattered to the ground as she wept and kicked at the door in a fury. Corin picked it up and let them in and then held her as she shivered and sobbed in the darkness of her pitiful home. Pulling herself together, she wiped her eyes and turned on the lights and the heating. She didn't have the faintest idea how she was going to pay the bill that was coming and was a little surprised it hadn't already been cut off as the red letter for the last one sat glaring at her from on top of the bread bin.

She turned her back on it and leaned against the kitchen counter as she remembered Carla, so very fragile, her hold on life slipping away as Océane's ploughed on relentlessly.

"You're sure she ... Carla, she won't ..." She stopped,

quite unable to finish the sentence, and looked up to find Corin standing close to her. He stroked her hair, tucking a strand behind her ear.

"You will see her again, I promise," he said. She nodded and laid her head against his shoulder. His arms went around her and held her close and the thought of losing this, of losing Carla and him ... She shivered uncontrollably and felt Corin kiss the top of her head.

"Darling, you're freezing. Go and take a hot shower and I will endeavour to make us some coffee."

She sniffed, looking at him in surprise. "Do you know how?" she asked. From what she had seen in their world, both Princes had been waited on hand and foot.

"I can make tea too," he said, amusement flickering in his eyes and she couldn't help but laugh at the pride in his voice.

"Such domestication," she teased. "Now you need only learn to cook and you will make a wonderful husband."

The atmosphere changed suddenly and she was very aware of his body pressed close, of the hard muscle just beneath her fingertips with only the thin material of his T-shirt between them. She wondered what it would feel like to put her hands on the skin beneath the fabric and heat bloomed under her palms. Her fingers spread out, smoothing over his chest and feeling the little nub under her thumb as it moved slowly over his nipple. He shivered under her touch and she knew the cold was not to blame as she looked up and took a shaky breath as his eyes darkened. For a moment he was utterly still and she hardly dared breathe. He looked away, releasing her, and began opening cupboards. "Go and have your shower, Océane."

She did as she was told and went to her room. Closing the door, she undressed as her skin prickled with goosebumps in the chilly air. Taking the two steps into the bathroom, she turned the water up as hot as she could stand it and stood under it, shivering as it sluiced over her body but failed to melt the ice in her heart or touch the chill that had taken root somewhere deep inside.

THE DARK PRINCE

When she was done she rubbed herself briskly with a towel that was more akin to sandpaper than the expanses of soft, warm material she had been given at the castle but at least it got her blood moving a little faster. She pulled on her threadbare cotton dressing gown and stood in her room with her hair dripping down her back, and she wondered what the hell was happening to her life. A few weeks ago she had been blissfully ignorant of the Fae and their land and now she wasn't sure how she felt. Their world was so terribly beautiful, the knowledge that it really existed so astonishing, and a part of her longed to return to it, but she wished she had never chanced upon Laen. She had been such a fool to think there was any kindness behind those black eyes after everything he had done to her. Yet she'd believed he had been sincere in his apology ... What an idiot she was.

Laen was a black-hearted monster and she was much safer staying far away from him. She swallowed down the misery that accompanied that decision. Instead she remembered how Corin had behaved. His quiet support and the respect and care with which he had treated Carla brought Laen's behaviour into such sharp focus in contrast. She would never forget what Corin had done for her friend. The effort he had taken to ease her and reassure her that there was no reason to be afraid made her heart ache and she felt tears spill down her cheeks all over again.

***

Corin stood in the shabby kitchen with the rich smell of coffee scenting the air and wondered what was taking Océane so long. It had been some time since he had heard her turn the shower off. His heart constricted at the fear he had seen in her eyes. She was so terribly afraid of being alone. Gods he knew only too well how that felt. Anger at Laen bloomed in his chest, though he knew how hard being in that room must have been for him. He could not condemn him for running out. That he hadn't explained himself though ... That he had just given up ...

He leaned on the kitchen counter and took a deep breath. Gods, what a situation they had created.

There was still no sound from the bedroom and he began to worry about her. He didn't like the idea that she was crying alone in her room. He picked up the coffee pot and poured her out a cup, hoping he'd remembered how to make it correctly. He added a generous spoonful of sugar, which he understood was customary to help with the shock of unhappy emotions and wished he could lay hands on a bottle of Ebony Fire as personally he needed something a great deal stronger to calm his own feelings. He stirred the cup with care and went and knocked on her door.

"Come in."

He walked in to find her sitting on the side of her bed, trying to comb the tangles out of her hair. She wore a simple white, cotton dressing gown and her eyes looked big and sorrowful against her pale skin. She looked so lost that he longed to take her in his arms and try to make her happy. Even knowing that she didn't love him, he wanted to try. He wished so badly that things could have been different.

What a damnable mess, all three of them breaking their hearts for no good reason.

He placed the coffee on the night stand by the bed and sat down beside her before taking the comb gently from her hands and combing her hair for her. Océane sighed and closed her eyes, her shoulders relaxing a little as he worked the comb gently through the thick tresses.

"Are you all right?" he asked.

There was a slight movement as her shoulders shrugged. "I don't know." The motion made the cotton slip a little, revealing the soft skin of her shoulder as the warm scent of vanilla drifted up from her body. She had turned towards him slightly and her wet hair dripped onto the worn dressing gown. The damp patches clung to her, showing the soft curve of her breast. How perfectly it would fit his hand if he were to reach out and touch her - slip his fingers under the fabric and caress that silken skin. The sodden material became transparent over her nipple and for a moment he imagined lowering his head to her breast and drawing it into his mouth, feeling the skin peak under the thin cotton as his tongue moved over her. The images came to him in quick succession, her hands on him, the sound of her pleasure under his touch, his name cried in rapture. His hand paused on the comb as hunger and desire burned under his skin and he swallowed hard before slamming the door on those careless emotions. She didn't want him and even if she did this was hardly the time. She was vulnerable and fragile. She needed a friend not some love sick fool too desperate for a taste of her to see sense. He stirred himself to resume his work with the comb and carried on, focusing diligently on a small knot for a moment before he could speak again.

"Everything will work out for the best I'm sure. You'll see," he said, though just at this moment he was far from being persuaded himself.

"Will it?" she asked, a tremor in her voice, and he cursed himself for not having been more convincing.

Corin put the comb down and turned her around to face him. He reached forward and took both of her hands in his and looked her steadily in the eyes. "I promise it will, Océane. My word of honour."

Her lip trembled and those lovely brown eyes filled with tears. "When she's gone ... I'll be alone. She's been my family since we were children. There just isn't anyone else."

He shook his head. "I'll always be your friend, Océane, and ... And you have Laen."

"Don't speak to me about him!" she snapped, tearing her hands away from his grasp. Corin frowned and opened his mouth anyway and she shouted again. "I mean it!"

He sighed and looked away from her, unsure what to do next.

They sat in silence and her head hung down, her face covered by the thick curtain of her hair. "You say you'll be my friend but you'll return home and I won't ever see you again," she said, her voice so quiet he could hardly hear the words. "And I'll be left here." She gestured at the tiny bedroom that had been her home ever since she had left the orphanage.

He felt a lump in his throat. No. No, he would not allow it. He would not let her stay here alone. "No." She looked up at him and he realised he had spoken aloud. "It doesn't have to be like that. Not ..." He hesitated. "Not if you don't want it to."

"What do you mean?" Her eyes were on him, and the fact that she needed him made his chest ache.

"I mean that you can come back with me. I will always have a place for you if you want it, Océane." He held out his hands to her. "Don't misunderstand me. I'm not expecting anything, please don't think ... I mean, you can come and go as you please, no strings, no tricks ... you have my word."

"Oh, Corin." The tears that had been trembling in her eyes began to roll down her face and Corin felt his restraint crumble.

"Please don't cry, Océane," he pleaded. "I can't bear it. I'll do anything, only don't cry."

"Anything?" she asked, her head tilting towards him with a look in her eyes that made his heart pound.

"Yes," he replied, utterly serious. "Anything."

She moved closer to him, the sweet vanilla scent of her skin curling around him like a caress. "Then kiss me."

His brain froze as the demands his body were making began to take over but he shook his head as the last vestige of sanity lingered. "Océane, I don't think ..." But before he could finish the sentence she had leaned forward and pressed her soft lips against his and the longing that had been growing within him ever since the day they first met overwhelmed everything else. He closed his eyes as her lips moved against his, and returned the kiss, his hand going to the back of her neck to draw her closer as she opened to him and his tongue sought the warmth he had been needing. He felt her arms wrap around him and pull him closer and he went willingly, reaching for her in return, caressing her. One hand glided around her waist as the other stroked her face with tender care and then slid down her neck, to her collar bone and then lower. He felt the softness of her breast under the worn cotton, and held himself firmly in check when all he wanted to do was rip the material out of his way like a spoilt child with a Christmas gift. The heat of her body seeping through his clothes chased away the chill in his bones from walking around Paris and replaced it with a fire that threatened to burn him up from the inside out. He tried to be restrained, tried to tell himself it was just a kiss. She just needed comforting ... it wasn't going anywhere, but then her hands were moving over him and her kisses became more intense, drawing him further towards the point of no return.

Her fingers found the edge of his T-shirt and her hands were upon his skin. He sighed against her as they moved in a slow glide over his back and he was too lost to even try to resist. Taking control, he moved her back onto the bed, pushing her down as his body covered hers and exalted in the way she held on to him, her body coiling around his as she responded to his touch. His hands dropped to her hips and pulled them against him before hooking his hand under her knee and pulling it around until there was nothing but clothes between him and where he needed to be. His blood surged in his veins as she moved against him and their bodies twined together. With her hand tangled in his hair, pulling his head down, she demanded more as she clung to him with desperation. He knew she was escaping, trying to outrun the grief and sorrow that was dragging her into a dark place, and understood probably better than anyone what she was feeling. He wanted to escape with her. She arched against him, grinding her hips against his and moaning against his mouth and he could think of nothing other than the need to get the wretched gown from her body as fast he could ... until a voice in his head reminded him of what was really going on.

He ignored it, pushing it away. Damn but he was tired of doing the right thing. What about what he wanted ... What he needed ... Except ... No.

"No." Leaving the warmth of her body was the hardest thing he had ever done but he pushed himself away from her. He moved fast, sitting at the end of the bed and breathing hard with his head in his hands.

"I ... I'm sorry," she said, looking horrified. "I thought it was what you wanted."

He gave a short bark of laughter swiftly followed by a furious tirade of swearing in the old tongue of his people. He should not in all conscience use such foul language in front of her but those words at least she would not understand, though from the look in her eyes he felt sure she understood the sentiment. He could not control the blaze of light and magic that flared around him however, which was so bright she had to shield her eyes and curl herself into a ball as the power burned against her.

When it had subsided and she dared to look up at him again he was standing in the doorway, one hand on each side of the jamb, his head hanging down.

"Of course it's what I want!" he said, biting out the words as he turned to look at her. He saw her find the need in his eyes and take a breath. He clutched at the door frame, afraid he would run back to her. "Oh, gods, you have no idea how much I want ..." He paused as a combination of passion and fury stole his own breath. "If you knew all the things I wanted, you would not be able to sit there so calmly."

She shook her head at him, clearly not understanding how he could want her so much and refuse what she was offering. "Then why?"

"Because I won't be a consolation prize, dammit!" He moved away as anger overtook him and he smacked the door with his hand, so hard that it banged against the wall and then slammed shut. He relented, his fury subsiding as he saw her jump in shock and wrap the dressing gown more tightly around her. He raked his hand through his hair and closed his eyes, his voice softer now. "Not even for you, Océane."

"I'm so sorry."

He nodded. "Me too." He stayed in the far corner of the bedroom, needing to put some distance between them, and leant against the wall. "Now listen to me and attend me well, because I swear to the gods this is the last time I mediate between you and Laen. If this ever happens again I shall take what I want and damn Laen, and you, and the consequences. I won't be a gentleman again, I swear it!" he cursed. "I will consider my own feelings in the future and no one else's." He crossed his arms and glared at her. "Do you understand?" he demanded.

She nodded and bit her lip and from the stain that coloured her cheeks he could tell she was embarrassed, but he could not be too kind to her or it would be his undoing.

"Good." He closed his eyes and took a breath. "Now you remember that I told you of the sickness that has come to the Fae Lands."

She nodded again and he looked away as the vulnerability in her eyes was killing him.

"It is still a very rare thing but for those whom it affects it is fatal. It mostly affects the weak- that is, those with little magical ability. In our world magic is power; the more magic, the more land you can claim; the more wealth you possess. This sickness is not only a threat to our world but it is becoming something to be ashamed of. Powerful families will do much to cover up the fact the disease took one of theirs as if it shows some fault in the line." He shook his head in disgust. "These are human diseases that we have no resistance to and our healers do not seem able to cure them. I thank the gods that I have not yet lost anyone I know of or care about but you have no idea of the terror it brings to our race." He paused. "How old do you think I am?"

Océane looked up at him, clearly puzzled by the question. "I ... I don't know, twenty six, maybe twenty eight?"

"I am one hundred and eighty seven."

She gasped and stared at him.

"By Fae standards I am a very young man." He smiled, amused by the shock on her face. "My father is over eight hundred and there are some amongst us who are older than you could ever imagine." He frowned and looked down at the nauseating swirl on the orange carpet at his feet. When he spoke again his voice was soft. "Can you understand then, the terror it creates when we begin to die so young?" He looked up and held her eyes. "Laen's mother was no older than me when she died and when that happened Laen was just six, Océane. She was the only one who ever protected him from his father and he watched her die. From the moment she was gone he was alone and in the tender care of a monster who despised him. Can you imagine perhaps what it was like for him to see your pretty young friend in the last hours of her life?"

He paused as his words took effect.

"When his mother died the manner of her death was deemed shameful and so she was effectively erased from the world. Her belongings, pictures of her, all of it gone." His voice quavered a little and he cleared his throat. "Laen came back, Océane. He wasn't running away, he wasn't disgusted. He was scared and he didn't want you to see." Corin watched the tears roll down her face as she realised what she'd done and knew he had been right. "He would slay dragons for you, my darling girl, but when it comes to affairs of the heart you are the one who needs to be brave, for he does not know how. But you see this is why you need each other. You will teach him to trust in you and in his own heart and he will give you the unconditional love and security you crave so badly. You must just be patient with him. It is all very well longing for the strong silent type but if you get him you must put aside too much hope of romantic declarations and pretty words. You cannot have it all ways."

"Oh." She put her hand to her mouth and smothered a sob and he closed his eyes. He knew he had done the right thing. He could never have kept her. Sooner or later she would have realised her mistake and if she had left him and run to Laen it would have caused a rift between them. He would have lost his closest friend as well as a lover and he didn't think he could have born that. It didn't ease the pain in his heart at all, though, or the longing to stop being such a damned gentleman and take what had been offered him. He was suddenly exhausted, tired of fighting the future on so many levels and feeling that no matter what path he took, the gods were laying their traps accordingly.

He pushed himself to his feet and headed for the door. "Get some sleep now, Océane, and in the morning we will set everything to rights."

"Corin ..." He paused but didn't dare turn to look at her. "I ... I am so sorry ... truly. I wish things were different. I ... I do love you."

His heart fractured slightly at the admission but he nodded. "I know, darling. It does help ... a little."

"You've been so ... I can never thank you enough ..."

He slammed his hand against the door as his anger flared again. "Don't! Whatever you do, don't make out like I'm some knight in shining armour, for the love of the gods!" he raged. "Right at this moment the only thought in my head is of the two of us naked in that bed. It is all I can think of and I still don't know if I am going to make it out of the room without taking my chances. So if you really want to know the truth, as much as I want you, the two of us would be a disaster. I have never been faithful in all my life and I don't believe I ever could be. Laen will. He would never dishonour you. Don't go thinking I'm something I'm not, Océane. I would break your heart just like every other woman I have ever encountered, so count your blessings!"

He heard her sniff and hated himself for being such a

bastard.

"I don't believe that," she whispered.

He hung his head and his voice was bleak as he answered her. "Then you are very, very foolish."

"Corin, we both know which of us has behaved badly and it certainly isn't you. I'm just so embarrassed," she sobbed. "I've never ...Oh, God I've acted like such a nasty slut."

A sigh escaped his lips and he shook his head. "Don't be absurd, Océane. You have had a traumatic day. You are tired and emotional and you needed someone to hold you." He paused and leaned his head on the door. "So did I."

"Will ... Will you tell him?"

He snorted. "Absolutely not and I forbid you to do so either! It will change nothing and he damn well asked for it, the blithering idiot."

"Oh, God."

He looked up and risked a glance in her direction. Her head was in her hands and where she had leaned forward the damned dressing gown had fallen open, revealing ... He turned swiftly away from her. "Goodnight, Océane," he said, his voice rough. He grabbed hold of the door handle and yanked it open. "Lock the door behind me please," he said without turning around and then went out, shutting it firmly behind him. He waited and did not hear the tell-tale snick of a key turning. "That was not a joke!" he shouted through the door. And he heard Océane jump up off the bed and turn the key in the lock.

Chapter 25

Corin stood on the wrong side of the locked door with frustration singing in his blood and he closed his eyes. Gods he needed a drink. He sank down into the ugly brown armchair and massaged his temples as the headache behind his eyes began to make itself known. Whispered voices called out to him and he rubbed his eyes with his palms, willing them to shut up and go away, knowing they wouldn't. Drowning them was the only thing that shut them up, at least temporarily.

He tried to concentrate on something else so that their pleading would drift into the distance but the only thing he could focus on with any clarity was the feel of Océane's body beneath his as she had arched up against him. Cursing, he stood up again as his arousal ached with the need for him to break the damn door down. He flicked the light on and began a methodical search of the room in the dim hope of finding enough alcohol to put him to sleep. Bearing in mind human booze was not half as strong as the kind the Fae made, his body would take far more abuse than any human could sustain without submitting to liver failure. He found a small bottle of gin with about half an inch left in the bottom, and slammed it down on the work top with distaste. Nonetheless he unscrewed the top and drank it down in a few large swallows. He put the empty bottle back down, shaking his head in disgust, though he wasn't sure whether he was more disgusted with himself or the weakness of the liquor.

"Shut up, shut up, shut up," he muttered as the pain in his head worsened, the ache behind his eyes increasing to a dull throb that pulsed along with the restrained desire of his body. He began to pace the tiny room as every muscle locked down tight. His lungs felt rigid as the rest of him, refusing to draw a proper breath, and images of Océane spread out for him, naked on the bed behind the flimsy door that separated them made sweat prickle down his back. Of course, telling her to lock the door had simply been to put her on her guard. With his powers it would take one hell of a security system to keep him out if he decided he was going to get in.

He increased the pace, stalking around the confines of the room as frustration burned. He stopped dead suddenly, right outside the bedroom door, convinced he could smell the sweet scent of vanilla perfuming the air. What if she was lying awake, thinking of him ... wanting him?

For a moment he stood still as the unlikely possibility warred with reality in his mind, the various scenarios of his welcome reception playing through his head like an in-house porn show. He clenched his fists, as he knew full well he had already made the decision. He could never betray Laen like that and she didn't want him - not now. He'd had his chance and rejected it.

Cursing with the filthiest language he could bring to mind, he wrote Océane a brief note assuring her he would be back. He put the note on the worktop, grabbed his coat and rushed out of the flat, hoping to be swallowed up by

Paris and her glittering cold embrace. It wouldn't be the first time.

Pausing to set a ward around the entrance to the flat to make sure Océane was secure, he looked around to check he wasn't observed before the shower of gold sparks flickered briefly around her door. He ran down the stairs of the building and out into the streets, satisfied that she would be safe until his return or at least safer than if he stayed.

As he was unfamiliar with Océane's area, he hailed a taxi and directed the driver to Boulevard de Clichy, the garish lights of the Quartier Rouge seeming as good a place as any to drown his demons. At least he would be in good company.

He paid the driver and got out, looking at the bright red windmill of the Moulin Rouge announcing with glitzy pride the new review *Féerie*. He snorted in amusement and wondered what the exotic dancers would do if a real live one appeared in their midst. Pulling his coat collar up against the cold, he turned his back on the polished face of the district, the acceptable porn served up for mainstreaming tourists, and headed towards Rue Saint-Denis.

Here girls in skimpy clothes braved the Arctic wind that blew car fumes and the toxic scent of the red light district in their pretty faces and cold, hard eyes. Balanced on high heels with slick movements far too practised to be erotic they tried to persuade him in to see a show ... a private dance ... just for him. They pouted and posed with a flick of long hair and sucked with lewd noises on red enamelled finger nails until he laughed and shook his head in amusement, walking on. When the obvious approach got them nowhere, they wheedled and looked up at him with cherry lip gloss and wide eyes, trying to look younger than their experience and making a parody of the innocent expressions they gave. He shook them off, polite but firm and they jeered him, cat calls directing him to the gay bars where he'd be more welcome.

He wondered what Océane would say if she knew he was just like them, only his whore-monger was the Queen and political power the coin that was paid for him. Not that he wasn't adept at the trade, and to be fair, his mother had only decided to profit from an already established lifestyle. It wasn't as if she had sold him into slavery.

Sinking deep and fast in a slick-sided well of depression, he passed an old man huddled in a shop doorway and could see only too well the disease that dawdled in his blood, slowly but surely poisoning a body already abused. He paused and the shabby creature looked up to reveal not an old man but a young one, though his eyes were dull and ancient. The two men looked at each other for a moment and Corin frowned as the pleading voices in his head cried louder. Stepping forward, he crouched down and the man jerked away, drawing a knife from the grey stained coat that covered his bones. With a flick of his magic, the knife disappeared and the man looked at Corin with real fear this time, not just the dull, habitual kind he obviously lived with day in, day out. Wanting to be gone already, Corin grasped his hand and set free the magic that passed through him, the faint golden glow lighting up his beautiful face with a softness that would not be found anywhere else under the neon illuminations.

"Ange," the old young man said with an awestruck voice and Corin gave him a hard look.

"Devil more like," he replied, dropping the cold, calloused hand. "Death isn't going to be kind now. It will be some time before it offers you any release from this existence. So what will you do? Live ... or go and kill yourself all over again?"

"Merci, merci, merci." The man clutched at his hand again and the eyes that looked up at Corin now were brighter, though there was nothing he could do to heal the weight of experience that still lurked behind his gratitude.

Corin nodded and pulled himself free. Reaching into

his pocket he found a bundle of notes and pushed them into the hand that was still outstretched towards him.

"Get out of here, for the love of the gods."

Turning quickly away, he walked fast, hearing the man still calling ange, ange as curious and calculating eyes regarded him in the darkness. He ducked into a dingy side street where the coloured signs gave way to a more dangerous obscurity and he found the building he needed. Outside, the shabby bar front boasted a dirty window and peeling paint and he grasped hold of the cold metal handle as a feeling of dread washed over him. Everything outside repulsed the senses, urged him to turn away. But he pushed the door open and stepped through.

Inside, the air was warm and sweet, the thick cloying scent of magic that he was only too familiar with inviting him into dangerous territory. For a moment there was silence even though the dull thud of music continued as every head turned towards him. He paused, convention making him await his due whether he wanted to or not, and then their heads bowed in deference, most of them at least. At a table in the corner a group of heavy-shouldered men raised their heads from their drinks and narrowed their sloe black eyes, shifting as hatred turned their auras a deep bloody red to Corin's vision; Dark Fae with their loathing burning savagely behind diamond hard stares. He laughed and smiled at them, blowing a kiss in their direction with a theatrical flourish. One of them cursed, the obscenity a harsh guttural sound from sneering lips as he hoisted his considerable bulk upright and slammed a gleaming dagger into the table top.

At the bar a large ruddy-faced man with a mop of dirty blond, curly hair and brilliant blue eyes smacked his hand on the bar. "No trouble!" he yelled and glared at Corin, who was regarding the men with an amused smile and anticipation glittering in his eyes. "Please, your Highness."

Corin waved his hand in a dismissive gesture. "Beck, my old friend, you know me better than that, surely."

"Aye." The blue eyes narrowed in a face that was grey and waxy and spoke of too long living this side of the gates and far from the Light Fae's realm he had originated from. Beck reached down behind the bar and brought up a black bottle with no marking but a red wax seal around the neck that covered the cork. "And I say again, we'll have no trouble, your Highness ... will we?"

Corin reached out and took the bottle but the big man kept it in his grasp until he had his answer.

Putting his hand over his heart Corin closed his eyes. "Word of honour, Beck."

Beck grunted, appeased, and handed over the bottle and a glass.

The Dark Fae grunted and muttered ribald insults about the *pretty golden prince* but it was the same refrain he had heard repeated and embroidered all his life. Sometimes in vulgar terms such as these, sometimes wrapped up in clever words that needed untying to find the insult hidden beneath the fancy layers.

As it appeared the show was over and there was to be no entertainment after all, the crowd returned to their drinks and the rumble of conversation mingled with the music as Corin drew the black bottle towards him. Stamped in the wax was the image of a flame and as he passed his hand over the top there was a flare of light and the wax melted, dripping in thick little rivers down the sides. He filled the glass with the black liquid, savouring the sweet honey aroma that belied the strength of the potent brew. Raising it in a salute, he gave a distant smile. "Laen, may you live long and happy with the lovely Océane and have many children to bring to you joy." He downed the drink and refilled the glass before adding, "And a good few headaches." Draining the glass once more he leaned against the bar as he felt the slow burn of the alcohol warming his blood. If there was one thing the Light Fae knew, it was how to make a drink that could fell an elephant.

THE DARK PRINCE

Better. Not much, but better.

He was half way down the bottle before the boy he knew was watching him from the corner of the room was courageous enough to approach. Blond and blue-eyed in the same manner as Beck, Corin watched the Light Fae male come and stand beside him. His peaches and cream complexion mirrored what Beck's would once have been, many years ago before the human realm had taken its toll. He had a cherubic face, his guinea gold hair falling in soft curls to his shoulders. The Light Fae were always too pretty, too good to be true in Corin's opinion. Too often he had discovered their angelic faces hid covetous natures and greedy appetites. He trusted them even less than they did him.

Corin's eyes flicked to the boy and looked him over. To human eyes they would have appeared the same age, vaguely late twenties. But that really was the boy's age, not just the way he appeared on the surface. To Corin he was little more than an adolescent.

"What?" he asked, wishing the lad would spit it out whatever it was he wanted to say.

The young man blushed and Corin sighed. "If you were hoping I would buy you a drink I'm afraid you are barking up the wrong tree." He glanced at the contemptuous expressions of the Dark Fae and snorted. "No matter what they may have implied." There was a chorus of jeers and whistles as they were seen talking together and the boy blushed a more profound shade of red.

"No, your Highness!" he said. "That was not it."

Corin shook his head. "Well then for the love of the gods speak up and get out of here before they decide to escort you to a dark alley. I'm afraid you are far too pretty for their tastes and talking to me will more than seal your fate. What the devil are you doing here anyway?" Corin looked him up and down and raised an eyebrow. "Does your mother know you're here?"

The boy stiffened at the insult. "I got out ... a year ago

and I was told you come in here sometimes."

"You've been waiting for me for a whole year?"

The boy nodded and Corin frowned at him. "I'm amazed you survived if you've been hanging around here."

"I usually wait outside but ... it was cold."

"Well now that you've found me, what of it?"

The boy reached into the pocket of his coat and drew out a large velum envelope. "I was asked to give you this."

Corin looked at the envelope but made no move to take it. "What is it and who asked you?"

The boy shrugged but there was a haunted look in his eyes. "I do not know who and he had not the time to tell me."

"Why?"

"Because ..." He lowered his voice to a whisper. "Because he died before he could say."

The boy flinched as the golden eyes flashed at him and magic prickled over his skin. Beck looked towards them from the far side of the bar and Corin raised his hand to reassure him before turning back to the young man. "Don't play games, boy. I don't like them."

"I--I am not, I swear it, Sire," he stammered. "He made me promise to give these to you and I swore on my honour. Now honour is served and I may be on my way." His voice trembled but there was integrity in his eyes. Scowling, Corin snatched the envelope from his hand and tore open the seal. Inside were half a dozen heart-shaped leaves, dry and dead. Corin took one out and it disintegrated in his hand.

"What is the meaning of this?" he demanded and the boy paled and looked around him, fear sparkling in his lovely blue eyes.

"They are from the Heart of the City, at Aos Si."

Corin shook his head and shoved the envelope back towards him. "Don't be ridiculous, that is not possible." He turned away, angry with the boy for wasting his time, and he poured another drink. This time the boy moved forward and grasped his arm, letting it go again abruptly as magic burned his fingers.

"Your Highness, forgive me but whoever he was, that man died trying to get this information to you."

Closing his eyes, Corin wished the boy to the bottom of a very deep ocean, but he turned to look at him again. "And supposing I believe this story? What do you expect me to do about it?"

The young man shrugged. "I do not know. To be truthful the fellow was half mad with sickness and I have no way of knowing if his story is true but ... I saw the Heart Tree in my own village sicken and die and the people grow weak. That was why my parents sent me away. There is something very wrong and yet the King does nothing. That was a year ago and since then I have had no word from my family."

Corin's face softened as he looked at the boy and understood his concern. "That doesn't surprise me. Tensions are rising. Most of your kind have left Alfheim and the Dark Fae's territory too. They have been summoned home by King Auberren. He has had all communications cut and the borders closed. No one gets through without a pass from his own hand. Trade continues for the moment as his greed still cannot overcome his paranoia at least, but I do not know for how long that will last." He looked down into the black depths of his glass seeing one golden eye reflected back at him. He fancied he saw accusation in its gaze. "I believe he is quite mad."

"But you must have people there, spies, someone who can ..."

The boy stopped with a squeak of alarm as Corin smacked his hand over his mouth. "This is neither the time nor the place, you little fool," he hissed. The boy stepped away, visibly shaken and Corin turned back to his bottle. "I will try to look into it but I don't see what I can do." He glanced back at the boy who hesitated before he spoke.

"The man was some kind of prophet ... a seer. He said it was you. That you were ..."

"Don't." He glared at the boy who could not have spoken a word even without the command as Corin's magic bound him tightly from toe to tongue. "Don't say it, don't think it and don't ever repeat it," he snarled. A slight movement of the boy's eyes seemed to agree to this arrangement and so Corin released him and watched as he slumped against the bar. "Go away, lad, and go fast." Corin's eyes settled on the Dark Fae who brooded in the corner, all coiled violence and malicious intent. "I'll make sure they don't follow you."

"Thank you, Sire," he whispered and moved quickly, escaping out of the door while five pairs of black eyes watched him go, and the gold surveyed them in turn, warning them to stay put.

Not long after the boy had left him, Corin felt a warm hand slide over his thigh and turned to find a pair of brown eyes looking at him, but not the ones he was longing to see. She was Elven, one of his race and her hair was dark like his. She leaned into him and her scent wrapped around him reminding him of home, and he felt a stab of loneliness.

"You're a long way from Alfheim," he observed as the hand slid a little farther up his leg. She nodded, looking up at him from under her lashes.

"You too, Sire, but I am sure I can make you feel at home ..."

He closed his eyes, feeling the alcohol spin in his blood, and wondered just how far his life was going to spiral out of control. The girl found her goal and a small but surprisingly firm hand caressed him through the denim as she pressed her lips to his neck. "Shall we go somewhere more private?" she murmured against his ear.

A wave of sorrow overcame him as he thought about Océane asleep in her bed. Not for him. That kind of happy ever after was not for him. An image came to mind, unbidden and unwelcome, of a small boy with golden eyes laughing and giggling as Corin threw him into the air and caught him safely again. Holding the boy tight against him he kissed the thick mop of chestnut hair and his son looked up at him with adoration.

He blinked fiercely, trying to rid himself of the image. After all it was nothing more than a lovely daydream. Pouring another drink, he drained it and smacked the empty glass against the bar top before picking up the envelope and stuffing it in his jacket pocket. "I can't think of a reason not to," he said, sliding one hand around the girl's waist and snagging his bottle with the other. "Lead the way."

Three hours later and the bar was almost empty save for some hard core drinkers and Corin blinked as Beck slapped his face gently with a meaty hand.

"Sire, forgive me for noticing, but you're drunk."

"Thank the gods," Corin mumbled against the surface of the bar.

"Thank who you like, Sire, but I'm closing up and even the Prince of Alfheim needs to get his arse off my property."

Peeling his face from the polished wood, Corin frowned and tried to focus on the barman who appeared to be swimming in and out of view. "Beck, I have noticed you do not treat my title with the respect it deserves," he slurred as he got off the stool and stood holding onto the bar for a moment as the room appeared to be moving around him at an unreasonable speed.

"True enough, Sire, and title or no you have my utmost respect for the fact you are still standing, but in my experience a drunk is a drunk whether a noble or a street sweeper."

Corin grinned at him. "What an elegant observation and what a devilish pity. I believe I would have made an excellent street sweeper."

Beck grunted but made no comment as he escorted the

Elven Prince Regent to the door. "Go down there and you'll find a taxi waiting for you."

"Beck, you are a fine man," Corin said, smacking him on the back. "None better." He chuckled as Beck rolled his eyes at him.

"Whatever you say, your Highness, whatever you say. Now just stay out of trouble, will you."

Corin executed what he considered to be a surprisingly elegant bow bearing in mind that he had left an empty bottle of Ebony Fire on the bar top, and straightened to shake his head at Beck. "That, my friend, is something I am quite unable to promise."

There was a snort of amusement from the barman. "You do surprise me," he said drily as Corin turned away and headed for the taxi.

***

Océane unlocked the door to her bedroom with nervous fingers and wondered if Corin was still going to be angry with her for the appalling way she had behaved the night before. She really hoped not because she did not know how she was going to get through saying goodbye to her best friend without him. She opened the door cautiously and frowned as she looked around and didn't see him. Stepping a little further into the room she looked down at the dishevelled figure curled up on the floor of her kitchen. She ran to him and sat on the floor, checking him over. He was huddled into a ball, his leather jacket clutched tightly around him and she figured he must be freezing as there was a shocking draft coming from under the front door. She leaned down to rouse him and noticed first the strong smell of alcohol, and then the more subtle undertone of perfume, though the lipstick marks on his neck were the clincher. Well, somebody had been a busy boy. She stifled a stab of jealousy that he had found someone else with such alacrity before telling herself off. It was not for her to judge him. She hardly felt herself to be a paragon of virtue either just at the moment.

She gave him a gentle shake and he sighed sleepily. There was silence for a moment and then a deep groan as his hands touched his temples with delicate fingers.

"I have a feeling you deserve that," she said with a sad shake of her head.

"Oh, gods," he mumbled as the golden eyes tried to focus on her. They seemed to settle on her face and for a moment he looked relieved, peaceful even, and she thought he would smile at her. The expression faded and changed though, as if he'd remembered he had no right to look at her so. He moved - too quickly by all accounts as when he stood up he swayed a little and his normally honey gold skin paled. "Excuse me," he said and left the room with haste. She sighed and shut the bedroom door to give him some privacy but the paper thin walls could not muffle the sounds of retching from the bathroom.

A few moments later she heard the soft hiss of the shower come on and she began to move around the tiny kitchen on autopilot. With studied normality she opened cupboards and made coffee and hunted around for something that would pass as breakfast even though she couldn't possibly eat and she knew Corin wouldn't either. She would do anything, though, to keep her mind from Carla and the day ahead.

Just how did you say goodbye to someone forever? How did you say everything that you always thought you would have a lifetime to talk about? Perhaps it was possible to find some comforting, memorable moment to carry forward with you when all the time you were trying to act normal - when in truth nothing would be normal again.

By the time Corin came back she was no closer to answering any of the questions and a lot closer to curling up in a ball and howling at the unfairness of it.

With a great deal of concentration and rather less of his

usual elegance, Corin pulled out a chair and sat down. He winced visibly as Océane put a cup of coffee down on the table in front of him, and gave her a reproachful look when she asked if he wanted breakfast. He shook his head. "Not any time this century, thank you," he replied with a shudder. Océane snorted and threw a small box of pain killers on the table. The clatter made him close his eyes. "There is no need to be vindictive, darling."

"Who was she?" She turned her back on him to fill a large glass of water so that she didn't have to see his face. Turning back there was no escaping his golden gaze, however, placid with no apparent trace of shame.

"Does it matter?"

"Did you know her?" she demanded, wondering why she was asking.

"No."

"What was her name?"

He sighed and leant back in his chair, long elegant fingers circling the coffee cup. "I neither know nor care and I am at a loss to know why you do."

She slammed the water glass down on the table and smiled grimly as he cursed, the noise obviously having split his skull in two.

"So you think I like the fact that you said that you love me and yet run from my bed and go and ..."

She watched his jaw tighten as he trailed a fingertip down the side of the glass. "Go and what?" he asked, his voice flat.

Standing her ground, she glared at him and crossed her arms. "Go and ... And act like a slut."

"Ah." He nodded. His expression closed off and he looked up at her again. "I warned you, Océane, you don't know me. I am afraid you are just getting an uncomfortable glimpse of the truth." He dropped his gaze and picked up the pill box, turning it around and around in his hands. "Your observation of my character is perfectly accurate. I have been on my best behaviour for you, my dear, but I am sorry to say that it is just a pretty façade."

She shook her head, swallowing down the lump that had lodged itself in her throat and she walked over to stand beside him. She leant down and whispered in his ear. "You can't make me hate you."

He turned his head so that she was looking straight into his eyes and was taken aback by the sadness she found there.

"Don't worry, darling," he said with a bitter smile. "I can manage that quite well enough for the both of us."

By the time they were both ready to leave, Corin seemed to have recovered a little of his good humour or at least tried harder to cover his previous demeanour, but Océane felt a knot in her stomach that seemed to tie itself into tighter, more intricate contortions the harder she considered what the future might hold. Carla, Laen, Corin; their lives had touched and tangled together with her own and for the life of her she couldn't see how they were going to continue without twisting into an increasingly complex bind. Whether that was a good thing or something that would just continue to cause them pain, she didn't know. She was lost in the dark and all she could do was keep following the thread that had brought her into Laen's path and hope that it would lead her to where she ought to be in the end. She had no other choice.

Carla's life line was coming to its conclusion though and she needed to be there to help her complete it. So promising herself that she would be brave and strong for her best friend, they returned to Carla's flat where a different nurse opened the door to them.

"Hi, we're here to see Carla," Océane explained and watched in dismay as the nurse bit her lip and clasped her hands together before replying.

"Oh dear. I'm so sorry but I'm afraid ... she's gone."

Chapter 26

Océane's hand flew to her mouth in shock and the nurse gasped.

"Oh, my goodness, no! I didn't mean *she's gone*. She hasn't died." She looked horrified at the slip up but Océane's concern did not diminish as she continued. "At least ..." The woman blushed, clearly flustered. "I meant she's not here!" She wrung her hands together, looking anxious. "I checked on her when my shift began and she was still fast asleep. She looked really peaceful and to be honest ...well, I thought she would likely pass soon. I just sat down for a moment and ... I don't know. I must have fallen asleep." She frowned and put a hand to her forehead. "I never sleep like that, not at work - not without waking," she murmured, "but ... But I only woke up a few minutes ago and when I checked, she was gone."

Océane stared at her in disbelief. "How is that possible?"

The nurse shook her head. "It isn't! I just don't understand it. No one could have gotten in without me knowing and she was ... Well she was dying. There is no

THE DARK PRINCE

way she got out of here under her own steam," she insisted. "I'm going to call the hospital and the police." She turned and went into the flat and Océane moved to follow her.

"No, Océane." Corin grabbed her arm to stop her.

"What?" Océane glared at him. "Come on, Corin, we have to help."

He shook his head with a smile. "She's not here, Océane, but I think I know where to find her."

Corin would say no more, but insisted that she return to her flat and gather a few of her meagre belongings before they crossed back into the Fae Lands. The moment they got back to her place, he collapsed into the ratty brown armchair. Even hung over and crumpled it didn't disguise what he was. Like a gold Cartier watch slung down on a dirty Formica table. She dragged her eyes from him and scurried around the tiny flat as quietly as she could manage, shoving a very few precious items and necessities into a rucksack. Checking her wardrobe and finding absolutely nothing that she wanted to take, her eyes fell upon an old shoe box gathering dust under a disgusting pair of trainers.

She knelt down and chucked the shoes to the back of the wardrobe and lifted the lid. Inside was miscellaneous paperwork, an out of date passport from her time in the UK, and an envelope containing the very few photographs she had of her childhood. There hadn't been many to begin with but there were even fewer she had wished to preserve. That period of her life had been carefully boxed up and mentally shelved, very high up, in a dark place and the doors were locked tight. She found she didn't want to look at them now either, though the memories were happy ones at least, she and Carla together one summer. It seemed not only a lifetime but a world away now. One day she would want to see them again, but not now. She put the envelope in the bag, careful that they wouldn't get damaged, and was about to put the lid back on the box when she noticed the tatty red cover of a notebook. She paused as a forgotten sensation returned and felt anxiety lay its cold fingers against her back with a delicate touch. She wanted to slam the lid back on the box and put it away but ... something made her reach in and take it out. Her breathing sped as she told herself not to be so silly. It was only ever make believe. Except ...

She thought about the other story she had written so long ago, long before the one that had mirrored Laen's reality, and she felt her skin prickle with fear. All for a crown. A war for a crown. It couldn't be true, not possible, not twice. But she saw the flames, greedy and bright behind her eyes and the shadowy figure that screamed and burned as they devoured and consumed. So much death and destruction. So much power. So much power.

"Are you all right?"

She squealed as Corin's voice brought her back to reality, and then laughed, holding her hand to her heart. "Oh, don't do that, you frightened the life out of me." Suddenly her fears seemed ridiculous with his solid presence standing beside her. But somehow she couldn't leave the notebook behind, so she stuffed it in the rucksack. "Ready."

To her surprise Corin summoned the gateway in a dark corner of an alley behind her tower block. Apparently on this side of their world if you were powerful enough you could summon it anywhere. She asked if Laen could have done that as she had worried about him finding his way back to where they'd come through but Corin's silence seemed answer enough. She knew now that he was full of secrets and contradictions and his admission to Carla that he hid his power from his own kind seemed significant.

The thick skin that kept their world from hers pulled away from his hand just as it had for Laen, and she felt a rush of clean cold air as the Fae Lands came into view. The sight of the snow-capped mountains peeking out from behind thick cloud against a backdrop of urban Paris was enough to make her head spin, it was so absurd. Once again she felt the prickle and pull of magic against her skin.

The sweet scent wrapped around her and whirled in her brain until she felt quite dizzy and Corin reached out a hand to steady her as she stepped through, the tear in reality sealing off behind them. Corin instructed her to stay where she was as he walked away to retrieve their horses and she nodded and shivered, looking curiously at the meadow grass that was coated in a thick covering of frost.

It was much later in the day before Laen's castle came into sight. Océane trembled as she looked down the valley at it. Huge, intimidating and fiercely defended, it reminded her of the owner and she wondered what he would say when she returned. It was still daylight but the skies were bleak and the clouds so heavy she could believe they would fall to earth, crushing everything beneath. A thick, swirling mist surrounded the castle. It looked like some great ethereal snake had curled itself around the building, coiling the heavy grey stone within its sinuous embrace and enveloping it in gloom. The temperature had plummeted and was now even colder than Paris had been with a dense white frost that coated the entire landscape. The frozen covering gave the world a strange kind of sorrowful beauty, because she now knew what caused it. Océane's hands felt numb, her fingers brittle as they held onto the reins and the horse's coat steamed in the icy air, the beast huffing out great cloudy breaths as it bore her closer to Laen. She looked over at Corin, whose pallor matched the surroundings.

"Are you feeling any better?" she asked him and was rewarded with a look that clearly said what the hell do you think?

"Marvelous," was the reply he gave out loud.

"I was only asking," she muttered, burying her head further into her scarf with a shiver.

He sighed and his horse trotted closer to her. He reached his hand out and she offered hers so he could take it and give it a squeeze.

"Forgive me, darling. I am not very good company today, am I?"

She smiled at him and squeezed his hand in return. There were too many words in her head to find anything appropriate to say to him.

As the horse's hooves clattered over the cobbled surface of the stable yard, Océane wondered if she would have a heart attack before she made it inside the vast doors of the castle. Excitement, fear, longing and hope made up her state of mind, but she was in too much turmoil to settle on just one as her emotions bounced from euphoria to desperation.

When they got to the stables, some of Laen's men rushed over to help but Corin dismissed them. His voice was sharp and impatient and Océane felt another emotion add to the overload as concern for him layered over everything else. He turned to her and she saw the effort he made to relax his features and appear calm and composed as usual.

"Well then, here we are," he said with a smile.

"I don't understand what's happening, Corin. Why won't you explain?" she demanded for the twentieth time since they had left Carla's flat. Hope was alive and burning and she felt sure that if the news was bad he would have told her already. "Why would Laen bring her here? The journey here, in this freezing cold ... That alone could have killed her. What was he thinking?"

He just smiled at her enigmatically and dismounted, walking over and helping her off her horse. He lifted her easily by the waist and didn't let her go. She looked up into his tawny, golden eyes and sighed. "You have eyes like a lion, did you know that?"

"Well, thank you ... I think?"

She nodded, feeling a surge of affection for him. "They're very beautiful," she said, putting her hand against his cheek.

He sighed and closed his eyes, touching his forehead against hers. "Don't be nice to me, Océane, I beg you," he said with such quiet despair that her heart hurt.

"Oh, Corin, this is such a mess."

THE DARK PRINCE

***

Corin pulled her into an embrace. He knew it was the last time and hoped he would be able to leave without making a complete fool of himself. "No, my dear, I think you will find that things are going to work out quite well. He has broken the law, you know, bringing her here. You were a prisoner and that was one thing, but to bring a human into our lands as the law stands at the moment ... He could be disinherited for that. He could lose his title, the Kingdom - everything."

She frowned at him, perplexed. "Then why would he do it?"

He shook his head. He would let Laen explain what he had done and why. "Why don't you go and find out?"

She laid her head on his shoulder and he had to breathe hard and steady to remind himself he was going to let her go. "He loves you, Océane, remember that, and please, I beg you ... don't let him mess it up again. Don't let him push you away when he needs you." He put his hand under her chin, tilting her head and looking into her eyes. "Don't let him go."

She frowned, her soft brown eyes full of concern. "Why does it sound like you're saying goodbye?"

He shrugged. "I cannot stay here and watch the two of you together, and you do not want me around to make you feel guilty when there is nothing you can do."

"Oh, Corin, I don't want you to go." She held him tight and he swallowed hard. "I'm going to miss you so much," she whispered.

Corin smiled but didn't speak, afraid his voice would betray him. Instead he kissed her forehead and released her, gesturing for her to go inside. Océane kissed his cheek gently and began to walk away.

She turned back to him, anxiety in her eyes. "I will see you again, won't I?"

He nodded and tried hard to smile again. "Of course,

my dear, but ... maybe not for a while." She looked at him with such concern that he knew he had to get away. He had never felt so alone in his whole life as he did when he turned from her.

"Wait," she said suddenly and began to search in the rucksack she had brought with her. She pulled out the tatty notebook, looking at it as though it frightened her before handing it to Corin. "I wasn't sure what to do with this but I think ... I think you should have it." He took the book from her with a quizzical expression. "The Dark Prince, the book I was working on when Laen took me, it wasn't the original."

He stilled as he looked at the worn book cover and the childish writing that covered it, spelling out the same title as he had seen on Laen's story, and felt nausea swirl in his stomach. "Oh?" he asked, praying it was simply the hangover making him unwell and not a premonition of trouble.

She shook her head. "There was another version, much older. I was just a little kid when I wrote it and ..." She paused, shaking her head. "The story got too tangled, far too dark. I didn't really understand what I was writing and I think somehow it got tangled up with my nightmares. There was a fire you see, at the orphanage. No one was hurt but it must have played on my mind and ..." She pointed at the book, thankfully not looking at him because he could not now disguise the fear in his eyes. He heard her sigh and tried to remember how to breathe. "It's about a man who tries to become King, to save the Fae Lands ... I could never figure out how it ended so I gave up on it." She shrugged, looking awkward. "It's just that I think you should have it."

He held the book in his hands, feeling like it was burning his fingertips, like the fire waited for him just inside the pages. "Why?" he asked, hearing his voice, flat and emotionless, and wondering how that was possible when he wanted to scream.

"Open it," she said quietly.

THE DARK PRINCE

Corin looked down at the book as foreboding crawled over his skin. He had thought he could not feel any colder than he did, but fear sent a chill deep in his bones as the damp air clung to him. The only heat was where he touched the accursed book and he could almost smell the stench of burning flesh. He had the sure and certain feeling he did not want to see inside but he did as she asked and opened it, turning to the first page. There were two drawings, carefully wrought, though clearly in a childish hand. On one side of the book there was the drawing of a crown enveloped by flames drawn fiercely in thick red crayon and on the other ... A pair of familiar gold eyes looked back at him. He shut the book with a snap and handed it back to her. "I don't want it."

"But, Corin ..."

He shook his head, resolute, and pushed it back into her hands. "Please, Océane, take it away. Bury it, burn it, I don't care, but don't ever show it to anyone. Promise me." He knew she was shocked by his tone but he couldn't help it. He wanted to run, to leave now and keep on running. "Please, Océane, please ... Promise me." He wondered if she thought him quite mad. Judging from the desperation in his voice he wouldn't blame her. Running from a child's drawing - surely he was being a fool.

Nonetheless she nodded and gave him the promise he demanded, though she looked even more concerned for him than she had before. In normal circumstances he would think it beyond humiliating to have her know how low she'd brought him, but right now he could not muster the energy to care. He watched as she stuffed the book back in her bag and smiled at him sadly. She squeezed his hand briefly before turning her back on him and walking inside.

Corin watched her go with a yearning ache in his heart, and tried his hardest not to feel bitter. On top of everything else, the old stories about his golden eyes would continue to haunt him. Though surely his track record of hell-raising and debauchery should have long since extinguished any expectations of greatness for him. It damn well should have done. He gestured for the stable lads to come and take the horses now, and walked away across the yard, heading into the gardens. He would go in another entrance in case there was a romantic reunion going on in the great hall. He couldn't see her in Laen's arms - didn't need to torture himself any further. At least Laen would be happy now and for that he truly was glad. He was pleased for both of them, he told himself. They would marry and live happily ever after, like in all good Fairy stories. He snorted at the thought. Gods but he needed a drink, a lot of drink. In fact he thought it quite likely that he would not be sober again for some time. Maybe not ever. Anything to rid himself of the feeling in his chest.

He walked slowly through the gardens, as even though he was frozen and miserable he could not yet bring himself to go inside what he knew would become Océane's home. He looked up to find himself back in the dead orchard and sighed at the sight of the wisteria. All the flowers were gone and the stems were grey and bare with a rime of frost layered over them. From out of nowhere the murmuring voices began whispering in his mind once again and he grabbed hold of the branch of a dead apple tree, sick to his stomach. He stood with his eyes closed for a moment only to open them again and find that the branch he was holding was covered in buds, fat and green and spreading to all the other branches. He shouted with horror and leapt away. No! Not here. He should not be able to bring life to the dead here.

He stepped away, turning blindly back to the castle. He needed to get away - back to Alfheim. His heart pounded as he followed the path back to the castle. It was just because he was upset, he reassured himself. His powers were always the hardest to rein in when he was emotional and that certainly described his state of mind right now. His heart began to settle a little as he talked himself down. Of course, that would explain it. It was just a fluke, a burst of magic because he was not himself. It didn't mean anything. He just needed to get a grip, that's all. It *didn't* mean anything. He put his hand over his heart and massaged his chest. The pain and the tightness made it hard to breathe and he wondered if this was what it felt like to a human who was having heart trouble. Was this what a heart attack felt like? Never again, he swore. He would never, *ever* let another woman get under his skin like this again. It was just too painful. He had been right to always keep the women in his life at a distance and he would not be caught out again. Somehow he had let his guard down with Océane, but he had learned his lesson well. From now on his own needs were his priority - he would not live the same life his father had. Shutting his heart away as firmly as he could manage, he headed into the castle to gather his belongings and change his clothes before he froze to death. Though the only item he really intended to take was Océane's book. Even though it was Laen's story, not his ... It was all he had left of her, and with the darkness he sensed coming, he would soon need that comfort to hold on to.

***

Once inside the castle, Océane grabbed the first person she'd seen and asked where Laen was. The man who appeared to be a butler of some description frowned at her and said he didn't know. She narrowed her eyes at him and wondered if he was being deliberately obtuse. "Well what about a human woman, she's very sick?"

He frowned harder and pointed out reluctant directions.

Océane had flown down the corridor and flung the door open before the man had time to turn around let alone question who was asking. What she saw made her gasp in shock.

Carla sat by a roaring fire with a blanket over her knees and was tucking into a sandwich with Aleish sitting beside her.

"Carla!" she exclaimed and ran across the room to kneel beside her, almost flinging the sandwich to the floor as she tried to take hold of her hand. "Oh, my God! I thought you were dead!"

"Well I guess we're even then," Carla said with a laugh as she set the sandwich aside and grasped her friend's hands in return. "And so did I! I think ... I think I almost was."

Océane looked at her friend and was astonished to see how well she looked. She was still far too thin and frail but the colour and spark had returned to her eyes, and there was a pink flush in her cheeks. She reached out a hand and touched her face in wonder, trying to reassure herself it really was her. "How is this possible?" she whispered.

Aleish got up from her chair. "It is the effect of our lands and our magic. Carla will be quite well again, providing she stays here." She gave the two of them a warm smile and leaned down to hug Océane. "I am so glad you came home. This land would never have seen the sun again if you hadn't." She laughed as Océane hugged her fiercely in return and stood up again, smoothing down the perfect lines of her gown. "Now, if you'll excuse me, I think I will leave you two to talk." Aleish smiled again, wiping her eyes, which were suddenly shining very brightly, and left, shutting the door behind her.

Home, Océane thought to herself, Aleish had said she'd come *home*. She turned to Carla, wondering what on earth she was making of all this. "You have to stay here?" Océane asked. "Oh, my God. Carla, what will you do?"

"Yeah, cause it looks a really crap place to live!" Carla laughed. "Oh, Océane, that man ... My lord, he is one fine hunk of Fairy."

Océane opened her mouth and closed it again. "He's Fae, don't call him a Fairy. He doesn't like it."

Carla gave a dramatic sigh. "I'd call him anything he wanted," she said, looking wistful. Océane glared at her and she chuckled and shook her head. "Kidding! I guess you called dibs." She squeezed Océane's hand tightly, all trace of humour gone. "You know, I thought he was the angel of death when he came to get me?"

Océane sat up on her knees and leaned on the arm of the chair. "What happened?"

"I was in bed, just ... waiting for the end, you know," she recalled, sounding suddenly breathless, as though speaking of it made her chest tight all over again. "I was finding it hard to breathe and then suddenly he was there, sitting on the bed. He asked me if I wanted to live and I said, *hell yes!* So he gave me the choice. He said he could bring me here and that I would live. He said I'd live a long, long time ... but that I wouldn't be able to go home again." Carla squeezed her hand, her eyes alive with happiness. "You know what he said? He said I can stay here in the castle until I'm well enough and after that there is a little cottage in the village. He's giving it to me, Océane! He said no strings, I don't owe him anything and you know the best bit? He apologised that it didn't have much of a garden!" Carla laughed, until the tears ran down her face. "Not much of a garden ... After that shitty apartment, priceless!"

Océane looked at her friend, her heart aching with joy and regret. That Laen had done all that ...

As if she was reading her mind, Carla narrowed her eyes at Océane. "Now then, my friend. Tell me why he would do all of that for someone he doesn't know?"

"I ... I ..." Océane fought for an alternative explanation, just in case ... but she kept coming back to the same conclusion. Could it really be true?

Carla pouted and plucked at the warm blanket draped across her knees. "He asked me a lot of questions about you," she said, raising her eyebrows.

"He did?" Océane thought her voice sounded a bit wobbly and wondered if she was going to pass out. It was very warm in here, what with the fire blazing.

"Uh-huh." She patted Océane's hand. "He explained too, what he did - why you weren't there for me."

Océane felt tears spring to her eyes again. "Oh, Carla, I'm so sorry."

Carla laughed and waved away her apology. "He's apologised quite enough, thank you and it obviously wasn't your fault."

"He ... apologised?"

Carla paused as though she was considering her answer. "Well he never actually said *sorry*. In fact he kept building up to it and backing off again but ..." She chuckled at the astonishment in Océane's eyes. "Oh, that poor man is carrying around so much guilt at the moment. I don't know how he isn't drowning under the weight of it. Lord, Océane, can't you see he would do anything for you - anything to make you happy."

"Oh."

"Oh?" Carla rolled her eyes. "That's all you got? Good grief, Océane, get your backside off that floor and go find him. Tell him you love him and that you'll never let him go, because if you don't ... I sure as hell will!"

Océane just sat there, dumbstruck. She was too dazed to be happy yet and nothing was ever certain with Laen, but she was going to do everything she could to make sure he didn't frighten her off. Not again. She glanced up at Carla, who was clutching the arms of the chair in impatience.

"You do love him, don't you, Océane?" she demanded, and Océane looked up at her friend, at the pretty blue eyes that were going to sparkle and see life for a great deal longer.

"Yes." A smile spread out over her face and she laughed. "Yes, I do."

"Well, then! Go, woman, go! I'll be just fine. I'm going to live! And that gorgeous man loves you. He's just rescued your best friend from the jaws of death, what more do you need?"

"Nothing!" Océane squeaked and leapt to her feet. She had just reached the door when Carla called out to her.

"Oh, and, Océane, if you try to seduce that man

wearing those clothes and those ... Boots," she said, gesturing at her DM's with distaste. "I will never *ever* speak to you again."

"Yes, ma'am!" Océane laughed and flew out of the door.

Chapter 27

Océane took the stairs two at a time. She ran to her room with her heart beating too hard from excitement, at every moment convinced she would run into Laen around the next corner. She wasn't sure if she was relieved or disappointed as she arrived at her room without meeting him and paused outside the bedroom door. How strange it was not to have two burly guards standing outside. Feeling suddenly panicked, she opened the door slowly and stepped inside, wondering if maybe Laen had instructed all of the things Aleish had given her to be taken away. To her relief everything was exactly as she had left it and she opened the wardrobe doors with a happy sigh as she found the previously despised dresses hanging neatly just as before.

With a haste that had her tripping over her clothes, she stripped off and washed in record time to make sure she didn't smell of the wretched horse. She brushed her hair with hands that trembled, and even investigated the cosmetics Aleish had given her, adding a little colour to her cheeks and lips and a touch of perfume. She took out the prettiest underwear in a delicate white lace and then she went to choose a dress, wondering which one he would like the most. In the end it was an easy decision. Reaching into the wardrobe she hooked out the dark green one. It was the one she had worn the day he had kissed her neck, though frankly that seemed a poor description of what he had done considering the effect it had. Even now, just thinking about the feel of his lips made her skin flush and a yearning ache began to grow deep inside. She shook herself out of the daydream. She didn't want to just dream of him any longer. She wanted that for real - she wanted all of it.

With anxious fingers that simply refused to cooperate, she fumbled with the fastenings at the back of her dress. Stretching herself into knots to try and get the stupid things to do up, she cursed, almost screaming with impatience. Once she had the wretched things in place, she looked at herself in the mirror with critical eyes. Was this enough to make him want her again ... to forgive her? She bit her lip and sighed. Well it was all she had and she wouldn't find out standing around.

She left the room and decided she had better start her search for him up here. As she began knocking on doors it became harder and harder to breathe. With each door she knew she was closer to finding him and her worry grew. Perhaps everyone was wrong in their opinion of his feelings for her. Perhaps she was wrong. Maybe he didn't want her and never had. She scolded herself for being so pessimistic and remembered the way he had been in the café, the way he had looked at her, the way he had kissed her hand. But with yet another empty room open before her she felt tears prickle at her eyes as her confidence began to crumble. She had looked in around thirty rooms already without seeing a soul. She slammed the door shut with an oath and carried on, turning the corner into what appeared to be the south side of the castle. It was also much more luxurious with heavy brocade curtains and thick carpets, and her heart began to dance double time once again as she imagined his bedroom must be here somewhere.

At the end of the corridor a set of double doors waited, unguarded. She made herself stop and take a deep breath to try and settle her heart down and stop it beating in her throat. Standing right outside, she smoothed her dress down with care, rearranged her hair, licked her lips ... and knocked.

"Go away!" a furious and familiar deep voice responded through the door.

She took a breath and swung open the door, stepping through and shutting it behind her quickly, before she could lose her nerve.

Laen stood by the window, staring out. His bulk darkened the room as he blotted out what little daylight there was and she watched as he swung around, incensed by whoever had dared to interrupt him.

"I thought I said ..." The words died in his mouth as he saw Océane standing by the door.

She decided that this was a time when action was called for, in case they both tripped each other up by saying the wrong thing. So with hope burning, she ran across the room and threw her arms around his neck. Pulling his head down hard so that she could reach his mouth, she kissed him with all the desire that had been building up for what felt like an eternity.

He hesitated for just a moment and then his arms went around her and pulled tight, and she felt the joy of being in exactly the right place - where she belonged. They clung together as he kissed her back with just as much need as she had shown him. Slowly she pulled away, just a little, and he let her go, looking down at her with those fathomless black eyes.

"Thank you," she whispered before reaching up and kissing him again.

THE DARK PRINCE

***

Laen was lost. That she was here with him, that she had returned was everything he had needed but hadn't dared to hope for. The feel of her kiss, the softness of her body in his arms, was everything he had dreamed it would be.

He would never have pretended that he was a good man. He was antisocial and bad-tempered at best and he could never have acted as nobly as Corin had. There was no way he would have stepped aside if the tables had been turned. He would have done anything, said anything to have Océane love him. Even now he knew she was only here out of gratitude that he had saved her friend's life. It was wrong of him to take advantage of the situation but if this was the only chance he had to be with her, to know what it felt like to love her, then he *would* take it. Even knowing she would go back to Corin in the end, he would do his best to accept it and pray that Corin would find a way to forgive him. Rather that than spend the rest of his days regretting it and wondering what it might have been like.

Instead he would make sure it would be something neither of them would forget.

His lips left her mouth and kissed along the line of her jaw, down her neck, and he smiled against her skin as he felt her breathing hitch. He felt her hands at the back of his neck, tangling up in his hair and hoped he could be patient when every instinct demanded that he take what he wanted right now, this minute.

He pushed the fabric of the dress to one side and let his lips and tongue trail along her shoulder, and then returned his delicate attentions all the way back to her neck. Her head tilted to the side as he worked with exquisite care and turned her slowly in his arms so that her back was against his chest. Kissing and nipping at her skin, his hands travelled over her, dropping to her hips and pulling her against him, letting her feel how hard he was for her, so she would know just how much he wanted her. She leaned into him, her hands covering his and helping him pull her closer, arching against him, so brazen in her need of him that it was all he could do not to throw her down on the bed and bury himself inside of her.

Instead he released her and undid the fastenings at the back of her dress. His usually deft fingers seemed to tremble and fumble over every catch and he gritted his teeth to stop himself tearing the damn thing in two. Finally she was free of it and he watched with satisfaction as it slid down her body and hit the floor. He moved forward again and undid the clasp of her bra, slipping it from her shoulders as his hands moved around to cup her breasts. He sought her mouth once more as her head tipped backwards against him and his fingers caressed and toyed with the peaked skin that had grown taut under his touch. He wanted to taste them, to feel that tight skin under his tongue but his patience was fraying and his hands fell to her hips. He stripped the delicate lace from her with less care than he'd intended. She turned her head, looking over her shoulder at him, her expression fragile, and he knew the wrong word or the wrong move could break this moment into pieces.

He was desperate with the need to tell her how lovely she was, how much he wanted this, but it was suddenly hard to even breathe as he looked at her standing naked in front of him. She was so very beautiful. He realised that he would do anything she asked of him, be anything she wanted, if only she could love him ... even just a little. The words he needed clustered in his mind, everything he wanted to tell her clear and so very obvious but he simply couldn't speak.

Instead he swung her up into his arms. His eyes never left hers and he hoped that she could see in them everything he was feeling as he had no desire to hide it from her or anyone else a moment longer. He settled her on the bed with care before he wrenched off his boots and socks and began undoing his shirt. He yanked at it impatiently before deciding it was taking too long and left it on, turning his attention to what was waiting for him.

***

Océane thought her heart might actually give out as she watched him climb onto the bed. He was simply magnificent as he moved over her, his broad shoulders blocking the view of anything else, though there was nothing that could possibly be as captivating as he was. His shirt was all askew and gave her a glimpse of the massive chest she had begrudgingly admired so much the day she first saw him. She pushed the shirt aside with impatient fingers and ran her hands over the smooth skin of his chest, feeling the hard ridges of muscle along his stomach. The shirt fell forward and she snatched at the material again, wanting nothing to get in the way of the touch of his skin against hers. She saw Laen smile as she mirrored his own impatience and he helped her to pull the infuriating thing over his head. His smile broadened as she threw it across the room and reached for him again, sliding her hands around his body to the wide expanse of his back. When he lay down with her she gloried in the sensation, the fierce heat of his body against her as their mouths found each other again, searching greedily for more.

She pulled him closer still, as hard as she could, holding him tightly with arms and legs and leaving him with no room for doubting the fact that she wanted him. She locked her legs around his, raising her hips to meet him and found with frustration that his trousers and the cold clasp of his belt buckle were in the way. Yet she couldn't bring herself to turn away from him long enough to remove them. When his lips drew away from hers she almost protested until she felt his tongue draw a sinuous path down between her breasts. She held her breath with anticipation as his mouth moved over her, painting her with delicate touches that made her skin shiver with desire. Sinking her hands once more into the soft length of his hair, she gasped as the heat of his mouth engulfed her, his lips and tongue closing hard over her nipple. Her breath came in little gasps as his mouth continued to kiss and suck and nip with his teeth only to soothe again with the soft warmth of his tongue.

Writhing under his touch she drew a deep breath as his head raised and his mouth brushed teasingly over her skin to her other breast to begin his delicious ministrations all over again. She moaned, fretful and restless under his touch now as she had come to the limit of what she could bear. She could simply wait no longer. Putting her hands on his shoulders, she pushed him away from her and he looked down, a flicker of doubt in his eyes until he saw her hands fly to his belt buckle. With a very masculine smirk of satisfaction he helped her to rid them both of the last barrier between them.

Their bodies returned together immediately, like two magnets forced apart. She closed her eyes in bliss at the sound he made as he pressed against her, finding her slick and wanting and in such need of him. "Yes," she whispered against his cheek, scattering kisses over every inch of skin she could reach as their bodies moved together. She felt him surge against her, hard and insistent between her legs and she opened herself to him with no reservations, no doubt in her mind as to what she wanted. Her hips rose to meet his as his arousal pressed against her and sank deep inside and she threw her head back, making a sound somewhere between a joyous laugh and a desperate moan at the rightness of it. She closed her eyes, savouring the feel of him moving within her and with her and of the feel of his breath coming harsh and hot against her skin.

She looked back at him and found so much emotion in his eyes, so much desire that her heart swelled with love for him and she pulled his mouth back to her own. She knew he had been careful with her, gentle with his hands and considerate not to crush her under the weight of him, but she didn't want that. She didn't want careful ... She wanted rapture and demand and urgency and she told him as much with the way she touched him, finding that he was only too happy to give her what she asked as he lost all semblance of control. The sounds he made as pleasure overtook him made her want to laugh and cry with elation, though there was nothing she could do but gasp and sigh as her breath had long since departed. But as she heard him say her name over and over she finally knew the truth of what she had longed for. He loved her.

***

Laen was overwhelmed, consumed by sensation. There was no thought in his mind past the feeling of her skin against his, her mouth against his mouth, the uncontrolled heat of her body moving with his, and when Océane called out his name as she clung to him helplessly, he thought his heart might burst with the longing for this to never end. He saw the look on her face as she came for him, and gloried in the knowledge that she desired him so very much - even if desire was all it was. He held her locked against him as ecstasy untangled his thoughts and made everything so desperately clear. He would never be whole without her. He refused to let her move, even knowing he was probably crushing her as the heightened sensations drifted away, as elation faded into a bone deep contentment of having her close to him. He closed his eyes and savoured the moment and imagined a life where this would have been his, where she would have been his.

Eventually though their small eternity ended, and tangled in sheets and his own emotions, he watched her sleeping. Her dark hair spilled over the pillows and he reached over, gently taking a heavy lock in his hand and letting the silky strands twine around his fingers, wishing he could tie them together with a knot as tight as the one with which Océane had bound herself to his heart. He wanted more than anything to stay, to watch her wake and maybe to smile at him and be happy that he was still there with her, but he wasn't sure that would be what she wanted. She had given him a gift after all and he did not want her to think he had taken more than she had offered him. He brushed his lips against her shoulder, wanting to remember the softness of her skin, the smell of her. He would never forget any part of this day, not a single detail.

Carefully, so as not to wake her, he slipped from the bed, pulling the covers up over her shoulders so that she wouldn't get cold. He stood by the bed for the longest time, just watching her sleep and fighting the desire to climb back in and hold her again ... never to let her go - no matter if she loved him or not. He had forced his way into her life in the first place though, brought her here against her will. He would not do it again. He didn't want her to feel obliged to remain with him. He hoped maybe she would stay for a little while as Carla was here now. Maybe if he tried hard enough she would give him the chance to make her love him.

He dressed quietly, all the while watching her, smiling to himself as she murmured in her sleep and moved towards the place where he had been. With a last longing look, he tore his gaze from the bed and turned to leave.

Chapter 28

Océane sighed as she awoke. Her body was heavy, the lingering ache of Laen's passion a pleasure she hoped to become familiar with. In fact she never wanted them to leave this heavenly place. It had been everything she had needed and wanted and she hoped he felt the same. Sated and utterly content, she summoned the energy to snuggle closer to the warm body next to her ... only to find a cold space. With a flicker of unease in her stomach she opened her eyes and blinked as her eyes adjusted to the half-light the moon silvered the room with. Sitting up with a start, she looked around to see Laen dressed and with his hand on the bedroom door. Her heart gave a heavy thud as their eyes met.

"Where are you going?" Her voice was little more than a whisper, the sharp bite of disappointment already chasing her happiness away like a predator lunging for its quarry with rabid teeth.

"I ..." he began but said no more.

She stared at him. Couldn't he see her heart was on the

verge of breaking? Surely the cracks were visible. "You were just going to leave?" she demanded. She wondered if she really wanted to hear what he was going to say - if she could stand the answer or if the fractures would undermine everything and shatter her heart for good.

He stood in the doorway awkwardly. "No ... Well, yes."

She pulled the covers up to her neck, suddenly feeling exposed and vulnerable as though she had shown him the most private face of her soul and he had held it up for all to see. "Why? Why would you do that?" She couldn't see his face as he was standing in the shadows but she wanted to know what was in those black eyes. "Come here," she demanded, hearing her voice quaver, but resolved that she would not cry. Not yet.

Laen took a few steps back towards the bed. His blond hair fell around his face and brought to mind the frost she had seen covering the landscape outside when she arrived. Standing still in the moonlight he had a cold and terrible beauty, unreal and untouchable. She could certainly understand why Carla had believed he was the angel of death. But she found it hard to believe that his heart was really as frozen as it appeared. He just stood looking at her until she wanted to scream. Instead she asked him again, determined to make him answer the question.

"Why were you leaving?"

"I thought ..." He paused and shifted slightly, looking at the floor so his hair fell forwards, hiding his eyes. "I was not sure you would want me here." His voice was soft, quiet in the darkness, but she simply couldn't understand what he meant. After what had just passed between them, surely she hadn't got it wrong?

"What?" She frowned at him, clutching at the bed covers with tense fingers and willing him to explain this away. "Why not? Why wouldn't I want you here?"

"You ... You do not owe me anything."

She saw the uncertainty on his face, the hesitation before he spoke but his words made her so furious that for a moment she couldn't speak. She stared at him while the white hot fury of her anger overcame the ache in her chest. She gathered up the bed sheet, wrapping it around her and climbed off the bed, walking up to him.

"You thought that was ... gratitude?" she demanded, trying hard to keep her expression neutral and her hands to herself instead of slapping his stupid, handsome face. What was he thinking? She knew all too well what she was feeling herself, but to have the words illustrated under his skin as she looked at him was almost more than she could bear.

He shrugged. "What else could it be?" He sighed and swept his hand through his hair. "I know you love Corin."

She gritted her teeth for a moment before hitting him with the flat of her hand. "Of course I love Corin!" she said, and then stopped and took a breath, wanting to rant and rage, fury blazing inside her at his words. She opened her mouth again to vent her feelings and then she saw the hopelessness in his eyes. She took a deep breath and swallowed down her anger. For a moment she just stood there, breathing in and out in a bid to lower her blood pressure. She really didn't want to fight with him but seriously ... the man may have looked like a fallen angel but he was an imbecile if he couldn't see what was in front of his damn nose.

"Anyone in their right mind would love Corin and I know you do too. He is a good man, a good friend. He is my friend." Once she felt she was calm enough to carry on without screaming, she chose her words carefully. "If I was in the habit of sleeping with men just out of gratitude, Corin would have been in my bed a long time ago." She saw him flinch and knew that she had hit home. His eyes lifted to hers as her meaning filtered through. "Did you read the end of the story?" she asked, keeping her voice gentle when she wanted to shout with frustration.

He shook his head, his eyes still wary and she was put in mind of some wild, untamed creature that had learned by experience not to trust or get too close. "Why not?" She took a step closer, searching his face. "You've been demanding to know ever since I came here; you dragged me all the way back to Paris to get it. Why haven't you read it?"

He stood looking at her and she could see there was some kind of internal struggle going on in his mind and suddenly Corin's words came back to her. *Don't let him mess it up'*. She stood beside him and slipped her hand into his, reassured as his warm fingers closed around hers. She looked up at him, her voice soft but insistent. She would have an answer. "Why didn't you read it?"

He looked at her, hesitant. "I did not want to," he admitted.

"Why?"

He didn't reply but now it didn't matter, she knew why. She tightened her hold on his hand and leaned her head on his shoulder. "Shall I tell you a bedtime story?"

"Will it give me nightmares?" He said it jokingly but she could tell there was a real question there. He was afraid of what she might have written for him.

Standing on tip toe she reached up and brushed her lips against his, smiling against his mouth as his eyes closed and he drew in a sharp breath. "No nightmares," she said, "I promise."

She led him back to the bed and made him sit down, perching beside him and still holding his hand. "Are you sitting comfortably?" she asked with a smile, but he stayed quiet, looking at her with those deep black eyes that could no longer hide the feelings he held. "Then I'll begin," she said with a hint of humour, but her expression grew serious as she spoke. "After his mother's death and his treatment at the hands of his cruel human step mother, the dark prince was angry with the mortal world and decided he would have his revenge." She began her story watching his face and his eyes with avid attention, thirsty for every expression, every clue to how he was feeling. "He didn't care what he did or who he hurt ... He wanted retribution for the life that had been taken from him." Laen shifted uncomfortably beside her and she squeezed his hand.

"He went through the gates for the first time alone to investigate their realm and make plans. He would decide where he would begin, where he could cause the most damage. But he had no knowledge of the mortal world and its dangers and the gates brought him out onto a busy road. From out of nowhere a car appeared and bore down on him. He was faster than any human and leapt out of the way but the car struck him a glancing blow and he fell dazed and bleeding. He got to his feet and began to stagger away, hurt and disorientated when a woman rushed to his side. She was young and alone and he could tell she was afraid to help him but she went to him anyway and asked if she could take him to the hospital. He shook his head but the girl could see he was in pain. She gave him a drink of water and began to search for something to clean away the blood. When she came closer to him to tend his wound she saw his face clearly for the first time and knew that he wasn't human. She gasped, terrified, but the prince could not risk her screaming, so he picked her up and ran back through the gates to his own land, taking the girl with him." She paused and looked at him. "Do you really not know how this ends?"

He shook his head, his eyes never leaving hers.

She leaned into him, whispering. "It ends like all good Fairy stories."

She saw him frown. "I am not a Fairy," he muttered and she hid a smile.

"No, I know that." She soothed him, stroking his broad back with her hand. "Have you never heard of Beauty and the Beast?"

There was a snort of amusement. "I take it I am the beast?"

She chuckled and nodded. "Well if the cap fits ..." She leaned over and kissed his cheek and he looked back at her with such longing that it stole her breath away.

"Tell me how it ends," he asked, his voice husky, his lips so close to hers that she didn't want to continue, but she forced herself to stay still and carry on to the end.

She took a short breath before continuing, each word slow and precise. "The Prince takes her home and even though she has shown him kindness, he is cruel to the girl. He locks her away in a high tower and will let no one see her." He stiffened beside her, dropping his gaze and looking at the floor but Océane pressed on. "The girl is made of sterner stuff than he can imagine, however. She will not let him see how very afraid she is and she defies him, raging at him for his treatment of her. The Prince has never met anyone like her before and he is intrigued and makes excuses to spend more and more time visiting his prisoner. The girl can see now that he is not a bad man, he is just angry and hurt and afraid, and ... she falls in love with him."

Laen looked at her intently. She could feel his gaze like a caress, warm and full of desire, and see the hope burning in his eyes. She smiled and got up, pulling him to his feet. "Come over here." She took him over to a large mirror that stood in the corner of the room. "Look in the mirror." She watched, never taking her eyes off him as he looked at his reflection and saw the words that were in her heart flickering under his skin. He gasped and stepped forward to look closer to be sure he hadn't been mistaken. Océane smiled as he saw what she was feeling.

He turned, looking at her in amazement, and pulled her into his arms. "How can you love me ... after everything I have done to you?"

She smiled up at him, smoothing her hands over his chest. "Well, I figure you've got plenty of time to make it up to me."

His face became serious, his eyes intent as he put one hand to her face, his thumb stroking her cheek, careful and tender. "I will spend the rest of my days making it up to you if you will let me." He paused and closed his arms around her waist, holding her tight. "I love you, Océane."

"I know," she said with a sigh, quite unable to keep the smile from her face as she touched her fingertips to the words she was going to say as they illuminated his face. "I love you too."

He traced the curve of her bottom lip with a gentle finger. "Can you really forgive me?" he asked. "I swear on my honour, on my life, I will never hurt you again. You need never be afraid of me. I would rather cut my own throat than hurt you again. When I think of what I did, the way I thought about you - about anyone human ... I had no idea. I was wrong. I was so wrong and I'm sorrier than you will ever know." He paused and looked down at her. "I am sorry."

She felt her heart swell as she looked at him. "You said it!"

"For you," he replied and brought her hand to his lips. "I can and will do anything you ask, anything you need - anything at all ... for you."

He cupped her face in his big hands and kissed her, covering her face with the gentle brush of his lips until he settled against her mouth and stole her breath and with it any doubts she may have had about the way he felt. When he finally let her go she reached up and stroked his face. "So no war with the human race then?"

He held her tighter still, his eyes burning with emotion. "Never, I swear it."

"I know that our world is a mess, Laen. We all know it, but there are people who care, who would care terribly if they knew what they had done to your world too. We are just like the people here I think ... not all good but not all bad either."

"I know. I understand that now."

She sighed, settling herself into his embrace. "And you'll agree to open the gates?"

"Yes," he said, not sounding as though he gave a damn

what happened to the gates as he buried his face in her hair, breathing in the scent of her.

She grinned and pushed on, determined to have her answers now. "And you'll agree to the Fae marrying into the human race, if they wish to."

She looked up to see a frown cross his face and she swallowed a tremor of alarm. "On one condition," he replied, his voice stern.

"Oh?" she asked, clutching at his shirt with nervous fingers.

He looked down at her, his eyes filled with everything she knew he felt. "I get to show them how it's done."

THE *dark* HEART

LES FÉES: THE FRENCH FAE LEGEND

Book 2 Coming Summer 2015!
Sneak Peek:

Corin felt the brush of a soft pair of lips against his cheek, the press of a naked, warm body against his back but he kept his eyes firmly shut, his breathing even. He felt the sigh of her disappointment against his skin and it fluttered over him like most things did now; he was aware of it but it didn't really touch him. Nothing could, not any more. He listened to the girl moving around his elegant bedroom, gathering her clothes in the dim light like the regrets she would likely find weighing on her conscience the moment she closed the bedroom door. He wished he could be moved to find some pity for her but his compassion appeared to be long used up. He was done with feeling sorrow for another's plight, had enough of feeling anything at all. All he wanted now was sedation, an anaesthetised indifference to everything. It was the only way to get through the day and shut out the demanding voices that plagued him and kept him awake at night. No matter how much he drank or how far he lost himself to the dark, they were still waiting for him when he came to, a little louder, a little more insistent.

He heard the soft whispering of silky underwear and the rustle of skirts as the girl got dressed and he saw the pale daylight edging cautiously around the edges of the curtains as if aware it was unwelcome. She would have to hurry to get down to the kitchens where she worked or the other girls would talk. He wondered if he would have to move her on. She had looked at him with too much affection and he couldn't stand it when they cried.

He closed his eyes again as she moved towards him and felt her gaze on him as he feigned sleep. He knew she was trying to find the courage to wake him and knew too she would leave without a word. Not because she wanted to but because she knew he was done with her and she didn't want to see it in his eyes. He wondered if he had always been so callous and had just hidden it better with gentle words and pretty lies. He had certainly never hated himself more.

He heard the door shut and opened his eyes. They felt dry, as if they'd been rolled in sand and he closed them again. His head throbbed, a dull insistent ache which had become his usual prelude to the day. Generally he drank some more and went back to sleep until late afternoon. It was a routine of sorts.

He lit the candelabra with a dismissive flick of his fingers and blinked even in the soft light it cast. Hanging an arm out of the bed he reached for the black glass bottle he had left on the floor and picked it up, giving it a shake and cursing as he discovered it was empty. He let it drop from his fingers where it fell among his discarded clothes with a gentle thud. He groaned again as there was a soft knock at the door, and wondered what the devil Alsten was playing at. He never usually disturbed him this early, he knew better.

"Come," he said, laying his arm over his brow and praying his valet had brought something for his head, ideally a full bottle.

Alsten came in bearing a tray. His elderly retainer navigated the darkened room with unerring surety, moving around stray boots and clothes and placing the tray down beside the bed where Corin gave it a scathing look.

"That smells remarkably like peppermint tea," he said,

his disgust perfectly illustrated by his tone of voice.

"It is, your Highness," Alsten replied with dignity.

"Why, Alsten?" Corin demanded. "We have had a perfectly amicable working relationship since the day I was born, why spoil it now?"

"Your Mother, Sire." The cryptic reply was enough to give the old man Corin's undivided attention. He stilled, looking uneasy.

"What about her?" he asked, his tone wary.

"I regret to inform you ..." The old man sounded apologetic. "Queen Audrianne on her way, Sire."

The old man winced at Corin's volley of profanities and handed over the cup, which was snatched from his grasp as the Prince clambered out of bed and made his way to the bathroom. Well wasn't this a splendid way to start the morning. It looked as though a perfectly miserable day was about to go to hell.

An hour later and Corin was staring out of the window at yet another unremarkable day. He watched grey clouds hanging over the beautiful gardens in front of the grand house that had been his childhood home and felt guilty at the treatment they had suffered from the recent weather. The gardens were usually a spectacular sight, but endless rainstorms and months without sun had taken their toll. The clouds pressed damp caresses upon the tree tops and hung so low to the ground he felt as though they would smother the land and him with it. It felt increasingly hard to breathe and he wondered if it really was possible to die of boredom. He glanced at the half empty bottle on the cabinet beside him and sighed. He didn't dare have a drink. His mother coming to visit this morning was news enough to sober anyone. Besides, he needed his wits about him. The Queen did not visit without good reason and he had a fair idea what her reasoning was likely to be. He very much doubted he was going to like it. He closed his eyes against the dull thud of his headache and wished he could go back to bed. Not that he wanted to sleep. Sleep brought dreams and they were worse than the voices. No, he wanted to drink himself into a comfortable stupor where his brain was too sodden to think at all. Maybe that way he'd hold onto his sanity a little longer.

It had been a particularly depressing week, which was really quite remarkable against the now familiar landscape of depressing weeks. The downwards spiral had been triggered by the arrival of an invitation to Laen and Océane's wedding. Laen was Prince of the Dark Fae and his estate bordered Corin's in Alfheim, the part of the Elven Lands over which Corin had domain, being the only son of King Albrecht.

Laen had been his best friend since they were small children but he would not be attending the wedding and no amount of persuading was going to change his mind. He heard the sound of wheels on gravel and opened his eyes to watch his Mother's carriage being drawn inexorably towards the house and wondered just how hard she was going to try.

He heard a commotion outside on the wide stone steps that led up to the main entrance which was undoubtedly his wolves giving the Queen a royal welcome. Corin stifled a smile; his mother hated them.

"Get away from me, you idiotic creatures!" she yelled as she entered the room in a sweep of stunted majesty. She cursed and tried to hold the skirts of her dress out of the way of their massive paws. "Corin, control these wretched animals."

Corin gave a sharp whistle and the five black wolves ran to their master's command. He flicked his hand in the direction of the fire and they obediently sat down beside the hearth's flickering warmth.

She glared at him, brushing black hair and muddy paw marks off her silk dress. "Well if they are that well trained, why did you let them run riot when I arrived?"

"They were just so pleased to see you, dearest." He smiled at her as he bent down to caress the ears of one of the wolves who looked up at him adoringly.

Audrianne snorted with amusement at the idea. "I can imagine. Just about as pleased as you are I suspect."

Corin bit back a sarcastic comment and decided it was prudent to be polite rather than honest. "Mother, my house is yours. You are always most welcome."

There was a sound of amused sarcasm that might have been a laugh and she narrowed her eyes at him. "Pull the other one, my dear ... it's got bells on."

Sighing heavily, Corin got to his feet and raised his eyebrows. "You know I shall stop bringing you books from the human world if you are going to pick up such uncouth language. I cannot begin to imagine what they think of you at court."

"Oh as if I give a damn." His mother chuckled unrepentantly and sat down in one of the large chairs by the fire, nudging a wolf's tail gently out the way of her feet. She was still a stunning woman despite being over five hundred years old. In human terms she didn't look a day over forty, with long, glossy chestnut brown hair which was styled in an elegant chignon, and wide brown eyes. The colouring was usual for the Elven race but she was considered one of the most beautiful women in the Kingdom and took full advantage of the fact whenever she deemed it necessary. In a male dominated land, she had not become Queen simply by a chance of birth. A fact which Corin knew disgusted her on the one hand. At the same time however he had often seen her at work and knew damn well she got off on twisting powerful men around her finger simply because they desired her. She had married Corin's father, the King who had been bewitched by her startling beauty and had arranged the marriage with her parents and little consultation with his bride who was not only decades but centuries younger than him. She had been far more than the King had bargained for however and succeeded in wresting the power of land from his grasp. He was still besotted and utterly in her thrall and she was now the Sovereign. The King could do little but watch as she led her court by the nose and a good many of them via her bed.

"So, to what do I owe the pleasure of your company?" he asked, deciding he'd rather get it over with quickly. Rather that than suffer the verbal games his mother delighted in while she wound him up to the point where he wanted to throw her bodily from the house.

She pulled off her fine leather gloves and fixed him with a steely expression that had been known to make lesser men gibber and shake with nerves. "You know full well why I am here and don't pretend you don't."

He stood by the hearth and leaned one arm against the ornate, marble mantle piece as the flames leapt higher up the chimney. He looked down at the fire and steeled himself for an argument. "I'm not going."

"What? Oh, that." She waved her hand dismissively. "I know you won't attend the wedding," she replied, sounding resigned to the point of boredom.

Corin looked up at her with suspicion. "You mean you're not going to try to blackmail me into going?"

She raised her eyebrows, returning a haughty expression and looked down her nose at him with distaste. "I do not blackmail, I merely... persuade."

Corin gave a short bark of laughter which had his mother scowling at him. "I'm sorry, Mother, but I have seen the guard use more subtle means of persuasion than you."

She shrugged and arranged the deep purple swathes of her dress into more agreeable drapes. She soothed the fine silk with her long, slim fingers as diamond rings sparkled in the firelight. "And I have never known one of them to work on you, so I'm not about to waste my breath. Everybody knows why you're not going anyway ... Still moping around after that human girl."

Corin gave her a dark look, the gold of his eyes flashing amber with annoyance. "I do not mope!" he said, biting out the words.

Audrianne sighed and pursed her lips, looking him over carefully for a moment before she spoke. "So you're telling me this isn't the first morning you've been awake, shaved and sober for some months?" she demanded, folding her arms and allowing her gaze to travel to the half empty black bottle on the drinks cabinet and pointedly back at her son.

"That is a gross exaggeration," Corin lied. He turned his back on her and stared at the fire to stop himself casting another longing glance in the same direction.

"Is it indeed?" she said, and he heard the incredulity in her voice clearly enough. "I don't think so, and I am telling you it is time it stopped." He glanced up at her and gritted his teeth as she sat forward in her chair and pointed one perfectly manicured finger in his direction. "There is nothing wrong with you or your heart. She was not the one for you and what's more you know it."

"Damn it, Mother," he shouted, while the flames blazed and sent white hot sparks dancing around the hearth as his anger flared. "I will take a great deal from you but do not presume to tell me what is in my heart."

She shook her head sadly before starting in on him again. "My darling boy, I know you better than anyone else in this realm or the next and I know you did not truly love her." She watched him placidly, making no remark on the expressions of exasperation and incredulity that he knew were on his face.

"How?" he demanded, not bothering to moderate the anger in his voice. "How can you possibly know that?"

Her face softened and she reached forward and took his hand. "Because she is not here."

"That is because she loved Laen ... not me." Corin could not hide the bitterness of his words and as he looked down he saw the compassion on his mother's face. He looked away again, pulling his hand from her grasp. The last thing he wanted or needed was pity or kindness, especially from her, it was unbearable.

To his surprise the Queen laughed. "Oh, Corin, if you had loved her enough nothing would have stopped you. You would not have cared about a war in the Fae Lands or anyone or anything else. If she had been your heart's desire, nothing would have stood in your way. I know this, Corin ... I know you. That you didn't fight for her speaks for your heart." Corin opened his mouth to protest but she held up her hand to silence him. "I didn't say you didn't care for her or that you were not hurt but she wasn't the one for you. That woman is still out there and you need to go and find her."

Corin shook his head. "No. I don't." The idea of letting anyone have the power to hurt him like that again was unthinkable. He would marry if he must but his wife would never have his heart.

Audrianne sighed and he watched the steely glint in her eyes with growing apprehension. "Do I have to remind you that you are our only son and that we are growing old?" She folded her arms and he knew damn well what was coming next. "You have to provide the kingdom with an heir."

"I am well aware of my obligations," he snapped, making the wolves look up at him questioningly. Varge, the alpha, sat up and gave a low growl but Corin hushed him. He stroked the big male's head as he leaned into Corin his eyes closing with bliss, the massive wolf's solid presence a comfort to him as he sank his fingers into the wiry fur.

"Are you though?" his mother demanded, bringing his attention squarely back to the matter at hand.

Corin tried to take a breath but his lungs seemed to have turned to stone in his chest. The image of a small boy who looked just like him filled his mind and he felt his chest ache. "Yes, Mother," he said, his voice low and resigned to this fate at least. "I am fully aware of my obligations and I will provide you with a future Queen and an heir in the fullness of time."

Audrianne stood and walked over to him and a familiar uncompromising expression in her eyes bode ill. "No my son, your time is up. I am tired of waiting for you to settle down as are our people. You will find a bride now. You have three weeks to announce the engagement or I will do it for you."

He caught his breath. His mother had never failed to surprise him with just how far she would go to get her own way. This though ... He looked at her with undisguised horror. "You wouldn't!"

She smiled at him but it was a hard look, the one she gave when she was going to give him a spell in the palace cells for defying her at court - for his own good. "If you do not do it yourself then yes I will, and I might add that does not include seducing the staff or any other pretty face that takes your fancy in your usual manner, you are looking for a suitable wife who is capable of bearing you sons. Otherwise your father and I have the power under Elven law to choose for you."

"That law goes back to the beginning of bloody time!" he raged, as the fire in the hearth roared up the chimney and thunder exploded over the great house. Varge shifted next to him, his eyes on the Queen and his lips drawn back in a silent snarl. Corin was more than tempted to give him the nod.

Audrianne looked at the wolf and then at Corin, her face impassive even though he had no doubt she was aware of his train of thought. She was as adept at reading people as he was. "Nonetheless," she said with a tight smile, "it is still legal, and do please try and control yourself. Why you cannot keep a tighter rein on your magic I don't know."

He ignored the accustomed dig at his control, too furious to focus on anything but her ultimatum. "If you do that," he warned her, his voice vibrating with suppressed anger, "I will never forgive you." He had suffered much at the hands of his mother, forever being dragged into some nefarious plot or other but that she should blackmail him into marriage ...

His mother sighed, and her expression changed. Suddenly she was all softness and pretty sparkling eyes and he turned away in disgust. He had seen the routine too many time to fall for it. "I don't want to do it, my darling," she said with regret. "If you go and find yourself someone then I won't interfere further." Her voice hardened and he gave a bitter laugh, knowing she would continue to interfere in his life until the day she died. "But if you continue to wallow in self-pity you simply give me no choice."

He gave her a scathing look. "So you did come here to blackmail me after all." He headed for the bottle and snatched up a glass. He was now far from caring what she thought of him and so he poured out a large measure, the black liquid glinting red as it splashed up the sides.

"I wouldn't call it blackmail," she said, watching him knock back the drink with distaste. "But I'll tell you what is ..."

He froze with the bottle still in his hand and looked at her, foreboding growing with every second. "Mother ... what have you done?"

The Queen laughed and snatched the bottle away before he could refill his glass; she rushed to open the window and poured it outside where it gushed in a black puddle onto the sodden ground.

"No! Don't ..." Corin blanched and reached to grab it from her but was too late. "Gods, Mother. That was over two hundred years old!" he shouted. "Now stop trying to aggravate the hell out of me and tell me what in damnation you're up to."

Audrianne gave him a smug smile as she closed the window again and set the bottle down. "Oh nothing much." She pursed her lips and looked innocent which was enough to alarm him before she even opened her mouth. "I just invited Elswyth to come and stay with you. I told her you needed ... looking after."

Corin felt his jaw drop open. "You did what?" he croaked, as horror seemed to have stolen his voice.

"Yes." The Queen laughed at his appalled expression, quite unrepentant. "In fact I think she should arrive ... oh, in an hour or so."

"Of all the low ..." Corin began to think of a lot of things he would like to say to his darling mother but if what she said was true, then time was of the essence. "I can't believe even you would do such a wicked thing to me." He headed for the door, wrenching it open and yelling down the corridor. "Alsten! Pack my things ... immediately! I'm leaving in twenty minutes."

His mother chuckled. "Well, my darling, I shall leave you to get ready and your father and I will look forward to meeting our future daughter in law in due course."

Corin cursed under his breath as thunder rumbled over the house. Audrianne seemed oblivious to his temper however and walked up to him with a sweet smile. Corin dutifully kissed her proffered cheek, all the while staring daggers at her. She walked to the door and opened it and then paused. "By the way, darling, I hear the Countess was quite delighted by your ... attentions."

Corin grimaced. "I'm so relieved she was satisfied," he said with disgust.

Audrianne nodded, apparently oblivious to his discomfort. "It seems that she was so pleased she persuaded the Count to change his mind about signing the agreement. Isn't that good news?"

Corin stared down at the hearth, at the flames dancing as they consumed the dry logs with voracity and wondered how long it would take to burn his own body to nothing more than cinders. As it was in his dreams. "I am simply thrilled for you, Mother," he replied, his voice dead and empty of emotion. He needed a drink. He needed to numb himself until none of this mattered a damn.

He heard her bid him goodbye and walk away and he crossed the room slamming the door hard behind her as she departed.

He stared at the door for a moment and not for the first time wished he had been born to one of the farmers families. He could have worked in the stables ... It was an old and familiar daydream and one he and Laen had often played at as children. Pretending they were brothers with no one watching with expectations of them being future Kings. Free to live their lives as they wanted. He snapped himself out of his reverie, remembering Elswyth was on her way. Wrenching the door open again he took the stairs two at a time, cursing under his breath. He had to get out of here and fast before he was submitted to the tender mercies of a waspish woman who had been determined to reform and then marry him since they were children. He would take refuge in the human world where she would not follow and if his parents wanted him to find a wife ... well he may as well get it over with while he was there. He'd find a girl and use all the Elven tricks at his disposal to bring her to the Fae Lands where he would explain the deal, and it would be exactly that, a business arrangement. The girl could then return home and only need show her face for the usual events where the royal family was expected to appear. There was the matter of the heir of course but he didn't intend to choose someone who he didn't have at least some attraction to and he knew that he would have no problem with the reverse. So there it was, a workable plan ... and he had just the girl in mind.

Discover the prequel series to The Dark Prince...

Book #1:
The Key to Erebus

The truth can kill you.

Taken as a small child, from a life where faeries, sirens and mythical creatures are real and treacherous, Jéhenne Corbeaux is totally unprepared when she returns to France to stay with her eccentric Grandmother.

Thrown headlong into a world she knows nothing about she seeks to learn the truth about herself, uncovering secrets more shocking than anything she could ever have imagined and finding that she is by no means powerless to protect the ones she loves.

Despite her Gran's dire warnings, she is inexorably drawn to the dark and terrifying figure of Corvus, an ancient vampire and master of the Albinus family.

Jéhenne is about to find her answers and discover that, not only is Corvus far more dangerous than she could ever imagine but that he holds much more than the key to her heart...

ACKNOWLEDGMENTS

There are many people to thank as always ...

My amazing editor, Gemma Fisk. I'm actually loathe to put her name here as now people know who she is, they'll go and poach her and she's mine. Mine I tell you!

My right hand gal and the replacement for that bit of my brain that mysteriously disappeared when I had children. Varsi Appel at mission control. I <3 you.

Alys Arden. I've said it before ... Awesomeness in a person sized package. She is too talented and this book wouldn't be available without her. Make sure you check out The Casquette Girls to see just how amazing she is.

Keevz Coleman for the original cover design of The Dark Prince. Thank you, honey!

My beautiful betas. Varsi, Kim Brown, Eloise 'Hellvis' Wayne-Gacey and Linzi Clarke. As always thank you so much for your advice and support.

My incredible Street Team! I am blessed indeed to have so many dedicated readers going out into the world and shouting my name. You guys are too wonderful for words and I adore you.

To the Dark Addicts and my wicked Angels (you know who you are), to see your ranks growing daily and to hear all of your amazing comments and receive such unstinting support is more than I could ever have hoped for. You make my day, every day.

To my husband, Pat. For putting up with my frequent disappearances into the Faelands and always believing.

ABOUT EMMA V LEECH

I was born in Kent in the UK and moved to France in 1998. I currently live, according to my husband, in LALA land but the rest of the time in the middle of nowhere in darkest Dordogne, as far from the real world as possible. I'm married with three daughters and a wild imagination.

As a child I spent more time than I'm going to admit to wishing I was Samantha from Bewitched. Yet despite hours spent perfecting the nose twitch; sadly, so far at least, no magical ability has been discovered. Now I have to say it's looking unlikely, but remain hopeful.

I like Tarot cards and anything creepy... except spiders. I worship at the altar of Florence + the Machine and am addicted to music, as long as it's LOUD! I love chocolate, think The Wizard of Oz is the scariest film I've ever seen and still believe in faeries

Want more *darkness?*

Join the Dark Addicts and instantly download free short stories, characters interviews, and other goodies!

Sign up at:
www.emmavleech.com

Printed in Poland
by Amazon Fulfillment
Poland Sp. z o.o., Wrocław